Murder
on the London
Underground

By
Malcolm C. Brooks

MAPLE
PUBLISHERS

Murder on the London Underground

Author: Malcolm C. Brooks

First Published in 2025

ISBN 978-1-83538-756-6 (Paperback)
        978-1-83538-757-3 (E-Book)

Book Layout by:
        Maple Publishers
        www.maplepublishers.com

Cover design by Artist Jean Davey

Published by:
        Maple Publishers
        Fairbourne Drive, Atterbury,
        Milton Keynes,
        MK10 9RG, UK
        www.maplepublishers.com

A CIP catalogue record for this title is available from the British Library.

MURDER ON THE LONDON UNDERGROUND

Metropolitan Police Scotland Yard

Special Operations

OPERATION LIVE WIRE

Main Character List

- Chief Commander Police Security and Protection.

- Matt Gibbons.

- Assistant Commander Special Branch.

- Simon Harris.

- Special Branch Detectives.

- Andrew Brown.

- Gino Fernandez.

- Zoe Williams.

- Ravidid Bhatir.

- Police Constable Brad Evans.

- Team secretary Val Mitchell.

- Neasden Underground Train Depot Manger.

- Don Walker.

- Metropolitan Transport Manger.

- Tony Edwards.

- London Synagogue Chief Rabbi.

- Ethan Bennouitz.

- Birmingham Synagogue Chief Rabbi.

- Yosef Kahane.

- Manchester Synagogue Chief Rabbi.

- Zacharies Baeck.
- Birmingham Police Crime Commissioner.
- Peter Johnson.
- Manchester Police Chief Constable.
- Alan Edwards.
- Two Police Detectives in Manchester Police Station.
- Dave Robinson and Asrov Khan.
- Chief Police Officer for Drugs and Gun running
- Clive Dawson.

- Andrew Brown's wife Chloe and son Dimitris.
- Gino Fernandez's wife Sophia and twin girls
- Eve and Becky.

CHAPTER ONE

Out on the busy streets of London where the late November air carried a crisp chill, the city hummed with its usual uncontrolled energy. Yet, within the depths of Holborn underground station, an entirely different atmosphere enveloped the underground network of passageways.

Holborn underground station, nestled 41 metres beneath the surface, boasts an architectural marvel—the towering escalators that seem to descend into the depths below. Every day it is a rush hour connection for the commuters traversing the Piccadilly and Central lines, offering swift access to dynamic places like Tottenham Court Road and Covent Garden.

Inside Holborn underground station, the rumble of the trains echoed through the tunnels, each carriage a beacon of passage for the throngs of passengers eager to reach their destinations. With eight carriages per train and three doors per carriage, capable of accommodating up to 1,100 passengers, the station pulsated with the ebb and flow of London's restless masses.

Yet, amidst the flurry of activity, an air of anticipation lingered—a silent foreboding that eluded the unsuspecting commuters. Little did they know, concealed within the many corridors, an incident of grave consequence loomed on the horizon, poised to disrupt the ordinary rhythm of their daily commute.

Detective Gino Fernandez was sitting on the platform floor his sharp eyes scanned the noisy crowd, his presence disguised amidst the rush of commuters and travellers. His gaze flickered with purpose, honed on the mission at hand. Beside him Detective Andrew Brown remained vigilant, both poised to spring into action at the slightest hint of their targets.

The platform buzzed with activity, Gino Fernandez remained focused. His keen instincts guided him as he awaited the arrival of the suspects, a man and a woman whose appearance had set the gears of their investigation into motion.

Their objective was clear: track the movements of this elusive pair, believed to be integral members of a secret arms smuggling syndicate. With each passing moment, the tension heightened, anticipation mingling with the electric atmosphere of the station.

They knew the risks involved, the delicate balance between observation and intervention. But as dedicated officers of the law they were prepared to navigate the shadows, to pursue justice wherever it may lead.

As the minutes ticked by Gino Fernandez couldn't help but wonder about the twists and turns that lay ahead. Would their targets attempt to evade detection, slipping through the city's streets? Or perhaps they would brazenly rendezvous with their superiors, their next move shrouded in mystery.

Amidst the commotion at the station one thing remained certain, it was beginning to happen, and Gino Fernandez was determined to see it through to its conclusion.

With steely resolve, he awaited the next chapter in this gripping tale of cat and mouse, ready to embark on whatever path lay ahead in the pursuit of justice.

Meanwhile aboard the incoming train the man's grip tightened on the sleek sports bag slung over his shoulder, its contents veiled in secrecy, a silent guardian of untold mysteries.

Within the sports bag whispered rumours danced amidst the fabric, tales of contraband and concealed dealings hidden from prying eyes. Each zip held the promise of revelation, each pocket a potential cache of illicit goods waiting to be unveiled.

Beside him the woman radiated an air of sophistication. Her fingers were tracing the contours of a lavish leather case which exuded an aura of opulence, its fine craftsmanship a testament to wealth and privilege. Yet beneath its elegant facade lurked the possibility of danger, a hidden compartment whispering secrets of firearms and ammunition carefully concealed from view.

As the train approached the station, their burdens were heavy with the impending uncertainty.

Behind the façade of ordinary travellers lay the shadows of suspicion, their every movement scrutinized by watchful eyes. In the depth of deception and intrigue, the sports bag and leather case stood as silent sentries, guardians of a truth waiting to be revealed. With the train fast approaching the station, the duo moved closer to their destiny, their fates intertwined with the pulse of the city and the relentless pursuit of justice.

Simon Harris, the Assistant Commander of the Special Branch, received an intriguing tip-off from the railway police stationed at St Pancras International station.

According to their report, a mysterious woman was spotted wearing a striking green cashmere skirt paired elegantly with a matching sweater. Completing her attire was a rich brown coat and footwear to match.

In contrast, the man accompanying her seemed to embody a more casual, yet still distinctive style. Sporting classic blue jeans, a crisp white polo neck jumper, and a snug black winter coat, he strutted confidently in his white Nike trainers, exuding an air of urban sophistication in his wake.

But amidst this number of everyday commuters there lurked a figure of intrigue—Gino, draped in a disguise that seemed plucked from the pages of a detective novel. Concealed beneath a weathered green tweed coat, his appearance was further marred by its evident neglect, marked by patches of grime and dirt. His choice of attire, including his trusty black jeans, hinted at a life lived on the fringes of society.

Yet it was not merely his attire that drew attention, but the captivating spectacle of his unkempt mane—long brown dreadlocks cascading haphazardly over his shoulders, intertwining with his matted hair.

Seated upon a worn blanket at Holborn underground station Detective Gino Fernandez seemed unperturbed by the commotion around him, his muttered Italian soliloquies creating an aura of mystery.

Despite the railway police's attempts to coax him away Gino gruffly rebuffed their offers, preferring the solace of his solitude. Left to his own devices he remained seated upon the station floor, an enigmatic figure amidst the crowds—a testament to the diverse tapestry of life that unfolded within the confines of the Holborn underground station.

Detective Andrew Brown stood amongst the Arsenal and Liverpool football supporters, his disguise expertly crafted, blending into the sea of red and white colours. A vibrant red wig perched on top of his head, a bold declaration of allegiance to the Arsenal club, whilst an oversized Arsenal scarf was draped around his neck, billowing in the crisp evening breeze like the flag of a devoted fan. His attire, a striking ensemble of bright red jeans and pristine white trainers completed the transformation, ensuring he would pass undetected among the passionate supporters flooding the platform.

As the station platform swelled with the excited chatter of the football supporters anticipation crackled in the air like electricity before a storm. Tonight's match against Liverpool promised to be a spectacle of sporting prowess, the Emirates Stadium poised to bear witness to the clash of champions at 7:45 pm sharp.

In the sea of red and white Detective Brown's keen eye caught sight of a figure standing near the platform edge, a man of the Jewish faith distinguishable by his traditional attire.

The black kippah perched atop his head served as a beacon amidst the vibrant crowd, while his dark clothing of a short black coat and trousers, coupled with open-toe sandals, offered a stark contrast to the sea of Arsenal and Liverpool regalia.

Also it was the peculiar length of the man's trousers that drew Detective Andrew Brown's attention, the hems grazing his ankles in a fashion both curious and out of place amongst the fervent energy of the football crowd.

In the middle of the busy platform this enigmatic figure stood out like a lone beacon, and in the confusion a mystery waiting to be unravelled.

Amongst the many Arsenal and Liverpool supporters stood this man with an air of mystery. His hair, cropped short save for a small ponytail, hinted at a story untold, while his restless movements betrayed a mind in turmoil. Clutching a small leather-bound book he muttered to himself, lost in the pages of what Andrew suspected might be the sacred scriptures of his faith.

With the train's imminent arrival tension hung thick in the air, the man's agitation intense. Andrew's heart quickened with apprehension as he observed the man edging closer to the platform's edge, his demeanour fraught with distress. It was a precarious situation, the threat of tragedy looming ever closer, yet Andrew dared not break cover, his duty as an undercover detective binding him to the shadows.

Meanwhile, in the group of the Arsenal and Liverpool supporters, inconspicuously blended another man with a black beard in a blue boiler suit bearing the printing of Express Removals on the back, his presence unnoticed amidst the fervour of the football crowd. A nondescript lunch box tucked under his arm he moved with purpose, his intentions shrouded in mystery.

Behind Andrew a figure of refinement stood poised, a city gent exuding an air of sophistication amidst the chaos. His attire spoke of wealth and privilege, his polished facade betraying nothing of the turmoil unfolding around them.

With a small briefcase clutched tightly to his chest, he observed the scene unfolding with detached interest as well as watching the man in the blue boiler suit.

As the train emerged from the tunnel with a deafening roar the sound of a gun shattered the air, sending shock waves rippling through the crowded platform.

In an instant tragedy struck as the Jewish man fell beneath the oncoming train, chaos erupting in its wake. The screech of brakes pierced the confusion as the train ground to an abrupt halt, half of the train still in the tunnel, the aftermath engulfed in a mayhem of screams.

Amidst the chaos Andrew and Gino both exchanged a glance, their resolve steeling as they assessed the situation. Soon they would hear the sound of approaching sirens echoing in the distance, they knew time was of the essence. Swiftly they made their escape, slipping away unnoticed during the extreme disorder, their identities concealed by the artifice of disguise.

In a quiet corner, away from prying eyes, they shed their disguises, transforming to a different style with their easy reversible clothes. As Andrew's red jeans turned to blue denim and he took off his red wig and Gino's dreadlocks vanished into his duffel bag they emerged anew, ready to face whatever challenges lay ahead in the pursuit of justice.

With a nod of agreement, Andrew and Gino surveyed their transformed reflections in the gents toilet mirrors, reassured by the unfamiliar faces that stared back at them. Gone were the traces of their former selves, replaced by the guise of anonymity crafted in the wake of their daring escape.

Emerging from the sanctuary of the toilets, they were met with a scene of the controlled emergency responders flooding the station in a flurry of activity. Police officers, firefighters and ambulance technicians dashed down escalators, their urgent mission unfolding before their eyes. Outside, fire engines and ambulances lined the streets, a testament to the gravity of the situation they had narrowly escaped.

"Let's blend in and take a leisurely stroll," Andrew suggested, his voice calm amidst the turmoil. "We'll catch a bus to Covent Garden."

The journey passed without incident, the rhythmic hum of the city bus soothing their frayed nerves. Soon, they found themselves in Covent Garden, in search of solace and information on the Holborn underground train accident.

Spotting a familiar coffee bar Andrew led the way, his familiarity with the locale evident as they entered. With a nod of approval he gestured towards the large TV screen mounted on the wall, a beacon of information amidst the confusion.

Seated with their cappuccinos in hand Andrew wasted no time in contacting Simon Harris from Special Branch, eager to relay the events that had transpired at Holborn underground station. When the call connected he was soon recounting the harrowing ordeal they had just narrowly escaped.

With a heavy heart Andrew related the grim details of the incident, the crack of gunfire still echoing in his mind amidst the disarray at the station. As he spoke he could feel the weight of the situation pressing down upon him, the uncertainty of what lay ahead casting a shadow over their precarious existence.

Yet amongst the turmoil one thing remained clear, they had narrowly escaped tragedy, but the threat of danger still loomed large on the horizon. With each passing moment the stakes grew higher, and Andrew knew that the road ahead would be fraught with peril.

Andrew's urgency painted the air with tension as he understood Simon's instructions, each word conveying the weight of impending chaos. "Simon praised our decision to change our appearances and evacuate the station," he said, "It's bedlam down there—people shoving, howling, and practically wrestling with the train doors. A large number of the train passengers are seriously injured, from the sudden emergency stop."

"And where is our rendezvous, set for tomorrow?" asked Gino.

"We meet Simon at the coffee house in the City Hall, right by the London Eye," Andrew replied, his mind already mapping out the course for the day ahead.

Recognition flickered in Gino's gaze. "Yes that place brings back memories! Remember when we took Eve and Becky during our London Eye adventure?"

Andrew's smile held a tinge of nostalgia. "Indeed, a spot steeped in cherished moments. One day, we'll whisk our young Dimitris there when he's old enough to appreciate it."

With an unspoken agreement, they drained their cups, the anticipation for the hurdles ahead mounting with each ticking second. Tomorrow promised new challenges in their ongoing pursuit, they found comfort in the familiar embrace of their surroundings and the unbreakable bond of camaraderie propelling them forward on their mission.

Gino nodded, understanding dawning in his eyes. "And now we will see what instructions we receive from our meeting tomorrow?"

The atmosphere in the coffee bar grew tense as people gathered, their faces etched with a mixture of shock and sorrow, gripped by the unfolding tragedy at the Holborn underground station in London.

Whispers swirled like steam from freshly brewed cups as the latest TV News updates painted a grim picture of the trapped passengers. After a quick arrival the firefighters were wielding axes against unyielding carriage doors, and they could see frantic efforts of paramedics administering CPR to the stricken train driver.

Inside the station a sombre realisation hung heavy in the air - the toll of injuries could be severe with many passengers in dire need of medical attention. The urgency of the situation was intense as all emergency services who had entered the station worked tirelessly to rescue survivors and recover the fallen.

As the hours passed the coffee bar became a refuge for those seeking solace in the face of tragedy, a sanctuary amidst the turmoil of the outside world. But even within its walls, the weight of the events unfolding underground cast a shadow over every conversation, a reminder of the fragility of life and the unpredictability of fate.

In the chaotic aftermath of the incident at Holborn underground station tension hung heavy in the air like a thick fog. The scene was a frenzy of activity as emergency responders battled against time and adversity.

The once tranquil coffee bar had transformed into a hub of disbelief and sorrow. The chatter of shocked patrons mingled with the urgent commands of rescue personnel.

On the platform the firefighters waged a fierce battle against the unyielding carriage doors, their axes swinging with determined force as they fought to breach the metal barrier that held precious lives captive within.

As the hours dragged on the true extent of the tragedy became painfully clear. Wounded and dazed passengers were led to safety, their faces etched with expressions of shock and disbelief. Many would require urgent medical attention, their injuries a stark reminder of the fragility of life.

In the midst of it all, the police grappled with the grim task of retrieving a body trapped beneath the train—a reminder of the price paid in the confusion of the train accident.

Through it all the spirit of resilience burned bright as emergency services standing together in a united front against adversity and despair. A community standing together by a shared sense of loss and determination to emerge from the darkness stronger than before.

With the urgency at the scene, brave firemen swiftly navigated through the accessible carriages, their determination unwavering as they rescued passengers in distress, their bodies battered and minds reeling from shock.

Urgent whispers of medical assistance echoed through the air, a stark reminder of the gravity of the situation as wounded travellers were carefully extricated, their fate uncertain, hanging in the balance of impending medical care.

Meanwhile, in a sombre interview with the authorities, the collaborative efforts of emergency services were highlighted as they grappled with the daunting task of retrieving a life lost beneath the weight of the train.

Each moment felt like an eternity as they worked tirelessly, a tragic testament to their unwavering commitment to every soul affected by the tragedy.

In the chaos the ambulance report delivered a chilling revelation: the train's valiant driver had succumbed to a sudden heart attack. With skilful hands and frantic urgency paramedics worked tirelessly to free him from the confines of the drivers cab, administering life-saving CPR in a desperate bid to snatch him from the clutches of fate. Each beat of his heart echoed the collective hope of those on the scene, a beacon of resilience amidst the darkness that enveloped them.

In the busy streets of Covent Garden, a sense of trepidation hung heavy in the air, as whispers of potential victims enduring life-altering injuries spread like wildfire.

Andrew and Gino navigated their way through the main roads of the London buses like urban explorers charting unknown territories until they arrived at the London Borough Market. Hidden within its depths was their sanctuary, a discreet lock-up unit where an array of disguises awaited them, ready to transform them into unrecognizable figures on their hidden stakeouts. With neat hands they stashed away their street clothes, ensuring their identities remained concealed.

In the blink of an eye, they shed their disguises and slipped back into the familiarity of denim and jackets, blending seamlessly into the crowd once more.

As the evening descended Andrew secured the unit, the click of the lock signalling the end of their secret operations for the day. They boarded separate buses, each bound for their respective homes

Gino's journey took him through the affluent streets of West Brompton while Andrew's path led him to the sleek high-rises of the South Bank.

"Until tomorrow, my friend!" Gino's voice echoed through the departing bus, a promise of another day of intrigue and mystery awaiting them with Simon's plans on the horizon.

The next morning, as the sun began to stretch its rays across the cityscape, Andrew and Gino found themselves outside the majestic City Hall, punctual as ever at 8:10 am. Early birds by nature they relished the quiet moments before the day erupted into a flurry of activity.

It was their ritual to exchange anecdotes from the previous day, steeling themselves for whatever inquiries Simon, the dapper Assistant Commander of the Special Branch, might throw their way.

At precisely 8:30 am Simon strode onto the scene with an air of authority that matched his impeccably tailored attire--a light grey suit complemented by a crisp blue shirt and a daringly pink tie, all accentuated by his trademark gleaming black shoes.

"Morning gentlemen," Simon greeted them with a hint of admiration in his tone, noting their timely arrival with a nod of approval. Andrew and Gino exchanged knowing smiles, their camaraderie unspoken.

"Well, well, well, what a spectacle yesterday turned out to be for you two!" Simon remarked, his voice carrying a mix of amusement and intrigue. "The Metropolitan incident department is combing through every shred of information with the precision of a surgeon, diligently compiling their reports for our Chief Commander Matt Gibbons. Rest assured, I'll be keeping you both abreast of any developments as they unfold.

In the early hours of the morning Matt called me for a whirlwind meeting that sent shock waves through our veins. According to him, the latest updates painted a harrowing picture: 148 passengers taken away to the hospitals each with their own tale of survival etched in cuts, bruises, and shattered bones. Tragically, one man's journey on this mortal coil came to an abrupt end right there on the train, leaving a solemn silence in its wake.

As dawn broke, the uncertainty loomed over us like a heavy fog. How many lingered in the sterile wards of hospitals, clinging to life's fragile thread?

The news channels buzzed with sombre confirmation—the valiant driver of the London underground train, now lay in the embrace of CPR, his heart stilled momentarily, his family keeping vigil by his side.

Then there was the tale of the Jewish man, a grim chapter etched in tragedy. His final moments played out on unforgiving concrete, pierced by a merciless bullet in his back, his identity shrouded in mystery. No phone, no wallet, no trace of his existence save for the gaping wound in his back, a cruel testament to life's unpredictability.

Our quest for closure hinges on a single image—a photograph to breathe life into our inquiries, to grant this nameless soul the dignity of recognition. Until then we're left to scour the many reels of all the CCTV footage for more details of a passenger who met his fate at the crossroads of chance and circumstance.

The enigmatic man and woman, elusive as ever, embarking on a train journey shrouded in mystery. As the train chugged into Holborn underground station whispers of their presence circulated. But alas, the details remain murky. Were they unscathed, slipping away unnoticed to another platform, or were they whisked away to the hospital, their fate veiled in uncertainty?

Ah, but here's the twist: the authorities from Eurostar, ever vigilant, revealed some very interesting news—false passports! Like a thread unravelling from a grand tapestry, the investigation unfolds, weaving through the searching of the CCTV cameras dotting every platform.

"But hold your breath, here comes the latest." said Simon, with a sly grin and a twinkle in his eye, will he unravel the couple's disguises? Or will they remain cloaked in secrecy?

"I have new codex mobile phones for you both.

They look and work like any other mobiles with the addition of a series of coded numbers.

Okay, If you press and hold number 1 for ten seconds

This confirms to me you have arrived at your destination.

Now press and hold number 2 for ten seconds.This confirms you have made contact and are both safe.

Next press and hold number 3 for ten seconds. It tells me you have located a gunman and are in danger.

Now when you press and hold number 4 for ten seconds I know you are requiring backup urgently.

Now press Number 5 and I will have your post code

It's very important you use this codex mobile and keep in contact with me at all times.

I can change the codes at any time and would inform you if I need to make changes".

"Yes Simon, we will".

"Okay guys, brace yourselves. Matt just dropped a bombshell. We are off the gun running case for now. I know, I know, it stings. We were really hitting our stride there. But don't worry, our talents aren't going to waste. We're getting a new case, and it's a juicy one. Ever heard of the murder mystery on the London underground?

So many questions, I need you to find me the answers.

First things first, let's dive into the intriguing area of London's synagogues.

Picture yourself uncovering their hidden corners, each with its own story and spirit. From the historic streets of the East End to the busy heart of the city, we're on a mission to map out every address, every phone number, every email – unlocking a treasure trove of connections.

1 Who is he?

2 Why did he have no identification at all on him?

3 Is he really a Jewish priest? If true which Synagogue was he from?

4 Could he be from one of the London Synagogues , or maybe from Birmingham or one the larger cities in the UK?

5 Or is he an imposter?

6 Has he any family in the UK ?

7 Why was he shot in the back at the London Holborn underground station?

8 Who shot him?

9 Has he any enemies?

10 Why was he behaving so erratically quoting the scriptures and walking round in circles and standing close to the platform edge?

So many questions we need to answer.

But wait, there's more to this thrilling puzzle. Imagine receiving snapshots, like pieces of a jigsaw revealing the mysterious figure caught on CCTV at the station. With each image, a new lead emerges, beckoning you to embark on a journey through London's synagogues, where secrets lie in wait.

Now, picture this: a secret rendezvous with an unmarked police car, awaiting your command. It's a scene straight out of a spy novel, filled with suspense and anticipation. When the time is right, you'll be ready to pursue justice down the many streets of our city.

And let's not forget the stakes. With a gun in play, the danger looms large. But fear not, for you'll be fitted out with the latest gear – bulletproof vests and a trusty 9 mm gun, authorised and ready to defend against any threat that may arise.

As the conversation turns to the chilling encounter with the assailant, tension fills the air. Andrew, you were standing just feet away from the scene of the crime, the weight of caution heavy on your shoulders. With every step, every decision, the need for backup becomes clear – a reminder to stay vigilant, to trust in each other's instincts, as you navigate the shadows of uncertainty.

Well, guys I think we've pretty much covered everything at the moment. I've got to get back to the Metropolitan station. As soon as those CCTV photos come through, I'll be sure to forward them to you. You're going to need some crystal-clear photos as you start contacting all the London synagogues."

After Simon left, they flagged down the waiter for two more cups of coffee and searched Google, exploring every nook and cranny of London's synagogues. Gino's eyes widened as he unearthed a staggering 454 synagogues across the UK.

"Blimey!" Andrew exclaimed, taken aback. "I never realised there were that many. Quite the revelation."

"Nor did I," Gino admitted, scratching his head. "This is going to be a real slog Andrew a proper marathon of synagogue sleuthing."

"Absolutely," Andrew agreed, casting a glance around the busy cafe, "it's getting a bit crowded in here. Time to relocate I reckon. The office in my apartment in Hammersmith boasts a couple of large computer screens. We'll be able to blitz through this research in no time."

As they prepared to depart, Andrew turned to Gino with a mischievous gleam in his eye.

"You know," he began, "before we were married. Chloe and I used that apartment as our little sanctuary. We decided to hold onto it even after we moved to those towering high-rises along the South Bank. It's proven to be quite the gem, especially when friends or family drop by unexpectedly."

With a plan in mind, they caught a bus, their journey unfolding amidst the vibrant pulse of the city. Thirty-five minutes later, they reached their destination, Andrew carefully punching in the security code to grant them access.

"Okay, Gino, let's get started," Andrew declared, switching on the pair of imposing screens that dominated the room. "I will tackle East London while you take a look at the North."

Their mission commenced in earnest as they meticulously compiled lists, the hum of productivity filling the air. Printed addresses, phone numbers and emails began to materialize before them, though they couldn't help but be taken aback by the absence of email addresses for many of the London synagogues.

"We should stop for lunch Gino." Andrew suggested, breaking the focused silence. "There's this charming Greek deli just a stone's throw away. They serve up some of the finest coffee and mouthwatering Greek Feta cheese sandwiches."

Gino didn't hesitate for a moment. At the mere mention of food he sprang into motion like a coiled spring, eager and ready to tackle whatever lay ahead.

As lunchtime rolled around Gino found himself lost in contemplation, his mind buzzing with thoughts. Suddenly, breaking the silence, he turned to Andrew with a curious glint in his eye.

CHAPTER TWO

"What do you think Andrew about the shiny new codex mobile phones Simon bestowed upon us?" Gino inquired.

Andrew's eyes lit up with enthusiasm. "Absolutely fantastic Gino, they're a marvel of modern technology, with the pace at which advancements are happening it's incredible to think that help is just a few taps away, ready to swoop in within seconds of our call."

After a satisfying lunch they returned to Andrew's cosy apartment, eager to dive back into their exploration of all London's synagogues. With renewed vigour they delved into their task, quickly compiling lists of these sacred sites. Their efforts bore fruit, yielding a tally of forty-three synagogues spread across London and the southern reaches of England. Among these, the vibrant communities of Golders Green, along with Edgware and Hendon stood out as the largest and most active.

Andrew was on the brink of updating Simon on their progress when his mobile phone rang, interrupting the moment. With a curious glance he answered, only to be greeted by Simon's voice on the other end. "Hi Andrew, eager to hear the latest on your exploration of London's synagogues, and I've got some intriguing information to share with you."

Andrew's voice crackled through the phone, filled with an intense sense of urgency. "I was going to call you Simon! We've been very busy this afternoon. We now have a long list of all the synagogues across London and the South of England. Tomorrow, we hit the ground running!

We're now in Hammersmith, at my old apartment.

It's a nice little setup here in my apartment complete with not one, but two massive screens. Makes our work a breeze," he chuckled.

"Have you had any luck with those CCTV photos?" Andrew queried eagerly.

"Absolutely, Andrew. We've got some very good photos of the guy we need to name, clear as day," came the confident response. "I'll forward them over to you. He's doing this peculiar dance, pacing in circles, nose buried in some tiny scripture book. We fished it out from the rail tracks it's got 20 pages , it's leather bound. My tech team's on it, trying to crack the code.

Oh, and about you two? The CCTV caught some cracking photos. Gino's there, chilling on the ground, flaunting his dreadlocks like he's in a reggae music video. And you. Well, you're mingling with the Arsenal supporters, blending in like a chameleon in a sea of red and white. No worries Andrew you're incognito. Although, according to the local police, you both pulled a Houdini act disappearing into thin air after a quick sprint up a couple of escalators. Not a trace left behind. Top-notch vanishing act if you ask me.

We won't be getting any photos from the mortuary just yet, but word has it he's a ghastly sight, marred by the brutal plunge from the platform and a forced journey along the tracks. They estimate him at around 40 years old, standing a towering 6 feet tall. With a bullet in his back.

I received a call from Matt Gibbons and we chewed over the idea of getting you a police unmarked car.

So, I called Tony Edwards, our transport manager and he has located an old Ford Mondeo. Says he'll have it primed and ready for you to pick up at the crack of dawn, 8:30 sharp. I know, I know, you're eyeing up that sleek new silver BMW but we figure an older set of wheels might serve you better in some of the dangerous areas you could be visiting.

Tony did ask about parking. He's not keen on having it hauled back to the Police compound every night. Have you a garage at your apartment?"

"We don't have a garage at our apartment but we've got a lock-up secure garage over here in Hammersmith," Andrew explained.

"Sounds good, just text me the post code so I can keep tabs on you both," came the reply.

"And once you're behind the wheel and driving to your first call, remember to dial in with your new codex mobile, numbers 1 and 5. That way, I'll know you have arrived, and I will know exactly where you are.

Oh, and about those synagogues you're looking at , have you settled on which one gets the first visit?"

"Yes" replied Andrew "I think we should make the large one at Golders Green our first call.

I will make a call to the Chief Rabbi Ethan Bennouitz to confirm a time before or after their morning prayer meetings with the office administrator Hannah Lachman."

"That's fine Andrew, let me know if you have any problems when you collect the car in the morning."

"Sure Simon we will."

With a satisfied nod Andrew felt they had accomplished enough."Let's call it a day, Gino," he suggested, a sense of accomplishment evident in his voice. "We've made excellent headway with our list of synagogues. I'll lock up, and then we can hop on a bus and go home to our families. How are your girls?"

Gino grinned. "All good, thanks. We're immersing them in Italian, they'll be fluent before we know it."

"That's fantastic," Andrew replied with genuine enthusiasm. "As for our little Dimitris he is still mastering the art of crawling. Once he's talking, Greek lessons are next on the agenda, and Chloe has grand plans for our holidays – she's plotting a getaway to Cyprus, staying at one of her mother's hotels."

Their conversation flowed effortlessly as they boarded their respective buses – Gino heading towards West Brompton, Andrew towards London Bridge.

Within 45 minutes, Andrew was back in the comfort of their high-rise apartment. Chloe greeted him with a smile, pleasantly surprised by his early return.

"Could you take Dimitris up to his room, Andrew? I'll prepare dinner while you read him his bedtime story," Chloe requested, her appreciation evident in her tone.

"Of course, Chloe. It's a rare treat to be home early enough for story time; usually, he's already fast asleep by the time I get in," Andrew replied warmly, eager to partake in a cherished evening routine with his family. "Ah, Chloe, my culinary partner, what delectable delights shall grace our plates this evening?" inquired Andrew.

"Why, only one of your special favourites, Andrew! A tantalizing Greek Moussaka paired with a crisp, green salad," replied the chef with a flourish.

"Marvellous! I suppose you'd fancy a glass of that divine Cypriot wine, Viana Vidiano, whilst I opt for a refreshing Coca-Cola" Andrew declared with a twinkle in his eye.

With the kitchen a hubbub of activity, soon the sounds of Greek conversation and Andrew's melodic serenades to Dimitris filled the air. As the little one drifted off into dreams, Andrew descended the stairs with a grin, announcing,

"Chloe dear, our prince slumbers soundly! My crooning seemed to work its magic."

"Indeed, Andrew, I couldn't help but overhear. It appears Dimitris has quite a liking for your singing; he was lulled into dreams before we knew it," Chloe chuckled softly, a warmth in her voice as she spoke of their cherished family moments.

As Chloe hovered over the bubbling Moussaka, her attention was suddenly diverted by the blaring interruption of a news flash. "Andrew, quick! Look at this," she exclaimed, her voice cutting through the ordinary hum of their evening. "It's breaking news, interrupting the main program. A bomb has detonated on a London underground train.

Did you catch today's paper? There was another incident on the London underground yesterday," Chloe continued, her eyes wide with some concern. "Someone fell onto the tracks, causing serious injuries to many passengers. Did you hear about that?"

"Yes, we heard," Andrew replied solemnly, his mind already processing the gravity of the situation.

Andrew's phone rang, signalling an incoming call from Simon. "Excuse me, Chloe," Andrew said, stepping away to answer the call. "It's Simon. He might have urgent news."

"Hi Andrew, have you seen the news about the London underground train explosion?" Simon's urgent voice crackled through the phone. "It's the same train involved in yesterday's incident at Holborn underground station. Thankfully, no one was on board when the bomb went off. London transport moved it to their Neasden repair depot. I suspect the bomb was meant to detonate yesterday."

"I'll send you the details," Simon continued swiftly. "When you pick up your car tomorrow, head straight to the Neasden depot. I'll text you the post code and the name of the repair shop manager. And remember, use the codex phone so I know you're safe."

"Got it, Simon," Andrew replied, his mind racing with the weight of the situation. The mundane evening had taken an alarming turn, and the urgency in Simon's voice only emphasised the gravity of the situation.

Chloe's concern hung in the air like a thick fog, swirling around the conversation as she turned to Andrew with a furrowed brow. "Andrew, is everything alright?"

Andrew's response came as a beacon of reassurance amidst the uncertainty. "No problems, Chloe. Simon checked in on the aftermath of the train explosion. Thankfully, it was only a stationary mishap in the repair depot. No casualties, no harm done."

Chloe let out a sigh of relief, her shoulders relaxing as tension melted away. "Thank the stars for that, Andrew. We can't afford any more chaos on the underground. People will be too spooked to even think about commuting until the authorities can 100% guarantee complete safety."

"Absolutely," Andrew concurred, nodding solemnly. "On that note, I've been meaning to ask about parking. Would it be alright if I kept an old unmarked police car in our secure garage overnight? I need to pick it up with Gino in the morning. It's discreet, you wouldn't even know it's a police vehicle."

Chloe's agreement came swift and decisive, a practical solution in the face of uncertainty. "Of course, Andrew. It's the smartest move, especially since we don't utilize the garage when we're not around. It could serve as a deterrent for any would-be intruders. But let's set aside these worries for now. Come, let's indulge in this moussaka before it loses its warmth. Oh, and did you pour my wine?"

Andrew's response came with a smile, a silent promise of comfort amidst the chaos. "Indeed, Chloe. Your wine awaits, perfectly chilled just as you prefer."

The next morning dawned with a crisp freshness in the transport compound nestled at the rear of the Metropolitan Police Station. Andrew and Gino, two seasoned officers, found themselves crossing paths with Tony Edwards, the senior transport manager.

"Morning, gentlemen," Tony greeted them with a knowing grin. "Simon's got a special request for you today. We've had quite the debate on what would suit your needs best."

With a raised eyebrow, Andrew leaned in, curious. "Oh? And what's the verdict?"

Tony's eyes sparkled with mischief. "An older, unmarked car with a beast of an engine. Simon's adamant it's the way to go."

Gino chuckled, nodding in agreement. "A bit unconventional, but we trust Simon's judgment."

Tony gestured towards a sleek Ford Mondeo as mentioned by Simon, its polished exterior gleaming in the morning light. "Well then, here's your unmarked car. Simon briefed you on the reasons, I assume?"

Andrew and Gino exchanged a knowing glance before nodding in unison. "Indeed he has," they replied, ready for whatever the day may bring in their unconventional but powerful ride.

"Alright, guys, gather round," said Tony. "I've got to give you the info on our latest project with this beauty of a car. Now, I know it might seem a bit retro at first glance, but let me tell you, we've increased the engine power, it's now big time. Picture this: a roaring 2,000 cc engine under the bonnet.

But wait, there's more! Ever wished you could activate some slick, undercover blue flashing lights at the flick of a switch? Well, guess what? We've got that covered too. Hidden so cleverly, you'd think it's straight out of a spy movie. And get this, with the keys in your pocket, the doors practically roll out the red carpet for you, swinging open like magic for a swift entry.

And let's not forget about navigation. No more fumbling with clunky gadgets. Our little secret? A state-of-the-art satnav snugly nestled in the console, just waiting for your command. Simply utter 'satnav,' and voila! It pops up like a trusty sidekick, ready to guide you wherever you please. And when it's time to bid adieu, it gracefully retreats back into its hiding spot.

Clear as crystal, guys? Keep this beauty under wraps, just as Simon instructed. Secured tight in your fortress of a garage over in Hammersmith."

"You bet, Tony! Simon's orders, locked up tight."

Tony casually passed the keys to Andrew with a grin, a silent plea embedded in his gaze. "Make sure I get it back in mint condition guys.Tank's full, so you're all set to go."

"Got it, Tony. We'll take good care of it," Andrew replied swinging the keys with a confident nod.

He couldn't help but broach a heavier topic, "Hi Gino, did you hear the news last night? There was a bomb blast on an underground train." Gino's expression darkened momentarily. "Yes, I heard about it. Turns out it was a decommissioned one, under repair at the depot."

"Exactly," Andrew affirmed, his tone tinged with concern. "When Simon rang me last night he said he wants us to go to the Neasden repair depot first thing.

He thinks it might be connected to yesterday's chaos at the Holborn underground station." "Right, then let's not waste any time." Gino agreed with a sense of urgency.

As they strolled toward their sleek car, a faint click echoed, and suddenly the entire vehicle burst into illumination, its doors gracefully swinging open as if beckoning them in. With a shared glance of "surprise " they eagerly sat in the plush seats.

"Hello ! Looks like this car's got some tricks up its sleeve," exclaimed Gino, getting into the driver's seat. As they closed the doors, Gino said satnav and like magic a sleek device gracefully emerged.

"What's the postcode, Andrew?" Gino inquired.

"NW10 GBO," Andrew replied.

With a few deft keystrokes, Gino punched in the code, bidding farewell to Tony with a wave before setting off.

"Smooth ride, Gino. I'll hand over the keys when we have arrived at the first synagogue " Andrew remarked with a grin.

"Sounds like a plan, Andrew. Sharing the driving duty is only fair," Gino agreed.

After a scenic 45-minute drive, they arrived at Neasden.

Gino said, "I will be responsible for the coded phone." He pressed No1 and No5.

However, their journey hit a minor snag as they approached the imposing security gates, where uniformed officers stood watchfully. Stepping out of the car, they proudly showed their warrant cards to the vigilant police.

Once their credentials were verified, the police officers inquired about their purpose with a mix of curiosity and caution.

Andrew sauntered in, his demeanour exuding authority as he introduced himself and Gino. "We're from Security and Protection," he announced with a subtle air of mystery, "we've come to pay a visit to the depot manager, Mr Don Walker. His words hung in the air, carrying a weight of purpose.

He leaned in closer, his voice dropping to a conspiratorial whisper, "You see, we've been directed by none other than Assistant Commander Simon Harris." The mention of the esteemed Assistant Commander added a layer of urgency and importance to their mission.

Meanwhile, a police officer's gaze lingered on their somewhat weathered Ford Mondeo. "Quite the relic you're driving," he remarked casually, unable to resist a jest.

But Gino, ever quick-witted, responded with a twinkling in his eyes. "Yes, but appearances can be deceiving, my friend. We've just retrieved it from the clutches of the Metropolitan Police compound." His words held a hint of mischief, as if daring anyone to underestimate their capabilities.

The other police officer, nodding knowingly, chimed in with a touch of admiration. "Ah, Tony Edwards' handiwork, no doubt. Remarkable what that man can do with older cars." There was a subtle reverence in his tone, acknowledging the skill and ingenuity of the compound manager.

In this exchange, the mundane was transformed into a scene filled with intrigue and camaraderie, where every word and gesture hinted at a deeper story waiting to unfold. "Okay, guys, consider yourselves granted access, but here's the deal: stick to the right side of the train carriages. You won't be able to overlook the bomb squad stationed near the centre of the first train. Don's office lies just beyond them. I'll give him a call to expect you and don't forget to show your warrant cards to Don, he's a bit on edge after the train explosion mishap,"

"Understood, much appreciated," replied Andrew.

As they cruised to a halt near Don's office, the man himself emerged like a character from a suspense thriller, ready to unravel the mystery. Andrew and Gino showed their warrant cards with the flair of seasoned detectives, introducing themselves as Security and Protection operatives on a mission to crack the case of the recent bomb blast that rocked the stationary underground tube train.

"Come on in lads. The kettle's singing a tune. Fancy a cuppa, tea or coffee?" Don's hospitality was as warm as the glow of a crackling fireplace on a chilly night. "Coffee sounds good thanks," they chimed in unison, eager to fuel their investigation with caffeine.

"Is this the same train tangled up in the Holborn underground station chaos?" Andrew inquired, his curiosity as sharp as a freshly honed blade. "That's the one," Don confirmed with a nod, his eyes reflecting the weight of the situation.

"So, what so far have the bomb squad managed to uncover?" Gino asked.

"Well, according to the latest information, a small explosive device went off around 6 pm last night. The tricky part? The blasted thing was set to detonate yesterday at Holborn station, but the timer had other plans.

It sent shock waves, blew doors and windows wide open, turning the train into a chaotic canvas," Don explained, his words painting a vivid picture of the scene.

"It's a real mess in there. Bags and holdalls scattered about like pieces of a sinister puzzle. They're combing through them with a robot before they can even think about moving them off the train," he concluded, his tone tinged with concern for the unfolding chaos.

"Alright Don, thanks for the update," Andrew acknowledged, their minds already racing with strategies to piece together the puzzle. "We wondered why those stubborn doors refused to budge when the driver slammed on the brakes in a panic?" "Well you see," said Don. "When the driver hits the brakes hard, whether in the eerie depths of a tunnel, or as the train arrives at the platform, only the driver or a vigilant platform guard holds the key to freedom. It's all about safety.

Those doors stay firmly shut until every last spark of electricity has been snuffed out from the system and the train has been moved fully onto the platform."

"But wait," interjected Andrew, his curiosity aroused, "I don't understand why the platform guards couldn't rush in to move everyone out once the brakes screeched to a halt."

Don relayed with a furrowed brow that a malfunction had occurred, prompting his team to delve into the depths of investigation once the bomb squad had given them the green light.

With his affable demeanour, Don regaled them with tales steeped in the rich history of the railway, painting vivid pictures of its past glories.

Then, after a very interesting 55 minutes, the Chief bomb squad engineer disembarked from the train, cradling a sleek leather case in his grasp. Upon entering Don's office the engineer looked astonished as he laid eyes on Andrew and Gino, who promptly showed their warrant cards, outlining their affiliation with Metropolitan security.

With the air thick with anticipation, they explained their mission: tasked by the Assistant Commander of Special Branch to ascertain the contents of a leather-bound case suspected to contain secret weaponry—information gleaned from the vigilant Railway Police at St Pancras station.

With a flourish the engineer unveiled the contents of the case, revealing only 3 bullets , yet bereft of the anticipated firearms. Traces of three small firearms left their ghostly imprints within the confines of the case, a testament to its cargo.

The Chief engineer explained how the case had evaded detection, its insides swathed in a cloak of soft lead shielding, ingeniously concealing its deadly payload from the prying eyes of the x-ray cameras stationed at the Eurostar's arrival from France.

"Fortune favours you this day," the engineer remarked, his tone tinged with a mix of admiration and caution, "for within this innocuous case lies the potential for mayhem—a stark reminder of the constant vigilance demanded in our line of work.

Our robot x -ray scanner is one of the latest designs and it can detect a wide range of metallic and non- metallic in a few seconds. They will soon have them installed at all airports, train stations and ports.

So here you are, do you want to take it now? We have kept our cotton gloves on so you won't have any of our fingerprints on the case."

"Thanks" replied Andrew as he put on his cotton gloves.

"We will take the case with us to the Metropolitan armoury. Only one question, what type of case was the bomb that exploded in?"

"It was in a small backpack, we have found evidence of leather strapping and silver buckles."

"That's clear thank you, we will go now. Thanks for the coffee Don and your interesting chat about the history of the railways."

On the way out they said "cheerio " to the two uniformed police at the gates.

Andrew leaned in close to Gino. his voice low and urgent. "Gino, make the call to Simon. Let him know we're en route, but make sure to emphasise: no guns, only 3 measly bullets."

As they pulled up to the Metropolitan Armoury, tension hung heavy in the air, but Simon waiting for them provided a small comfort.

With a solemn nod, Andrew passed the smart leather case into Simon's hands, launching into an explanation of their harrowing encounter. Each word was punctuated with a weighty sense of urgency as he detailed the intricate workings of the robot scanner, the treacherous bomb nestled within a backpack, and the malfunctioning timer that had averted catastrophe.

"Okay, listen you two. I need your presence to emphasise the situation. I'll need to run this through the lab for fingerprints before it goes anywhere near the Armoury" he declared, his tone resolute.

As they discussed next steps, Simon's gaze flickered with determination."I've got my team combing through CCTV footage as we speak," he informed them, his voice tinged with a hint of optimism."With any luck we'll uncover the faces behind this mess."

"Off to Golders Green are you?" Simon inquired, a note of understanding in his tone. "Yes "Andrew replied. "When we have made another appointment with Chief Rabbi Ethan Bennouitz."

Simon's response was understanding, his words calming their frayed nerves."Go now, back to your Hammersmith apartment," he urged, his voice laced with concern."It's been a long day. Take some time to regroup, maybe explore the hallowed grounds of the City Hall coffee bar at the early hour of 8:00 am. We've got ourselves a rendezvous for a debriefing session before you head off to Golders Green and whichever other London synagogues strike your fancy. Is that agreeable to you both?"

"Absolutely," they chorused in unison.

The following morning, as the clock ticked toward 7:45 am, Gino and Andrew rendezvoused, the anticipation palpable in the air. They engaged in a quick recap of the previous day's escapades. "I can't help but wonder what Simon has up his sleeve," mused Gino.

"Likely, he's got us on the agenda for plotting our synagogue visits, or perhaps probing our failure on those elusive firearms that have conveniently slipped off our radar,"Andrew surmised.

Gino agreed.

"I did a bit of digging into the inter-synagogue communication scene," Gino piped up, "and you'll never guess how they're keeping in touch these days.

It's all gone digital—emails, fancy apps, Twitter, or as they're calling it now, X. Turns out the pandemic thrust them into the cyber realm, with Zoom becoming the lifeline connecting the scattered threads of the Jewish community."

"Yes Gino, the mystery awaits us!"Andrew exclaimed with a grin as he gestured towards the entrance. "Look, here comes Simon accompanied by a mysterious lady."

As Andrew and Gino greeted Simon with the warmth of the morning, Simon reciprocated, his voice carrying a cheerful melody."Good morning, good morning, my dear fellows! Let us secure a table and summon the taste of coffee!"

They swiftly secured a table in the bustling café, where Simon, with a flourish, ordered four steaming cups of coffee.

"Now," Simon declared, leaning in with an air of intrigue, "before we delve into our plans, allow me to introduce our newest ally Detective Zoe Williams. Hand picked by our Chief Commander Matt Gibbons himself."

Simon's eyes twinkled as he continued. "Detective Zoe Williams will be our guiding light in navigating the complications we have with both cases.

Assigned to man the incident room she'll meticulously document every detail, from the underground incident to the elusive missing firearms.

Fear not," Simon reassured with a confident nod, "Detective Williams will remain in constant communication with us, ensuring no stone is left unturned in our pursuit of justice.

Armed with the entirety of knowledge regarding the underground skirmish and the looming threat of an unexploded bomb, she's our beacon of hope in these murky waters.

Detective Zoe Williams is about to embark on a surveillance extravaganza! She will have her fingertips on every single CCTV camera perched across the sprawling platforms of the Holborn underground and even at the exits.

But wait, it gets better. She's not stopping there. Oh no, she will extend her eagle-eyed vision to the next train stations down the line, all in the noble quest to aid you in your pursuit of the elusive man and woman, who we suspect are gun runners.

So guess what? You're not alone in this adventure. You've got a direct line to Detective Williams and, might I add, yours truly. Yes, that's right, consider me your trusty sidekick in this escapade.

I would like to regale you with tales of Detective Williams' prowess. She's not just any detective; she is a fully-fledged sleuth with credentials to make Sherlock Holmes proud. Oh, and did I mention her sharp shooting skills? Top scores from the shooting range guys. Impressive guys?

But hold onto your hats because there's a twist. Our dear Matt, bless his heart, has sent a decree from on high: steer clear of our humble abode at the Metropolitan Station. Why, you ask? Well, it seems Matt has this uncanny belief that you're destined for solo missions. And guess what, he couldn't help but commend those brilliant disguises of yours. Kudos!

Now, onto the nitty-gritty. When it comes to your chats with the Chief Rabbi in each of their sacred synagogues, discretion is key. Matt's got a gut feeling about these cases. So as you venture forth keep your wits about you and, for heaven's sake, watch your backs.

Oh, but fear not! Matt's not one to send you off without a plan. It's imperative, he insists, that you work with the local Police Chiefs in every nook and cranny you visit. After all, we wouldn't want a chorus of complaints flooding his inbox from other high-ranking officers, now would we?

Detective Zoe has suggested she would take care of that provided she was given all the information.

Any burning inquiries, guys?"

Andrew's and Gino's voices broke the silence.

"No, crystal clear," they chimed in unison, nodding in agreement. With a warm smile, Andrew extended his welcome to Detective Zoe Williams."Delighted to have you on board! I have a feeling we'll make quite the team. Oh,and congratulations on the shooting award! Reminds me of the time I qualified." Gino, agreed vigorously, adding "Absolutely! Same here."

Exchanging approval of acknowledgment, they swapped mobile numbers.

"So, what's the plan for today? " Zoe inquired, her curiosity aroused.

"We're starting off with a visit to the grandest synagogue in North London, Golders Green, at 10:30 am. We've got an appointment all set," Andrew replied. "I might be able to lend you a hand guys. Did you know most synagogues are now wired up to the internet?" Zoe offered, a glint of helpfulness in her eyes.

"Indeed yes, we were discussing it earlier. Still, there's quite a number that remain unplugged," Andrew admitted, his interest now fully engaged.

"We're gearing up to make a start with this investigation! We're planning to enlist the Chief Rabbi's help in spreading the word to as many synagogues as possible, emailing out the photo of the Jewish man who tragically fell under the train. And for those synagogues without internet access, we'll try all the phones, reaching out far and wide. We're pulling out all the stops to track down any leads on his potential whereabouts among the community."

"Now, before you leave guys, let's make sure we're all on the same page. I want to ensure we start things off with a bang, working in sync. So, let's backtrack and go over everything we've got on this case.

1) First off, we're still in the dark about the identity of the Jewish man who met his end under that train. Forensic analysis has confirmed he was shot in the back with a 220 Swift, the kind of bullet that doesn't mess around. It's the fastest killer out there, indicating a small handgun was used. And remember, the shot rang out loud and clear over the train noise, ruling out any silencer. The weapon likely came in a compact package, possibly tucked away in a bag or a box.

2) Right guys, listen up for the latest update on our little mystery thriller. Simon's got his eagle-eyed squad combing through every pixel on those CCTV feeds, scouring every platform and station in the vicinity. Meanwhile, our forensic wizards are deep-diving into DNA samples like they're solving the crime of the century. So far, the plot thickens, but the resolution remains elusive.

3) We might have a break in the case. Seems like we're closing in on the trigger-happy culprit. Rest assured, guys, I'll be your faithful narrator, keeping you on the edge of your seat with every twist and turn in this gripping saga.

4) Do you have those riveting snapshots of the gentleman who found himself on the wrong end of a bullet? Are they sharp enough to provoke a ripple through the synagogues, bouncing from one corner of the internet to another?"

"Absolutely," both Andrew and Gino gave their approval.

"Fantastic , expect a steady stream of imagery from me henceforth. But between you and me, I can't shake this inkling that we might be staring at a clever impersonator.

One can never be too certain in these murky waters! As this drama unfolds beneath the vibrant streets of London, where a tiny bomb decided to defy its schedule, much to the dismay of our bomb disposal experts, who would have thought of mischief aboard an underground train and for what sinister purpose?

We're in dire need of a swift intervention; is there a trail linking this explosive ordeal to our previous shooter? And could there be a rendezvous between the mysterious duo with the smart cases?Now the saga unfolds, fear not, for I shall craft meticulous accounts of every twist and turn.

5) The factual accounts will all be in the iCloud, they will be the responsibility of Val Mitchell our team secretary, she will up load all our reports and they will only be accessible to Chief Commander Matt Gibbons, our main contact, Simon Harris, myself and, of course, you two guys.

6) Okay now take note and prepare for <u>Operation Live Wire</u>," Zoe declared, her voice tinged with a hint of excitement. "The mere mention of it sends shivers down my spine."

Zoe continued, her eyes scanning the room, "it's paramount that we unite our efforts to untangle the web of intrigue spun by these three incidents. Who knows what shadows lurk behind them."

With a knowing smile, Zoe leaned back, her gaze flickering between Andrew and Gino. "But enough of the formalities," she said, her tone suddenly lighter. "When we're on our own please call me Zoe. Let's keep it casual, shall we?"

Andrew and Gino agreed in unison, their expressions a mix of determination and gratitude. "Of course, Zoe," they chimed in together, their voices a harmony of compliance and camaraderie. "We'll stay vigilant and await your guidance."

Now with their plans in motion, Andrew wasted no time, his urgency sensible. "Gino," he said, clapping a hand on his colleague's shoulder, "let's go. We can catch a bus to my apartment in Hammersmith. There, we'll retrieve the keys to our Ford car and embark on our journey."

"Well guys , how's the car treating you? Is everything alright ?" Simon inquired.

Andrew flashed a grin."Oh, it's a breeze! Smooth sailing all the way. This car's got some serious zip when we need it, and all the gizmos are ticking away perfectly, though," he added with a wink, "we haven't had the chance to flash those blue lights yet!"

Simon chuckled."Glad to hear it's working out for you guys. Take good care of it."

With farewells exchanged, Andrew and Gino bid adieu to Zoe and Simon, departing from the cosy confines of the City Hall coffee bar, venturing forth into the streets of London.

As they reached Andrew's Hammersmith apartment, he proposed a quick double-check on their computers for the postcodes of various London synagogues they may have to visit.

"Smart move, Andrew. We've got time before we leave, having those postcodes handy for our satnav is crucial," Gino concurred.

With a few clicks Andrew powered up both computers, swiftly pulling up the lists they needed, all with the aid of their trusty internet connections.

"Okay, Gino, let's print out that London area list real quick, we might need it, especially when we go to Golders Green. We want to make sure we've got the right postcode.

"Absolutely, Andrew, I've got it all set. We're heading off to NW11, cruising down the North Circular Road. It's about 50 minutes until we reach Dunston Road."

"Brilliant, Gino, let's go." Andrew secured his apartment, then smoothly reversed the modified police car out of the garage, with Gino eagerly getting in. With a definitive click, Andrew locked up the garage signalling their departure.

Gino summoned the trusty satnav, its familiar glow emerging from the console as if on cue. Inputting the postcode, they were off on their adventure.

"So, Gino, what's your take on our new addition, Detective Zoe Williams?" Andrew inquired, breaking the silence as they navigated through the city's main streets.

"I reckon she'll fit in all right Andrew. She's got that spark, she'll definitely make it easier for us to sync up, especially considering our occasional struggle with reaching Simon."

Traffic was heavy on the North Circular Road but they manoeuvred through the chaos with expert finesse.

"Ah, finally we've arrived Andrew," Gino announced with a hint of satisfaction.

"Good spot for parking just ahead, by the synagogue," Andrew noted, as the satnav gracefully retreated back into its console sanctuary.

Gino said "looks like we've struck lucky with this trusty old Ford. Tony's really worked wonders on this old car Andrew."

Andrew nodded in agreement. "Right, Gino, let's punch in those codes, keep Zoe and Simon in the loop. It's crucial they know our whereabouts."

"Consider it done Andrew. No problem," Gino assured, tapping away on his codex mobile.

As they approached the front door their breath caught in their throats at the sight of the magnificent gardens sprawling before them. Each flower seemed to vie for attention, painting the air with a kaleidoscope of colour. The paths winding through the gardens were meticulously kept, weaving a tapestry of perfection around them.

With a loud knock, Andrew announced their presence on the imposing oak door. A hush enveloped them as they awaited a response.

The door creaked open, revealing a figure straight out of a storybook.

An elderly man greeted them, his long grey beard framing weathered features, while a black coat draped his form like a cloak of shadows. On top of his head sat a broad-brimmed hat, adding an air of mystery to his presence.

After a moment's pause, the old man ushered them inside, promising to lead them to the sanctum of the Chief Rabbi. As they followed him through the long corridors, Andrew and Gino found themselves spellbound by the architectural marvels surrounding them. Details of the craftsmanship were superior in the creation of the synagogue.

"It's like stepping back in time," Andrew remarked, his voice filled with wonder as he traced a finger along the ancient walls. Gino nodded in agreement, memories of his own home town in Italy flooding back to him. "I remember a church much like this," he murmured, lost in nostalgia.

Andrew replied "yes once, in Cyprus, I attended a funeral in a Greek Orthodox church that seemed to echo the same timeless age." As they neared the entrance of the office, a figure caught their attention—a lady engrossed in her work, her fingers dancing on the keyboard with purpose. With a flicker of curiosity she glanced up, her lips curling into a welcoming smile, like a secret invitation to their quest.

The ambience of the room shifted as the old man, a weathered guardian of the synagogue, motioned for them to take a seat, promising the imminent arrival of Rabbi Bennouitz. Time ticked by in anticipation until the old man reappeared, his steps echoing a sense of importance.

Then, in a moment draped with tradition and reverence, Rabbi Bennouitz entered, his presence commanding respect. "Shalom," he greeted Andrew and Gino, a bridge between worlds as he introduced himself as Ethan Bennouitz, the custodian of this sacred place.

Andrew and Gino rose in acknowledgment, each extending their hand in a gesture of mutual respect. With a hint of formality, Andrew, and Gino showed their warrant cards and revealed their purpose—a mission veiled in urgency and mystery.

The Rabbi, his smile a blend of curiosity and concern, invited them to share their burden. "Please be seated," he beckoned, a silent assurance that their concerns would find solace within these walls. "How may I assist you? It's not often we receive visitors of your nature, surely a matter of gravity."

With precision, Andrew presented the photo, a puzzle piece in need of placement within the fabric of their investigation. "We seek the identity of this man," he explained, his words heavy with purpose. "Time presses upon us, and the truth must be unveiled. Could he be among your congregation, or perhaps you may know if he could be from another synagogue?"

The Rabbi's eyes lingered on the image, his brow furrowing in concentration as he absorbed the details. "We will aid you in your quest," he assured them, his commitment unwavering. "Allow me to examine the photograph closely."

"Look at him, he's like a storm brewing, etched with lines of worry and strain. He's not one of ours, that's for sure," remarked Hannah, her gaze looking from the screen to the man in question.

"We'll do what we can to assist you," asked the synagogue Chief Rabbi. "Let me introduce you to Hannah Lachman our Office Administrator, and Caleb Meyer, my steadfast companion."

Caleb adjusting his glasses and shedding his hat said "I'm absolutely certain he's not part of our congregation."

"Thank you," Andrew and Gino chorused gratefully.

"Now, if you'll excuse me, duty calls for the mid-day prayers. Hannah will assist you further," the leader continued. "She'll send out the photo to all synagogues online, although I'm not entirely sure of their connectivity. Hannah will ensure you receive the information you need. I will arrange for Caleb to bring you some refreshments from the exotic lands of Israel and the enchanting flavours of Turkish coffee," he announced with a mischievous glint in his eye. "Shalom," his invitation carrying the rich cultural weight of centuries-old traditions. "I'd love to catch you before you embark on your journey, after my mid-day prayers."

With a nod of agreement, Hannah chimed in, her voice brimming with efficiency and determination. "Alright, gentlemen, let me just work my magic with this photo scan, and then I'll unleash a digital storm—emails, WhatsApp messages, and Twitter X blasts to every corner of the synagogue network.

Should I start with the esteemed Chief Rabbi in each of the synagogues and the administrators of the synagogues?"

"Absolutely, Hannah," replied Andrew, a hint of admiration in his tone. "And may we address you as Hannah?"

A gracious smile played on her lips as she affirmed, "of course you may.

As for our reconnaissance efforts," she continued, her focus unwavering, "we've unearthed approximately 38 synagogues in the sprawling expanse of London district alone."

"A fitting number, indeed," remarked one of the detectives, his mind already calculating the scope of their endeavour. "But let's not forget the broader reach, stretching all the way from the sunny shores of Bournemouth to the busy streets of Harlow" said Hannah.

The conversation turned to other major cities, their names resonating with significance. "And what of Birmingham, Manchester, and Liverpool?" they inquired, their curiosity driving them deeper into the intricate web of Jewish communal life. "In the realm of urban exploration, I've yet to venture into the depths of other cities. My estimation for the total count of synagogues in the UK hovers around 500."

"Are there many others out there still untouched by the digital embrace?" asked Andrew.

"Indeed, I can summon forth and prepare a list for your perusal," Hannah replied, her voice calm with a sense of hospitality. "Feel free to use the spare phones. Dial up and inquire directly, and unravel the mysteries of our absent congregants from the last fortnight or so." "Your assistance is invaluable, Hannah," remarked Andrew.

Then came the entrance of Caleb, bearing forth a tray with aromatic coffee, alongside a cherished trove of special Kichel biscuits! As they indulged in this sacred ritual of the coffee break, Hannah disclosed her current task of compiling lists of synagogues. The initial batch, meticulously crafted, spanned the East and West territories of southern England.

"Many thanks, Hannah," Andrew acknowledged, seizing the scissors to divide the lists amongst himself and Gino. Armed with their assignments, Andrew and Gino braced themselves for the journey ahead.

The passage of time was marked by the incessant ticking of the clock, and despite the earnest efforts invested in phone calls, the hunt for their missing flock yielded no fruit. Hannah found herself inundated with digital responses, yet none unveiled the whereabouts of the person they wanted information on.

After about an hour Caleb appeared again, bearing a fresh batch of coffee accompanied by an extra serving of Kichel biscuits. With a grin, Caleb inquired about their satisfaction with the latest supply of coffee, adding a touch of interest in their persistent search. "Marvellous!" they both exclaimed with gratitude.

As the aroma of freshly brewed coffee lingered in the air, Chief Rabbi Ethan Bennouitz entered the room, his presence commanding attention. With a smile he inquired about their progress, eager for any updates.

Andrew and Gino shook their heads apologetically, admitting they hadn't received any positive responses yet.

Then, like a burst of sunshine, Hannah sprang to her feet."Great news!" she exclaimed. "I've got a reply from Birmingham via email and another from Manchester on WhatsApp. They both recognise the photo as one of their missing congregants."

She swiftly promised to print out all the necessary information: addresses, phone numbers, and contacts of both synagogues, along with the names of office administrators.

"Thank you, Hannah. That will be immensely helpful," Andrew replied gratefully.

In no time, Hannah had the printouts ready, efficiently providing the support they needed.

Chief Rabbi Bennouitz turned to Andrew and Gino, offering further assistance through Hannah. "Feel free to reach out to Hannah for any additional help you might need. She'll be more than willing to assist you."

"Absolutely," Hannah affirmed. "Anytime."

"And make sure you prioritise visits to the synagogues in Birmingham and Manchester," Chief Rabbi Bennouitz advised. "They'll have all the vital information you need to track down the man you're seeking."

"Of course, Sir. We'll start there," Andrew affirmed.

As Andrew and Gino bid their farewells with a heartfelt "Shalom" and expressions of gratitude for all the assistance, they left the room, their mission renewed and energized.

As soon as they settled into the car, Andrew proposed they give Detective Zoe a ring for any further directives. The hum of anticipation filled the air as they dialled her number.

Zoe's voice greeted Andrew and Gino, her satisfaction justified as she commended their accomplishments of the day. "Marvellous work," she praised, promising to relay updates to Simon.

"Send me over all the main details—addresses, post codes, mobile numbers," she requested, her tone brimming with urgency. "I'll get in touch with the closest police stations to the synagogues right away. And remember, our Commander stressed the importance of keeping the Crime Commissioner informed."

"Alright, guys here's the plan," Zoe continued, her voice brimming with authority. "Go back home before dusk sets in. Pack an overnight bag, you may need one. Tomorrow, I'll secure two rooms for you at the Manchester Premier Inn, in case the Birmingham Synagogue visit doesn't work out."

With a nod of agreement Zoe assigned Andrew the task of disseminating the police station details later that evening, ensuring they'd be primed for an early start the next day.

"Crystal clear?" she concluded, seeking affirmation.

On the journey home, amidst the rhythmic hum of tyres on asphalt, Andrew turned to Gino with a mischievous glint in his eye and remarked, "Gino, tomorrow calls for a bit of sartorial splendour, don't you think?"

Gino raised an eyebrow, intrigued. "Oh? And what's the occasion?"

"Well, we're venturing into the unpredictable climes of Manchester, where the rain is said to have a permanent residency. I propose we dress ourselves in a crisp shirt, a smart tie, a dashing suit, and, of course, a trusty raincoat. Can't let Manchester's infamous weather catch us unawares!"

Gino chuckled. "Is that so, Andrew?"

"Absolutely," Andrew confirmed with a chuckle of his own. "Consider it a gentleman's decree."

"Very well then," Gino agreed. " Will you pick me up at 8:30 sharp?

I've already alerted Sophia as we speak of our impromptu adventure. She's preparing an overnight bag for me. "

"Excellent," Andrew nodded. "Preparedness is key."

As they arrived back in Hammersmith, they stowed away the car in Andrew's lock-up garage and caught the bus going towards home. With a friendly wave, Gino bid Andrew adieu, promising to be ready for their early morning escapade.

⁕

CHAPTER THREE

Meanwhile, upon Andrew's return home, he was greeted warmly by Chloe, who had just succeeded in lulling their young son Dimitris into a peaceful slumber and was now busy conjuring culinary delights in the kitchen.

Andrew, ever the thoughtful husband, cracked open a bottle of Chloe's favourite Greek wine and poured himself a refreshing can of Coca-Cola as they settled down for dinner.

Over the course of the meal, amidst the aromatic swirls of home made cuisine, Chloe inquired about Andrew's day.

"It was quite the adventure, Chloe," Andrew began, regaling her with tales of his first visit to the Golders Green synagogue. "We were on the trail of a missing person."

Chloe's curiosity was aroused."And did your sleuthing lead to any breakthroughs?"

Andrew shook his head sombrely. "Not yet. Our quest continues, and it seems the next leg of our journey will take us to Manchester and Birmingham. We may have to spend a night in the rainy city."

Chloe nodded understandingly, a flicker of concern crossing her features. "Well, be sure to take care of yourself up there, Andrew."

Andrew smiled reassuringly. "With Gino by my side, I shall weather any storm that comes our way.

So I will need to pack an overnight bag and wear a smart suit, shirt and tie. Oh and I had better take a raincoat"

"No problem Andrew. I will get everything ready for you, what time will you want to leave?"

"I will need to leave here before eight and catch the No 23 bus to Hammersmith, get the car from out of the garage, then collect Gino and get round to pick up the M25.

How did you get on with the other mothers at the new mothers club?"Andrew asked.

"Fine , it was good to get out and meet other people and make new friends."

"Did anyone ask you what work your husband did?"

"Yes several , I said you were a Policeman at the Metropolitan Station.

I didn't say any more as you know I'm very careful when talking to others about their husbands or partners."

"That's good, Chloe, I know it can be difficult for you."

"By the way, I was very impressed with the Golders Green synagogue. The building and grounds were magnificent."

"Yes Andrew I have been there. It's very similar to the Greek Orthodox Church in Cyprus where we had Mum's friend Dimitris's funeral if you remember"

"How could I forget," Andrew replied.

Next morning Andrew left home, said goodbye, and promised to phone when they were at the Premier Inn.

He then caught his bus, picked up the car from his Hammersmith apartment and went to collect Gino who was waiting for him with his bag and raincoat.

"Okay Gino let's go. I think this trip is going to be successful."

"I certainly hope so Andrew."

Gino called for the satnav.

"I have all the post codes you forwarded to me last night Andrew so we will start with Birmingham West Police Station and then we can proceed to the synagogue in the West Midlands."

"How long does the satnav say it will take us Gino?"

"About 3-4 hours subject to any traffic hold ups."

They were soon on the M25 then on the M1 and had a good journey.The roads were busy but they made good time.

Gino had been chatting on the journey.Andrew was mostly listening and concentrating on the road conditions.

When Gino was looking at the satnav he exclaimed ,"we are almost there," then about 5 minutes later the satnav said "you have arrived at your destination."

Andrew spotted the visitors car parking and found a space.

Then his mobile rang. It was Zoe.

"Hi guys are you anywhere near the West Midlands Police Station yet?"

Andrew replied "Yes Zoe, we have just parked in the Police car park and Gino was going to press 1 and 5 on the coded mobile."

"That's great guys. What I need to tell you is when you go into the Police Station ask for Peter Johnson, he is the Crime Commissioner for that area.

I have informed him you would make contact so he knows you are seeking the identification of a man who was murdered in London.

That's all he needs to know and you need to return to the Police Station and phone whatever the outcome when you leave the area.

Are you okay with everything guys ?"

"Yes fine with us," they both replied.

Andrew and Gino strode into the front reception and showed their warrant cards With a firm but courteous manner Andrew requested to see Peter Johnson, the Crime Commissioner.

The receptionist, a beacon of helpfulness, directed them to the waiting room with a warm smile. "Please, make yourselves comfortable. Mr. Johnson is expecting you," her words of reassurance.

Minutes ticked by like heartbeats as Andrew and Gino sat in anticipation. Then, like a scene from a suspenseful thriller, the door opened and in stepped the Crime Commissioner Peter Johnson.

"Thank you for prioritising us," he greeted, his tone a blend of respect and urgency."Time is of the essence in your quest to unravel the whereabouts of this elusive man."

Andrew and Gino listened intently, hanging onto every word like sailors clinging to a raft in a stormy sea. The Crime Commissioner offered his assistance, extending a lifeline in the form of his direct number, a beacon of hope in the darkness of uncertainty.

"Thank you for your advice Sir" they affirmed in unison, a symphony of determination resonating in their voices. With purposeful strides, they exited the room, their minds already racing with plans and strategies.

As they traversed the corridors back to the car park, Gino couldn't help but comment on the surprising welcome from the Crime Commissioner. "He was affable, wasn't he? Though I wouldn't want to cross him," he remarked, his tone a mixture of admiration and caution.

Andrew nodded in agreement, his thoughts already drifting to the daunting task ahead. "Indeed," he mused, "but I believe he's a valuable ally we can count on if the need arises."

As they approached the car in the Police parking lot it unlocked with a satisfying click, almost as if eager to embark on their next escapade. Gino deftly punched in to the satnav the postcode of the synagogue provided by Hannah, its screen lighting up with a digital roadmap to their destination.

"Will we be taking the A34?" Andrew asked, his tone brimming with curiosity.

"Absolutely spot on, Andrew. We've got about 15 miles of road ahead," Gino confirmed with a nod, his confidence in their route evident.

Andrew caught sight of a nearby garage and he couldn't resist the temptation for a quick caffeine fix."Ah, that's great," Gino remarked with a grateful sigh as they resumed their journey, the aroma of fresh coffee filling the car.

As they navigated through the heavy traffic and roadworks Andrew said "it's a pity we weren't allowed to put on the blue lights, we might have cut through this traffic a bit faster." Gino kept a hawk-like eye on the satnav and he couldn't help but feel a surge of anticipation."We're on the brink of arrival Andrew" he declared, his voice tinged with excitement.

"Absolutely, just a skip and a jump away now. I can practically smell it," Andrew concurred, deftly driving the car into the front parking lot of the synagogue.

Together, they strode towards the imposing oak front door, each step echoing with purpose against the pavement. "Refresh my memory, Gino, who's in charge here , the Chief Rabbi and the Office administrator?" Andrew inquired, a flicker of curiosity dancing in his eyes.

"Ah, let me consult the printouts," Gino quipped, producing a piece of paper with a flourish."The Chief Rabbi is none other than Yosef Kahane and the illustrious guardian of the office is Mrs Miriam Friedman."

"Okay, brace yourselves for the moment of truth," Andrew exclaimed, a spark of anticipation dancing in his eyes as he gestured towards the door. With a confident thud he knocked, each rap echoing through the quiet street like a challenge thrown down to fate itself. As the hinges groaned and the door inched open, it revealed a silhouette against the warm, beckoning glow of the interior.

"How may I be of service?" the woman's voice flowed out, a melody of hospitality, wrapping around them like a familiar tune.

In a well-rehearsed choreography, they both produced their warrant cards, gleaming symbols of authority in the dim light. "I'm Detective Andrew Brown, and my colleague is Detective Gino Fernandez," Andrew announced with a touch of flair, his words punctuated by a subtle nod of assurance.

"Step right in, gentlemen,"the woman invited, with her blend of curiosity and co-operation.

"Greetings"Miriam said, her voice carrying an air of authority softened by warmth. "I'm Miriam Friedman but you can call me Miriam. And you must be the two detectives Hannah from the Golders Green synagogue mentioned would be paying us a visit."

"Spot on, Miriam,"Andrew affirmed, his gaze unwavering as he surveyed their surroundings."We're here on a mission to uncover the truth. Hannah's been quite the informant, sharing her emails and Twitter X with us."

"Indeed," Gino chimed in, his eyes alight with curiosity. "We've been poring over those photos, trying to piece together the puzzle. But we thought a face-to-face chat with you might shed more light on the matter."

Miriam nodded knowingly, her expression a mix of concern and determination."Well, let's look into it, shall we? One of our members, Ezra Levin, has gone missing for a spell. Despite our best efforts to reach him, he's been as elusive as a ghost haunting the synagogue grounds."

"Oh, Ezra Levin," Andrew mused, his mind already connecting the dots. "We've got our suspicions, but we needed confirmation from the source. Your insight could be the key to cracking this case wide open."

"Thank you, Miriam," Gino added, a sense of gratitude with smooth words. "Your cooperation means the world to us. With your help, we just might bring closure to this mystery. Gino leaned in with an eager glint in his eye, his voice laced with anticipation, "May we trouble you for the address, including the full postcode?"

Miriam's face lit up with understanding. "Absolutely, I've got it all sorted for you. Here's a neat printed copy,"she said, passing it over.

"It's a bit of a jaunt, about 14 miles from here. Our Chief Rabbi Yosef Kahane sends his regards. He's out today, visiting a community member but he made sure I equipped you with as much detail as possible. He knows how pressing this matter is for you."

Gratefully, Gino accepted the document from Miriam, nodding appreciatively. "That's splendid! Your clarity is much appreciated, especially the postcode."

Andrew interjected, his tone decisive, "We'll be off then. Could we trouble you for your contact number? We'll ring you with the outcome, whether our man surfaces or not."

"Absolutely," Miriam replied with a warm smile. "I'll jot it down for you right here on your printout."

They bid farewell and headed out, expressions of gratitude echoing through the room. Gino soon punched the postcode into the satnav as they embarked on their journey.

Andrew glanced over at Gino, his admiration for Miriam evident. "She's been incredibly helpful but I can't shake the feeling that this lead might not work out. Nevertheless, we must explore every avenue."

After a 45-minute battle against the relentless forces of rush hour traffic, Gino and Andrew finally arrived at their destination. Gino punched in the numbers 1 and 5 on the codex phone, for Zoe.

"Ease off Andrew," Gino urged. "We're practically there. Take a left at the next corner."

As Andrew brought the car to a halt outside the house, their eyes were immediately drawn to a bold declaration emblazoned on a sign by the gate: SOLD, it proclaimed in letters large enough to be seen from space.

"Curiouser and curiouser," mused Gino, eyeing the house with a mix of anticipation and trepidation. "I wonder if anyone's still living here."

"We're about to find out," Andrew replied, his hand reaching for the doorbell with a sense of purpose.

The door creaked open, revealing a figure straight out of a psychedelic dream. "Well, hello my darlings," the man greeted them with a flourish, his attire a riot of colours that clashed with the ordinary suburban life. Tight green trousers hugged his legs, a bright red top threatened to outshine the sun and a jaunty yellow cravat completed the ensemble. But it was the shockingly vibrant red lipstick that truly stole the show.

Andrew and Gino exchanged a glance, momentarily taken aback by the flamboyant sight before them.

In keeping with their professionalism, they presented their warrant cards and inquired about the whereabouts of Ezra Levin.

"Oh, yes," the man chirped, his voice as colourful as his attire. "Ezra, darling, you've got visitors!"

From the depths of the house emerged a figure that seemed to defy categorisation. With no skull cap and a shaven head Ezra Levin made his entrance.

"How can I help you?" he asked.

Andrew's voice was apologetic yet determined. "We're very sorry to have bothered you. We're endeavouring to identify a missing Jewish man. Curiously, when we contacted your synagogue, we were informed of your absence for over four weeks. Miriam tried calling and even when Rabbi Yosef Kahane paid a visit, they couldn't seem to reach you."

Ezra's response was calm and decisive. "Yes, indeed Sir. I've been steering clear because I've undergone a religious transition. In fact, we've sold this house and I am planning to tie the knot with my partner, Jules. Our sights are set on a cosy little house in Kemptown, Brighton. I had every intention of contacting Miriam and Rabbi Yosef. I'll make sure to do so tomorrow."

"Alright, Ezra, we'll bid you goodbye for now and scratch you off our list. Kemptown ! I've got some memories from there myself, from when I was stationed in Brighton," Andrew chimed in, offering a farewell laced with a touch of nostalgia. "Best of luck with your move."

As Andrew and Gino retreated to the comfort of their car, Gino couldn't help but share his observation."I swear, Andrew, I've never seen a man with such bold lipstick as Jules."

Andrew chuckled, his mind already wandering. "Maybe it's time you took a day trip to Brighton ?"

Gino's response was swift and firm."No thank you, Andrew."

Andrew dialled Miriam's number, his excitement evident in the urgency of his voice as he relayed the news: they had finally met Ezra Levin, only to find out he wasn't the elusive figure they were searching for. "But don't worry," he assured her, "Ezra promised to ring you both tomorrow with his explanation."

Grateful for the update, Miriam responded with a touch of relief in her tone, adding, "Guess what? We've uncovered 12 more synagogues that aren't listed online."

"Fantastic!" Andrew exclaimed, his enthusiasm undimmed. "We'll call by your synagogue first and give them a call before heading off to Manchester."

As they journeyed back, Gino took the wheel while Andrew rang Detective Zoe to keep her abreast of the day's developments.

After about 50 minutes of travel, they arrived back and parked the car. Gino rapped on the aged door once more.

Welcomed inside by Miriam, they were immediately asked if they had eaten lunch.

"Not yet," they both admitted.

"Please have a seat," Miriam insisted. "Here's the list for you to tackle. And while you're busy, I'll bring you some salt beef sandwiches with a crisp salad, along with a refreshing lemon drink made from lemons straight from our gardens in Israel."

Andrew and Gino eagerly delved into their task of contacting the other synagogues, fuelled by Miriam's hospitality and the promise of a delicious meal.

They had started to phone some of the synagogues when Miriam walked in with lunch which they soon devoured and thoroughly enjoyed.

After a satisfying lunch that left their taste buds singing, they diligently worked through their list of synagogues, hoping for a break in the case. Yet, each call led to the same dead end – no missing members to report. As they bid farewell to Miriam, ready to depart, a mysterious figure in a flowing black coat materialized through a side door.

"Shalom," the man greeted them, his voice rich with warmth and authority."You must be the two London detectives Hannah spoke of."

Andrew and his partner Gino presented their warrant cards in confirmation."Yes sir" Andrew affirmed.

The man introduced himself as Yosef Kahane, the Chief Rabbi of the synagogue. "Has Miriam been attending to your needs?" he inquired.

Gratefully, they both said. "Yes, thank you. Lunch was delightful," they chimed in unison.

"And what of Ezra Levin?" Rabbi Kahane pressed, curiosity glinting in his eyes. "Is he still among the living?"

Andrew leaned forward slightly. "Yes sir. He's alive and well with promises to explain his absence tomorrow. We've crossed him off our suspect list."

"Thank you for your diligence," the Rabbi acknowledged. "Where to next?"

"We're off to Manchester," Andrew replied."Our journey through the Midlands synagogues is complete."

"Shalom and good luck," the Rabbi bid them farewell.

"Shalom," they echoed, departing the synagogue for their awaiting vehicle. Gino took the driver's seat, ready to tackle the winding road ahead. With Manchester on the horizon, the anticipation of the next leg of their investigation hung thick in the air.

"I will call Peter Johnson at the West Midlands Police station as we promised to update him with our visit although it was unsuccessful."

Andrew then dialled Zoe's number once more, anticipation bubbling within him like a pot ready to boil over. "Hi Zoe, Gino's at the wheel, steering us towards Manchester. Figured it's high time we had a chat."

"Thrilled you called, Andrew. What an adventure it must have been when you stepped into Ezra Levin's house! So, have you scoured all the synagogues in the Midlands now?"

"Indeed, Zoe. Miriam, the office manager, lent us a hand. We've reached out to every synagogue that's not online. Maybe we'll strike gold in Manchester." "Let's keep our fingers crossed, guys.

Oh, and here's the latest news for you. Our top man, Matt Gibbons, is being interviewed on the airwaves. He's appearing on the LB C 5 o'clock news and T V channel urging anyone from Holborn underground station that night to step forward.

Personally, I think he should've done that ages ago, but hey,what do I know?

As you know, we're still on the hunt for the sharp city man and the guy wearing Express Removals. CCTVs show they scattered like leaves in the wind, switching lines and destinations. We've spotted our city man on the New Elizabeth line taking a train to Paddington and catching a train to Bristol Temple Meads but whether he got off at Reading or ventured further remains a mystery.

And as for our delivery guy we trailed him all the way to Canning Town, then poof! He vanished into thin air."

"Sounds like you are making progress, Zoe. We're finally gaining some ground. How's the deciphering of those scripts from the Jewish man coming along?"

"No breakthroughs yet, I'm afraid."

Why don't you forward it to me Zoe. I can share it with a retired Senior Detective Harry Salter at Brighton. He is fantastic at cracking codes, it's worth a try. I'm sure he'd be thrilled to lend a hand."

"Thanks, Andrew! I'll send that over to you today," replied Zoe, a hint of relief in her voice.

"Okay guys duty calls. Give me a call once you get to Manchester," Zoe said before signing off.

"Gino, Zoe seems quite optimistic," remarked Andrew, his tone carrying a note of encouragement.

"Indeed" said Gino. "She's putting her all into this. By the way, how's our time looking?" queried Andrew, a touch of concern creeping into his voice.

"We're cruising along nicely... Oh, spoke too soon! Look at all those flashing lights up ahead," sighed Gino, resigned to the inevitable delay caused by an accident.

With the unexpected roadblock, their journey to Manchester stretched longer than anticipated. They finally checked into the Premier Inn after 6 pm with a sigh of relief.

"Wouldn't want to tackle that commute every day," Gino quipped, his voice tinged with exhaustion.

"Agreed. Let's find our rooms and then order a meal," suggested Andrew, eager to unwind after the arduous journey.

After some searching, they stumbled upon a new restaurant where they indulged in juicy steaks and crisp salads. Gino opted for a Chianti, his choice, while Andrew stuck to his trusty Coca-Cola.

Later, they caught up with their wives over the phone, and agreed to reconvene for breakfast at 8 am sharp.

The next morning, as they enjoyed their breakfast, Zoe's call came in, bringing news that a City gent had called her office after he had watched Matt Gibbons on the 5 o'clock news the day before. "He resides in Reading," she informed Andrew" with a mix of excitement and intrigue. "I will soon be boarding a train on the Elizabeth line bound for Reading, accompanied by Brad Evans, a Police Constable colleague. I have worked with him before and he is very keen to work for Special Branch.

Our mission? To delve into the depths of the harrowing incident. The anticipation tingles in the air as we embark on our journey.

Oh, but I almost forgot a crucial detail! A message from our boss Simon. The Chief Constable at the Moss Side station , Alan Edwards, is acquainted with our own Simon from their days at Hendon training college. The plot thickens," Zoe's warning resonated with gravity.

"Zoe, your caution is duly noted. We must tread carefully, for the paths we walk today are fraught with unseen perils."

After breakfast, they bid adieu to their hotel and set forth towards the Moss Side Police station. "Approximately 50 minutes, Andrew," Gino estimated, his voice a compass guiding their course through the urban maze.

En route, Andrew's reminder served as a beacon of caution, illuminating the dark alleys of Moss Side's tumultuous history. Gangs, violence, drugs and firearms—a tapestry woven with threads of danger. Yet, undeterred, they pressed onward, their resolve unyielding against the spectre of adversity.

Fortune favoured their journey, and soon they found they had arrived at their destination, pulling up outside the formidable office of the Police Station. Gino's eyes scanned the surroundings, seeking refuge for their trusty car. "Over there," he exclaims, spotting a sign beckoning them to the police parking.

"Excellent find, Gino."

Andrew squeezed his car into the last available spot, barely fitting as if he were completing a puzzle. As he and Gino emerged from their vehicle, two men materialised out of thin air, their voices booming with authority, demanding they vacate the spot. "Police parking only!" they bellowed, as if the words themselves were engraved in stone.

Andrew and Gino calmly stated their credentials. "We're officers from London Metropolitan," Andrew declared, his tone carrying the weight of legitimacy. "We're here to meet your Chief Constable Alan Edwards."

The challenge was thrown down like a gauntlet. "Let's see your warrant cards," the men retorted , their disbelief hanging in the air like a fog.

Without hesitation, Andrew and Gino presented their cards, each emblem a symbol of authority in its own right. "No problem," Andrew assured them, his voice steady and unwavering. "I'm Detective Andrew Brown, and this is my colleague, Detective Gino Fernandez."

"Fine, you can leave your old Ford here," they conceded, their words laced with a hint of disbelief."Though it does look like a relic from another era."

Gino smirked in response, his eyes twinkling with mischief. "Appearances can be deceiving," he quipped."Our HQ car manager is a genius with engines. This 'old banger' has been fitted up with a brand-new 2.0 litre engine and more modifications than you can count. I'd wager it could outpace your BMW any day."

The men exchanged a glance, a silent acknowledgment passing between them. "We'll keep an eye on your Ford while you meet with the Chief," they conceded, their tone softened by newfound respect. "But before you go, take a look at our warrant cards. We're Dave Robinson and Asrov Khan," they introduced themselves, their names echoing with a sense of camaraderie.

Andrew examined the cards with a practised eye, his gaze lingering for a moment before he nodded in approval. "Plain clothes detectives."

The men nodded in understanding, their shared mission uniting them in a silent pact."We're with the drugs and guns squad," they revealed, their words a testament to the dangers they faced daily. "I won't ask why you're here but the Chief will want to know. That is, if he doesn't already."

Andrew and Gino went into reception, exuding an air of purpose. At the desk, Andrew leaned on it, his gaze fixed on the receptionist. "We're here to see Chief Constable Alan Edwards.

We've got an appointment with him."

The receptionist nodded."Yes, that's fine," she said, her fingers tapping on the keyboard. "He's expecting you. Take the lift to level 5, top floor. His office is right in front of you."

"Cheers," Andrew replied with a nod and they strode off towards the lift, their steps echoing in the empty corridor.

As they ascended to the top floor, anticipation hung thick in the air. When the doors slid open, they found the Chief Constable's door already wide open. His voice floated out, welcoming them. "Please, come in. I've been expecting you. Take a seat."

Andrew and Gino entered, their eyes scanning the room. The Chief Constable leaned back in his chair. He seemed relaxed yet commanding. "I saw you in the car park," he said, with a knowing look, his tone sincere. "Thank you for your support," he said with a smile playing on his lips.

"Dave Robinson and Asrov Khan gave you a bit of trouble until you showed your warrant cards. I wanted to see how they'd handle it."

He leaned forward, his gaze shifting between them. "Simon Harris called me earlier. We go way back. He filled me in on your mission here in Manchester. I trust you will be able to identify the person from your London underground case."

Andrew nodded, his expression determined. "We're heading to White Lane Dukinfield, about 30 miles from here, Sir."

The Chief Constable nodded thoughtfully. "I know the area well. Text me the postcode once you've got the information from the Rabbi. And remember, keep me or my detectives informed. Your safety is our priority. Manchester's got its rough spots."

"We appreciate that, Sir," Andrew replied.

With a smile the Chief Constable rose from his seat, leading them towards the lift. "Good luck," he said, his voice echoing in the corridor as the doors closed behind them.

As they returned to the police car park the two detectives found their colleagues waiting by their vehicle, like two watchful hawks perched on the old Ford. Andrew and Gino stepped out, feeling the weight of the day's events still clinging to their shoulders and exchanged nods with their waiting companions.

"So, how did it go with the Chief?" one of the detectives inquired, his voice carrying the dignity of someone who knew the importance of every detail.

"Smooth as silk," Andrew replied, a hint of relief in his tone. "He was genuinely concerned about our well-being here in Manchester."

"Yes, he even went as far as insisting we swap numbers with you guys" Gino chimed in, fishing out his phone. "Let's snap a photo for the records?"

"Smart move, Gino," Dave remarked with a nod of approval. "We'll do the same. Stay safe out there, guys."

With a final farewell from Dave, they eased out of the police car park, the wheels of their vehicle spinning a tale of determination as they ventured back onto the city streets.

"Alright, Gino, punch in the post code for the synagogue that Hannah gave us," Andrew instructed as they navigated the main streets. "We should be there in 40 to 45 minutes if the traffic keeps moving."

Indeed, luck was on their side as they cruised through the city, the flow of traffic carrying them swiftly towards their destination. Before they knew it they were pulling up outside the synagogue. Gino was pointing out the parking at the rear of the building.

"Hmm, seems a bit weathered, this synagogue." Andrew mused, eyeing the building with a critical eye. "Not as smart as the one back in Golders Green. And look, only one car in the lot. Not as busy like some of the others."

Parking alongside the lone vehicle, they made their way to the entrance, knocking on the weathered wooden door. It creaked open to reveal a young girl, her curiosity shining in her eyes as she greeted them.

"How can I help you?" she inquired, her voice echoing in the quietude of the synagogue's halls. "Hi there," Andrew chimed, a friendly grin spreading across his face. "I'm Detective Andrew Brown, and my colleague is Detective Gino Fernandez," he gestured towards his partner with a wink. "We're from London, proud members of the law enforcement brigade, " he added, as they both showed their warrant cards.

"We've got a little mission on our hands, you see," Andrew continued, his voice carrying an air of anticipation. "We're here to see the Rabbi Zacharies Baeck or your office manager," he explained, his eyes scanning the room for anyone.

The girl's eyes widened in recognition. "Oh, yes!" she exclaimed, her words ringing with a hint of excitement. "He's been expecting you. Got a call from a lovely lady at a London synagogue, singing your praises about tracking someone down."

"But the trouble is," she continued, "Rabbi Baeck had to dash off to tend to a sick member of our congregation, and our office manager, Eliana Gella, has a transport problem. Her car was stolen last night." Sympathy laced her words as she recounted the unfortunate events.

"I scribbled a note this morning," the girl admitted, her voice apologetic. "Not the clearest handwriting, mind you. But I reckon you tech-savvy folks can work your magic with your 'sat thingy'," she teased, a playful twinkle in her eye.

"Oh, and Eliana insisted I give you his name from the register," she added, her brow furrowing in concentration. "It's Ahmadi Levy," she announced triumphantly, as if unveiling a crucial piece of the puzzle.

Andrew nodded appreciatively, his gaze shifting to the piece of paper in his hand. "Thank you kindly. Almost forgot the most important detail," he admitted with a sheepish grin. "And you are?" he inquired, realizing he hadn't caught her name in the flurry of information.

The girl chuckled softly, a self-deprecating smile playing on her lips. "Oh, silly me. I'm Emma," she replied, a touch of humour colouring her words. "Seems I'm becoming quite the scatterbrain these days."

"Before we leave, Emma, would you kindly cast your gaze upon the portrait of our elusive subject?" Gino presented Emma with a pristine print of the photograph.

Emma scrutinized the image closely, her brow furrowing with concern before she suddenly exclaimed, "Yes! I recognise that man. It's Ahmadi Levy, unmistakably. His face is rugged and I must confess, I found him rather peculiar."

"How frequently did your paths cross?" inquired Gino.

"I was a fixture at the prayer gatherings and more often than not, so was he, though not with the regularity one might expect," replied Emma.

"And how long has he been amongst your congregation?" Gino probed further.

"After consulting our records, it appears he's been with us a mere nine weeks. And though I hesitate to disclose, I recently overheard talking between the Rabbi and Eliana. They were deeply troubled, suspecting Ahmadi's faith and origins. They fear he masquerades as one of us, though his roots may extend far beyond our borders, perhaps even to Iraq or Iran," Emma revealed.

"Oh, intriguing indeed,"mused Andrew."Your insights are invaluable, Emma."

With that, Emma pivoted abruptly, inadvertently sending a cascade of papers sailing from Eliana's desk. She blushed profusely, swiftly offering her apologies amidst the fluttering flurry of documents.

Andrew and Gino helped her gather all the scattered papers. Emma thanked them both, adding with a sigh, "Eliana will be so cross with me when she comes in.

I just remembered something else," Emma said, pulling out a small note."Eliana asked if you could please phone her directly as soon as you can confirm anything. This is her mobile number." "Thank you, Emma. We'll give her a call," Andrew replied.

"We'll head out now, Emma. Take care and thanks again," Gino added.

As they stepped out of the synagogue, the rain poured down heavily. "Good thing we brought our raincoats," Gino remarked."

"Yes, Gino, they say it always rains in Manchester," Andrew replied with a grin.

As they pulled out of the car park, Gino glanced at the piece of paper with the postcode from Emma "15 Stocking Street, M16 17SE," he read aloud, squinting at the writing "Andrew, I hope this is correct. According to the satnav we're looking at 55 minutes to Moss Side," Gino said, glancing at the device.

"Alright, Gino let's go. And don't forget to forward the details to Chief Constable Alan Edwards, as promised."

"What do you make of everything Emma told us?" Gino asked. "Yes, it's very possible," Andrew replied. "I had my suspicions. Remember when we first met Zoe? She did mention he might be an imposter."

"Well, Andrew, we'll soon know. Once we find where he was lodging, we'll be making good progress."

The journey was swift and they made excellent time. "Hope we didn't get caught by any speed cameras!" Gino joked as the satnav confirmed they had reached their destination.

Driving down Stocking Street, Andrew searched for number 15. "Looks like we passed it," Gino pointed out. "There are some parking spaces further down."

"Let's park here and walk back," Andrew suggested. "There are some rough old cars and vans on both sides, so our old Ford won't look out of place. This area looks pretty run-down, all terraced houses with alleyways every few houses."

Gino nodded, noting the surroundings. "Let's keep a low profile. This place has seen better days."

Andrew and Gino strolled down the street, their eyes scanning for house number 15, which was just past a dimly lit alleyway.

"I don't see any houses with those new video doorbells," Andrew remarked, squinting at the doorways.

"No," replied Gino. "I'll just give this old knocker a try."

He reached out and rapped the heavy iron knocker against the wooden door. Almost instantly, it creaked open, and a woman with dishevelled hair and a fierce expression stuck her head out.

"Clear off!" she barked. "We don't want you bastards here!" She tried to slam the door, but Gino quickly wedged his size 11 boot in the gap and gave it a forceful shove.

Suddenly, a man's voice bellowed from inside the house. "Keep the bloody door shut, you stupid woman! Don't let the bastards in."

A gunshot rang out and a bullet whizzed past Gino's shoulder, narrowly missing him. The next moment was a blur, a loud crash echoed through the house as the man tumbled head first down the stairs, his gun clattering to the floor beside him. He lay there, dazed, wearing a tee shirt and jeans that were only half pulled up, with no socks or shoes on his feet.

The woman was hysterical, her voice cracking as she shouted "you bloody bastards have killed him!"

Andrew knelt beside the man, checking his pulse—it was steady but blood gushed from a head wound. Acting quickly, he noticed a door, dashed through it and grabbed some kitchen towels to staunch the bleeding. As he wrapped the man's head, he spotted the gun on the floor and swiftly kicked it under a cabinet.

Meanwhile, Gino was trying to console the woman, who continued to scream and curse. "I'll dial 999," Gino said, his voice steady despite the chaos.

"Yes, call them now, Gino! You have the postcode and street name," Andrew urged.

Gino got through quickly and conveyed the urgency of the situation—a man lying unconscious at the bottom of the stairs. He relayed to Andrew that the ambulances and police were on their way.

Suddenly, a thunderous crash echoed as the door burst open and the two Manchester detectives, Dave and Asrov, stormed in. "Okay guys, what's going on here?" Dave demanded.

Andrew and Gino stared in disbelief. "How are you here already? Gino only called 999 a minute ago!"

"When you phoned our chief earlier you left a message with this postcode. He was concerned for your safety and suspected you had the wrong code.

He ordered us to follow you, so we picked you up on our radar and kept a distance. We've been tailing you for the last five miles. You guys should use your wing mirrors more!" Asrov explained with a smirk.

Andrew and Gino exchanged looks of astonishment, trying to process the rapid turn of events.

"Well, you guys have really helped us," DI Dave said, his voice filled with a mix of relief and urgency. This is someone we've been looking for. We heard a gunshot. Who got lucky?" Dave asked.

"Me," Gino replied, breathless. " The bullet went right over my shoulder."

DI Dave turned to Asrov. "Keep hold of the woman," he instructed, nodding towards the captive, who was still screaming obscenities. Then, pulling Andrew and Gino aside into the kitchen, he lowered his voice. "I need to have a word with you two and she mustn't hear us."

As the kitchen door closed, Dave spoke quickly. "Listen, guys, you need to disappear quick. This is our territory and our Chief wouldn't want you here. Leave this to us."

The wail of sirens grew louder, urgency creeping into Dave's tone. "Go out the back door. There's a gate leading to the alley. Turn right, then another right past the block of six terraces and you'll be close to your old Ford.

We saw where you parked." He paused, making sure they understood. "Walk out slowly, don't run. There's always someone with a phone ready to snap a photo and sell it to the newspapers or a TV channel.

When you get back to the synagogue and they give you the correct postcode, don't forget to call or text Chief Alan Edwards.

He'll want to know where you are. I'm sure he'll be on the phone to your boss, Simon, soon enough."

"That's fine Dave ,thanks. We'll call you later."

As they stepped out of the back door, rain and sleet pelted down. They turned up their collars and slipped through the back gate into the alleyway.

Suddenly, the gate next door flew open. A man burst out, wearing white trainers, a black coat, trousers, and a black hood. He carried a blue kit bag and a large holdall, shoving his way through while shouting, "get out of my bloody way!' He turned left as Andrew and Gino turned right.

"Should we chase after him, Andrew?" asked Gino.

"No, definitely not, Gino. As Dave said, it's not our patch and we wouldn't catch him anyway. Once we're back in the car, I'll call him. We need to get away quickly before the local police start asking questions."

Andrew and Gino maintained a steady pace along the alleyway, turned right and spotted their car. As they approached, the doors unlocked and they quickly got in. Gino drove while Andrew entered the synagogue's postcode into the satnav.

"Let's hope Rabbi Zacharies Baeck or Eliana are around now,"Andrew said, settling into his seat as they sped away.

Andrew dialled DI Dave's mobile but it went straight to voicemail. He left a detailed message about their departure and described the man who had dashed out of the neighbour's gate, turning left and sprinting away. Andrew provided a full description of the man and asked Dave to call back if he needed any further information.

Gino drove expertly, though they encountered a minor delay, arriving about an hour and fifteen minutes later. As they circled to the rear car park at the synagogue, they spotted two cars.

"That's a good sign," Gino remarked. "Looks like someone's here." Gino parked next to a Fiat car and they made their way to the large weathered wooden front door. When they knocked, a man in a long black coat answered.

"Hello, 'Shalom' how can I help you?" he asked. "I'm Chief Rabbi Zacharies Baeck of this synagogue."

"I'm Detective Andrew Brown and this is my colleague Detective Gino Fernandez," Andrew introduced both. "We called earlier this morning, and a young girl named Emma gave us a postcode for the address of a man we're looking for. She said his name is Ahmadi Levy."

"Yes, of course, please come in," Rabbi Baeck replied, stepping aside. "Emma mentioned you called this morning. I apologise for missing you; I had to visit one of my congregation members who is very sick, and Eliana had her car stolen last night. Have you visited the house where Ahmadi Levy is lodging? Emma gave you a postcode and the street number?"

"Yes, sir," Andrew replied, " but unfortunately, it was incorrect, and we ended up at the wrong address."

"Oh dear, I am very sorry to hear that," the Rabbi said, sighing. "We do have a bit of a problem with Emma. She is very dyslexic, although she is incredibly keen to help people."

"Can you show me the postcode she gave you?"

"Yes," replied Gino, pulling a slip of paper from his pocket. "It's M16 17SE, 15 Stocking Street."

"That doesn't seem right," the Rabbi said. "Give me a few minutes to find Eliana's file. We've been quite concerned about Ahmadi.

He's missed several of our prayer meetings lately," the Rabbi remarked "In fact, we were discussing him, only yesterday."

Suddenly, the door burst open, and a woman hurried in, breathless and wide-eyed.

"Hello, Eliana! I'm sorry to hear about your car. Have the police found it yet, or has the insurance company given you a replacement?"

"Yes, they have," Eliana replied, a slight smile breaking through her worry. "I've got a nice Mini from the insurance company. The police called this morning to say they found my car on a disused building site, completely burnt out."

"That must have been a shock for you, Eliana," the Rabbi said, his voice full of concern.

"Yes, Rabbi, it was. When I looked out of my window this morning and saw it was gone, I couldn't believe it."

Before the Rabbi could respond, he caught sight of the two men in sharp suits standing at the entrance. "Oh Eliana, I should introduce you to the two detectives from London. Detective Andrew Brown and Detective Gino Fernandez, is that correct, gentlemen?"

"Yes, sir," Andrew replied, a note of determination in his voice. "We're here to get to the bottom of this."

"Did Emma give you the address for Ahmadi Levy?" Eliana inquired.

"Yes, she did," Andrew replied, "on a crumpled piece of paper. She scribbled it down for us before we left, but unfortunately, it was incorrect. We had to come back and I handed it to your Rabbi. He's checking the address files now."

Eliana nodded thoughtfully. "I have the address over here. I didn't pull out the file earlier because I wasn't sure when you would arrive."

She glanced at the paper Emma had written on and shook her head. "I can see the mistake. Emma wrote M16 17SE 15 Stocking Street, but it should be M61 17ES 51 Stockley Street."

Eliana sighed, a note of apology in her voice. "I'm really sorry for the mix-up. Did our Rabbi mention that Emma has dyslexia? I hope it wasn't too much of an inconvenience."

Andrew smiled warmly, waving off her concern. "Don't worry about it, Eliana. We understand completely. And may we call call you Eliana?"

"Of course, please do," she replied with a warm smile.

"Before we set off, would you both please take a look at this photo?" Gino asked, holding up an image of a man."This is who we've been searching for. Note any peculiarities you can remember about him."

Eliana and Rabbi Baeck leaned in to examine the picture. Almost simultaneously, they exclaimed, "Yes, that's definitely him, one hundred percent! We always thought he was a bit odd. He wore open-toed sandals with no socks, his trousers were short below the knee, and he frequently missed our prayer meetings."

Andrew and Gino exchanged knowing glances, their suspicions confirmed. "How long had he been a member of your congregation?" Andrew inquired. "About eight weeks," Eliana replied, "but we haven't seen him for over three weeks."

Suddenly, a loud knock echoed through the room, and Emma burst in, expertly balancing a tray laden with steaming coffee and a plate of special kichel biscuits. "I heard you talking and thought you might enjoy some coffee before you leave. I'm really sorry about giving you the wrong address. I hope it didn't cause too much trouble."

Gino's face lit up with a warm smile as he shook his head. "No worries, Emma. It couldn't be helped. Besides, we got to see another side of Manchester. Thank you for the coffee and biscuits; they look delicious."

Andrew then turned to Eliana, his curiosity aroused. "So, where is Ahmadi lodging?"

Eliana replied, "He's been staying with Mrs Mary Gallagher. She runs a lovely accommodation where several of our members have stayed. It's a tall house with three bedrooms to let, fronted by a well-kept privet hedge.

We've been trying to reach her for the past three weeks, but she's been away in Sligo, Ireland, caring for her mother. I called two days ago when we knew you were coming, and one of her lodgers mentioned she's expected back today. You might be in luck."

"That's very helpful, thank you. We should get going," Gino said, rising from his chair. Both Gino and Andrew said"Shalom."

As they drove down the main street, deep in discussion about the day's events, they unanimously agreed, Ahmadi Levy was the man they had been searching for. "Let's hope Mrs Gallagher is at home," Gino mused, "so we can have a chat with her. Then we can wrap things up and head home."

"We need to update Zoe and try to speak with DI Dave Robinson first," Andrew added. "She needs to keep our boss Simon informed before Chief Constable Alan Edwards calls him."

They were almost at the lodging house when Andrew suggested they call both Zoe and D I Robinson later with all the details.

He discreetly entered the code 1-5 on the codex, as they turned the corner and they arrived at 51 Stockley Street.

"This looks like a nice place," Gino remarked, admiring the clean and tidy exterior. "Much better than I expected." As they were about to get out, a taxi pulled up, and a lady with a suitcase stepped out. "This could be the woman we need to see," Gino said, looking towards her.

"Yes, Gino, let's go introduce ourselves," Andrew agreed.

"Hi," Andrew greeted her warmly. "Can we help you with your case? Are you Mrs Mary Gallagher?"

"Yes, thank you,"she replied with a weary smile. "I've had a hectic journey back from Ireland, and yes, I am Mary Gallagher. I'll get the door open; if you could leave the suitcase in the hall, we can talk. I can tell you're not from around here. Are you looking to book a room? I have one spare at the moment."

Gino picked up the case, and they made their way into the hall. Showing their warrant cards, they introduced themselves to Mrs Gallagher and explained their purpose.

"We'd like to ask you about Ahmadi Levy," Gino began. "We've already spoken with Rabbi Baeck and the administrator, Eliana Gella, at the synagogue. They provided us with quite a bit of information. Would you mind answering a few questions?"

Mrs Gallagher said "yes ,no problem," and Gino continued, "First, we need you to confirm if this is Ahmadi Levy." He handed her a photo.

Without hesitation, Mrs Gallagher responded, "Yes, that's him for sure. He had a rugged face, always wore sandals, and his trousers were perpetually short."

Her expression soured as she added, "When you catch up with him, let him know he owes me £800. The scoundrel disappeared without paying his rent. On the day he left, he handed me a large envelope, thanked me, and loaded his hefty holdall into a waiting van. He played a dirty trick on me. The van sped off, leaving a cloud of dust in its wake. My hands trembled as I tore open the envelope, only to find it filled with shredded newspaper clippings."

"What a rotten trick," Gino said, shaking his head. "Do you still have any of the pieces?"

Andrew exchanged a knowing glance with Gino, recalling the incident vividly.

"Yes, I kept a few pieces in the drawer. I put most of them in the bin. I'll check later. But first, come into the kitchen. How about a cup of coffee or tea?"

"Coffee, please," they both replied in unison.

"Okay, what do you need to know?"

"How long was he lodging with you?" Andrew asked, his voice serious.

"Did he leave a forwarding address?

How did he get along with the other lodgers?

Did you ever suspect he wasn't who he claimed to be?"

"And about the van," Gino added, "did you notice the driver or any markings on the vehicle?"

Mrs Gallagher thought thoughtfully. "I can answer all your questions. Let's get those drinks first. Coffee, okay?"

"Yes, coffee please ," they confirmed. Mrs Gallagher went into the kitchen, the aroma of brewing coffee soon filling the air as they prepared for a revealing conversation.

After Mrs. Gallagher brought in the drinks, she began answering the detective's questions with a weary sigh.

"He lodged with me for nearly nine weeks," she said, "but he left about three weeks ago. He didn't leave a forwarding address. Mentioned he might head to South London, but after not paying me, I don't know if I should believe him."

"Did he interact much with the other tenants?" one of the detectives asked again. "Not really. He was out every day. According to Eliana, he wasn't at the synagogue much. I didn't see him often myself—I've been over to Ireland quite a bit. To be honest, I didn't like talking to him. I even wondered if he was truly Jewish. I overheard him shouting on his phone a lot, and it sounded more like Arabic.

We had an Arab staying here for a long time, so I picked up some of the language."

"What about the van driver?" Andrew and Gino inquired.

"Yes, The driver was probably from the Middle East. I've seen him before. He had Express Removals printed on his blue overalls and on the back of the van."

Andrew and Gino exchanged astonished glances. This was more information than they had anticipated.

"Thank you for your answers, Mrs Gallagher," Andrew said. "If you could let us have the shredded newspaper, clippings we'll be on our way."

It didn't take long for them to gather the cuttings and get up to leave.

"Will you let me know when you catch him?" Mrs Gallagher asked, a hint of concern in her voice.

"We will," Gino assured her, and with that, they left her small, cluttered apartment, each pondering the puzzle pieces they had been given.

Andrew and Gino were sitting in the car, their minds buzzing with the latest revelation. "Well," Gino said, shaking his head in disbelief, "I never expected he would have a connection with Express Removals! We'd better call Zoe before we head home."

"Yes," Andrew replied, "but first, I'll call Rabbi Baeck and Eliana and then DI Dave Robinson and his chief, Alan Edwards."

Eliana picked up almost immediately. "We promised to confirm to you and Rabbi Baeck that he was the man we were interested in," Andrew began. "We also met Mrs Gallagher as she returned from Ireland. She told us he's heading to London and won't be coming back to your synagogue."

"Thank you for the update," Eliana said with relief.

"Please tell Emma not to worry—everything has worked out okay" Andrew assured her.

As Andrew was about to call Zoe, his phone rang. It was DI Dave Robinson. "Hi guys, where are you? Have you found the correct address yet? Any information on the guy you were looking for?"

"Yes, Dave," Andrew said, feeling a surge of triumph. "We visited the correct postcode—M61 17ES 51 Stockley Street, not M16 17SE 15 Stocking Street. The girl who gave us the address has dyslexia, so it wasn't her fault. It all worked out in the end, and we got a lot of useful information to help us when we get back."

CHAPTER FOUR

Gino glanced at Andrew with a knowing smile. "Looks like everything's finally falling into place," he said, his voice tinged with satisfaction.

Andrew nodded. "Yeah, it sure does."

Dave said "Well, guys, that's great news. I'll let our Chief, Alan Edwards know. He's actually been here to see what we've discovered."

Andrew raised an eyebrow, curiosity aroused. "Oh, what did you find, Dave? It must have been important for him to come out. And what about the guy who was unconscious on the floor and the hysterical woman?"

"When the ambulances arrived the medics treated his head wound. Once he regained consciousness, we handcuffed both of them. They're now locked up in a cell at our station," Dave explained, a hint of pride in his voice.

"The Chief was worried about Gino. Narrowly missing a bullet. Is he okay?" Dave asked, glancing at his partner with concern. Andrew replied."Yes, Gino's fine. But you still haven't explained why your Chief was there."

Dave was lowering his voice to a conspiratorial whisper. "I can tell you, but it has to stay between us. Our Chief Alan Edwards doesn't want this getting out to any TV news channels or newspapers. You were given the wrong address. Not only did we arrest two criminals dealing in guns and drugs, but we also stumbled upon something much bigger.

You won't believe what we uncovered: 40 guns and 300 rounds of ammunition. And not just any guns—these were 9mm Smith & Wesson and Glock 20, two of the most powerful handguns on the market. But that was only the beginning.

A strong smell of cocaine led us to the loft, where we found bags upon bags of the stuff. As if that wasn't enough, a hidden door revealed even more bags in the house next door. We estimated the haul to be worth a staggering £3.5 million. We were in shock; we'd been chasing this stockpile for months."

"Crikey, all that because of us!" Andrew laughed, astonished. "No wonder that guy from next door came running past us. Have you managed to catch him?"

"Not yet, Andrew. Thanks to the description you provided, we picked him up on CCTV near the bus station. We've got officers checking all the buses that left around that time.

By the way, Andrew our Chief has spoken with your boss, Simon Harris. So when you talk to or see him next, he'll already be aware of what happened here." "Thanks for the info, Dave. We're on our way home now. Is it alright if we contact you in a few days for an update?"

"Sure thing, guys. Have a safe trip home. And don't forget to use your wing mirrors—you never know who might be following you!"

Andrew and Gino exchanged a glance and replied in unison, "we definitely don't want to make that mistake again."

"Okay, Gino. Let's get going. You drive first, and we'll switch at a service station when we stop for something to eat. I'll call Zoe and give her the latest news. It's about 200 miles, so it should take us around five hours."

After a few miles, before he had phoned her, Zoe rang them. "What did you find out about our man?" Zoe asked.

"It's all good news, Zoe," Andrew replied, we've cracked it, he is our man. "After we went back to the synagogue and got the correct postcode, we headed to the guest house where he'd been staying for nearly nine weeks. Turns out, he left about three weeks ago without leaving a forwarding address.

But here's where it gets interesting—he mentioned heading to South London." "What !" said Zoe

"The guest house owner, Mrs Gallagher, shared a juicy piece of information. You won't believe this, he was picked up by a van with Express Removals painted on the back. The driver, a Middle Eastern guy, even had Express Removals printed on his back. And get this—the guy we're looking for, he had this peculiar look, wearing open-toe sandals with his trousers rolled halfway up his legs."

Zoe's eyes widened. "Seriously? What's his name?"

"Ahmadi Levy," he answered. "But Mrs Gallagher is convinced he's not actually Jewish. She thinks he's more likely from Iran or Iraq. He didn't attend many prayer meetings at the synagogue and was always shouting on his mobile phone."

Zoe, thinking back, processing the information. said "Interesting, very interesting."

"Alright guys, Simon filled me in on the mix-up with the post code. How are you holding up, Gino?" Zoe inquired with genuine concern. Gino gave a reassuring reply. "I'm fine, thanks, Zoe." "Great to hear that, Gino. We have a lot to discuss. I might have some information on the guy who planted the bomb on the train for you to follow up ," Zoe said, with determination.

"Any word from your retired S D I in Brighton about those scripts? Has he managed to decipher them yet?" she continued.

"He promised to call me tonight, so fingers crossed he'll have some answers," Andrew replied, glancing at his watch.

"That's promising. Have a safe ride back, and we'll meet at 8:30 tomorrow morning at City Hall," Zoe instructed.

"That's fine with us, see you in the morning, Zoe," Andrew and Gino said before heading off.

As they cruised down the M6, Andrew suggested, "If we stop at the service station before the M1, we can get a bite to eat. Then I will take over driving."

They chatted about the bomb on the train, speculating on Zoe's potential lead. "We'll find out tomorrow, Gino. What do you think? Could it be a young lad or an older person?" Andrew mused.

"I'd bet on a young lad with a grudge against the London underground," Gino replied thoughtfully.

"You might be right, Gino."

Pulling into the service station, they quickly purchased coffee and burgers and were on the road again, their thoughts swirling with the day's revelations as they headed home.

The traffic was surprisingly light, allowing Andrew and Gino to make excellent time. Before long, Andrew navigated around the M25 and out to West Brompton to drop Gino off. Both men felt a wave of relief to be home.

"Cheerio, and remember, don't mention that close call with the bullet to Sophia," Andrew reminded him with a knowing smile.

"No worries, Andrew," Gino chuckled. "I'll keep it under wraps. Lucky it didn't ruin my nice suit." They shared a hearty laugh before parting ways.

Andrew then headed to his Hammersmith apartment. After securing his car in the garage, he caught a bus home. Chloe greeted him warmly as he stepped through the door.

"I'm so glad you're back!" she exclaimed. "Dimitris

won't sleep until he knows you're here. Could you go up and say goodnight to him?"

"Of course, Chloe. I'd never miss a chance to see our lovely boy," Andrew replied, heading upstairs.

Once Dimitris was sound asleep, Andrew and Chloe settled down for an evening meal. As they ate, Chloe's curiosity got the better of her.

"So, how did things go in Birmingham and Manchester?" she inquired.

Andrew, bound by confidentiality, could only share limited details. However, he recounted their Birmingham visit, particularly their encounter with two men heading to Brighton to get married. Gino's reaction to the situation priceless, and Chloe, having spent a significant amount of time in Brighton herself, laughed out loud.

"Oh, Gino!" she giggled. "Brighton does have that effect on people."

As they finished dinner and Chloe was enjoying her wine, the phone rang, cutting through the relaxed atmosphere. Chloe picked up, recognising the number immediately.

"Hello, Harry," she greeted warmly. But before Harry could respond, Chloe cut in, her curiosity getting the better of her. "How's Mary doing?" Harry chuckled on the other end. "She's right here. Let me put her on."

For the next twenty minutes, Chloe chatted with Mary catching up on family news and exchanging stories. After they had finished, Harry turned his attention to Andrew, who was waiting patiently.

"Andrew, I think you'll be very interested in what I've discovered," Harry began, lowering his voice conspiratorially. "The man who's been reading those so-called scripts? I'm almost certain he's not Jewish. In fact, I suspect he's from Kurdistan.

The scripts are written in Kurdish, which is an Indo-Iranian language with various dialects spoken in the north mountainous regions of Iraq, Iran, and Turkey."

Andrew listened intrigued. "That's fascinating. What do the scripts say?"

Harry's tone grew serious. "I'll email my interpretation to you. It's not pleasant reading. The scripts talk a lot about killing people from other countries. For security reasons, I'll send it to your police email. When you're free, or even during a meeting, give me a call, and we can discuss it in detail with your superiors."

Andrew agreed, appreciating the discretion. "Thanks Harry that's invaluable information. We'll definitely need to follow up on this. How about we arrange for you and Mary to visit us for a weekend before Christmas? We could catch a match on Saturday, and you might even end up babysitting!"

Harry laughed, a warm sound that broke the tension. "That sounds like a plan, Andrew. We'll make it happen."

As Andrew hung up the phone, he joined Chloe , her eyes sparkling with the excitement of the conversation. "So, what did I miss?" she asked playfully.

Andrew grinned. "Only another day of unravelling mysteries, Chloe. Only another day."

The next morning, Andrew and Gino met up at their usual spot, the City Hall Café, at 8 a.m. As always, they were early. Andrew, brimming with curiosity, was eager to know how Sophia and Gino's family were doing and whether Gino had managed to keep their trip to Birmingham and Manchester under wraps.

"How's Sophia?"Andrew asked. Gino grinned. "She's fine. I didn't let slip anything about the shooting. She was more interested in the weather, actually. You know how hard it is for me to keep quiet about our plans."

Andrew chuckled. "Yeah, I get it. How about Chloe?" Gino asked.

"She was fine Gino, she didn't ask many questions.

We had a call from retired SDI Harry Salter. Chloe ended up talking to his wife, Mary, for a good twenty minutes. It gave me some time to speak with her later. I had already mentioned the two men in Birmingham, and she found it quite amusing."

Andrew noticed someone approaching. "Look, Zoe's here by herself. Let's head inside."

As they walked into the café, Zoe greeted both with a warm smile. "Hi, guys! Good to see you again. Let's find a table for four. Simon's going to join us soon. He got called into our Commander's office just as we were about to leave."

Gino quickly found a table and ordered three coffees. The café buzzed with morning energy, setting the perfect backdrop for their conversation.

"Alright, team, let's get started. First off, I'm incredibly relieved that Gino dodged a bullet, literally. How close was it, Gino?"

"Too close for comfort, Zoe. We never expected such a hostile reception. At least my best suit is intact," Gino replied with a wry smile.

"Simon said he had a lengthy chat with Alan Edwards, the Manchester Police Constable. Edwards was thrilled about the two arrests and the substantial haul of cocaine, guns, and ammunition.

Edwards mentioned the man who fled and brushed past you, Gino. He was genuinely concerned for your safety. He revealed that he could have ordered his detectives to intercept you before you reached the address, but he took a gamble and had them shadow you closely instead. You had no idea they were there, did you?"

"Not a clue," Gino admitted. "But it worked out well. We left it to them, considering it was their patch and they preferred handling it themselves."

"Well, after all your hard work, we finally know the identity of the man shot at Holborn underground station. He goes by Ahmadi Levy, though we're not sure if that's his real name. As I suspected, he was an imposter from the start."

"Have you had a call from your retired S D I in Brighton, Andrew?"

"Yes," Andrew replied. Before he could elaborate, Simon walked in.

"Hi, sorry I'm late. Matt asked me for a few minutes to make sure he had all the latest information on the cases we're working on. He went through all the iCloud files on <u>Operation</u> <u>Live Wire</u> and wanted me to tell you, Zoe, that he was very impressed with how clearly you and Val Mitchell had everything recorded. It was easy to understand."

Simon continued, "I reviewed a few files with him, and he's now up to date. He also asked me to check on you, Gino. He said you were lucky and is pleased with the outcome.

We finally know the identity of the man who was shot. Plus, he received valuable information from his TV news request about the two suspects.

Matt has promised to personally call Rabbis Ethan Bennouitz from London, Yosef Kahane from Birmingham, and Zacharies Baeck from Manchester to thank them for their co-operation and hospitality. So, Zoe, how far have we got with this meeting?"

"Well this is what I have obtained so far from the Manchester incident with detectives following Andrew and Gino, uncovering a significant stash of cocaine, guns, and ammunition.

Then once Andrew and Gino had the correct address, they unearthed the occupant's name, his residence there, and his abrupt departure in an Express Removals van. The files paint a clear picture."

"Yes, they're fine," Simon said, "though my mind lingers on the Express Removals van, possibly transporting Ahmadi Levy to South London. If that's accurate, it seems likely the shooter was from that very van. Sadly, we're short on leads. I'm planning to enlist the traffic police in South London for any sightings of vans marked Express Removals.

Andrew, did you hear from your old boss, the retired Senior Detective in Brighton?" Simon asked.

"I did. He called last night. I was starting to tell Zoe when you arrived. He's been digging into it and concluded that the suspect hails from Northern Kurdistan. The scripts found were in Kurdish, an Indo-Iranian language with various dialects spoken in the north mountainous regions of Iran, Iraq, and Turkey.

The scripts also mention plans to assassinate key figures from other countries. He wouldn't provide further details and requested to speak with either you, Simon, or our Commander, Matt Gibbons."

"Sure, Andrew. Give me his mobile number later, and I'll call him when I get back to my office."

"He also warned that, based on his experience, the area is very dangerous, and no one can be trusted. They have methods of infiltrating Europe, selling drugs and guns, and may be involved in extorting money from illegal immigrants by providing them with substandard small boats and dinghies.

Another point he mentioned was the Jewish man who was shot. He likely had a wallet, a train ticket and some cash on him. It's very probable that someone picked his pockets, so he suggested rechecking all the CCTV footage on the platform. Verify which entrance he used; there are two. Do the same for the Express Removals guy to see if they both used the same entrance. It might help determine if he was followed into the Holborn underground station."

"Thank you, Andrew. It was a brilliant idea to make contact with retired S D I Harry Salter. I hadn't known him, but when I mentioned his name to Commander Matt, he immediately recognised him and spoke highly of his skills as an S D I.

I'll update everyone once I've had a chance to speak with him.

Now, let's talk about our next steps. Given that we've now identified the man who was shot on the Holborn London underground station, I suggest we pause for a moment on this case. However, we're still at a dead end with the man and woman from the train. They've completely vanished, and we need to get a grip on this situation. This case might be bigger than we initially thought.

Why would a couple, dressed so impeccably and carrying such expensive luggage, leave the train with only their guns? Could the sudden stop of the train have forced them to disembark quickly, taking only what they could grab in the chaos?

We have a report in to follow up from a neighbour of a Mrs Murphy. The man we want to interview is lodging with her. We have a name. He is Oliver Jones who apparently worked for London underground and was dismissed for disruption and not following orders. He is a bit of a train geek who is probably in his late twenties. I understand he is on the top floor of her house in Wood Green and has a shed in the garden where he spends a lot of time.

So check him out and ask the local shops if they had any parcels for him to collect. When you have found out more about him call me and we will decide on arresting him on suspicion of bomb making and planting a bomb on a London underground train.

Be careful and don't take any risks. Is that clear, everyone?" "Yes, got it." "Zoe, do you have the address and postcode?" Andrew asked.

"Yes It's in Wood Green on the Piccadilly line and The postcode is N22 E77 Number 9 Holly Road.

I'm not sure how long it will take to get there, but you can find out easily." "Any questions?" Simon asked.

"No," they all replied.

Zoe's mobile phone rang. "Excuse me, I'll take this outside. It's my office."

"Okay," said Simon, "it's getting a bit noisy in here anyway."

Everyone noticed Zoe flapping her arms frantically, her face etched with concern. She burst into the room, exclaiming."You'll never believe this! My office got a call from Lewisham Police station. Apparently, on the morning of the underground shooting, around 5 :30 am., a bus driver from Bermondsey was cycling to Lewisham bus station along his usual route. He takes a shortcut through a disused builder's yard. As he neared a large skip, he saw a man struggling to push an enormous bag into it. The man was of Jewish appearance, he had a black hat which he described as a kippah, dark clothing short trousers and open-toe sandals. He's dressed the same as the man Ahmadi Levy who was shot on Holborn underground station.

He stopped to help, but the bag was extremely heavy. He asked the man what was inside, and the man casually replied, "oh, it's an old garden pergola."

When the bag was pushed into the skip, the bus driver got on his bike and made his way towards Lewisham bus station. Another figure left the scene in a van.

Early this morning, at 5:30 am, he was cycling once more. It was his first day back after a holiday in North Cyprus with his wife, and he had been blissfully unaware of any news since his departure.

When he got to the skip, a foul, putrid stench assaulted his senses, growing more unbearable with each breath. Alarmed, he detoured to the Lewisham Police station on his way to the bus station. The police responded swiftly, dispatching a patrol car to investigate the source of the unpleasant smell.

When the officers arrived and opened the bag in the skip, they were hit with the full force of the nauseating smell. Inside, they discovered a body. Unable to endure the stench any longer, they called for the forensic team, who quickly arrived and transferred the body to the mortuary.

Upon examining the corpse, the forensic team noted a grim detail: the victim had been shot in the back.

The police are deepening their investigation at the abandoned builder's yard, appealing to anyone who was in the area that morning for information.

They've already received a call from a man walking his dog who narrowly escaped being run over by a speeding white van.

When asked if he could remember the registration number, he apologised and said no, but mentioned that the van had Express Removals printed on the back.

So ! what do we make of that, and what's our next move, Simon? you've assigned Andrew and Gino to head to Wood Green, should I go to Lewisham?" "Yes, I think it's crucial you head to the Lewisham Police Station and the mortuary now. I suggest you contact the uniformed officer Brad Evans, who you worked with in Reading, and arrange for Tony Edwards to have an unmarked police car ready for you. Meanwhile, we'll let Andrew and Gino proceed to Wood Green. Is that okay with everyone?"

"Yes, Simon, that's fine," they all replied.

Andrew and Gino had left when Zoe sprang into action, making two crucial calls: one to arrange for a police car and another to contact PC Brad Evans.

"Gino, I think we should head over to my lock-up at the London Borough Market and change into something sharper," Andrew suggested. "We've got some nice black coats and hats there. After that, we can catch a bus to Hammersmith, pick up our car, and head over to Wood Green."

As they travelled, Gino turned to Andrew with a question that had been nagging him. "What do you make of that Express Removals van that keeps popping up?"

Andrew, lost in thought, took a moment before replying. "It's tricky to figure out the connection Gino. I'm confident that our investigation will uncover everything."

Gino nodded, satisfied. "Remember what I said about the guy we're checking out? I had a feeling he'd be a young lad with a grudge against the London underground."

"Looks like you were right, Gino," Andrew agreed, a hint of admiration in his voice.

They soon arrived at Borough Market, Andrew swiftly unlocked his storage unit. After a brief deliberation, Andrew proposed that they use fake moustaches to alter their appearances while they went around asking questions about their target.

"Good idea, Andrew," Gino agreed. Andrew picked a sleek black moustache, while Gino opted for a flamboyant ginger one.

Dressed in sharp coats and stylish hats, they perfected their disguises, exuding an air of sophistication and readiness for their mission. Andrew locked up the unit, and they boarded the bus to Hammersmith, their minds buzzing with anticipation and curiosity.

Upon arrival in Hammersmith, Andrew retrieved the car from the garage, and they set off. Gino had the postcode and sent the coordinates to Simon to inform him they were en route. Despite the slow-moving traffic, they pressed on and arrived at their destination.

The neighbourhood was charming, with abundant greenery and colourful flowers lining the streets. The road was lined with elegant, old, three-story suburban houses, each exuding a sense of history and charm.

They decided to drive past the target house and park further down the road, opting to walk back and scout the area more discreetly.

Andrew noticed a few shops on the corner and thought it might be a good place to start their inquiries. They headed there first. "Let's try this newsagent, Gino. We might get some information from Mr Sanjay Patel. I noticed the owner's name on the shopfront."

They both went in and had a look round, it was quite busy, two ladies were serving. When they got a chance they asked if they could have a word with the owner Mr Patel. "Yes of course," one of the assistants said, "I will fetch him for you."

Mr Patel came into the shop through a side door. "How can I help you?" he asked "and who are you? If you want me to buy more stock the answer is no." Andrew replied "we are police detectives, could we have a few words with you somewhere private please," and they both showed their police warrant cards. "Sure, follow me this way." Andrew and Gino followed Mr Patel through a couple of stock rooms to a large office at the rear.

"Please take a seat and I will see if I can help you," said Mr Patel.

"Thank you" replied Andrew, "we would like to find some information about a Mr Oliver Jones. He lives down Holly road at No 9, do you know him?'

"Yes, I know him." Mr Patel said with a nod. "He often chats with me when he's in the shop. He buys the Model Railways Magazine—12 issues a year. I always set one aside for him. He has a large train set at Mrs Joan Murphy's, the lady who owns Number 9, But he hasn't come in for this month's issue yet, which is unusual."

"Oh, that's interesting," replied Andrew. "Do you know if he worked for the railways? Also, have you had any parcels delivered here for his collection. I see you're an agent for U P S and D H L."

"He mentioned working shifts at Wood Green station," Mr Patel continued. "They seem to move him around a lot to other stations. He wants to be a line manager, but he hasn't said much about that lately. The last time we spoke, he seemed very angry about constantly moving between stations. Yes, he collects parcels here, and he's had a few in the last few months—some small but quite heavy."

Andrew thanked Mr Patel for his help and they left the shop.

"You're right Gino," Andrew agreed. "Maybe he keeps his model railway in a bedroom."

Determined to investigate further, they continued down the back of Holly Road and decided to look in the back of Number 9. As they turned into Holly Road, an older man walking by stopped them.

"Are you lost?" he asked, eyeing them suspiciously. "I saw you looking at the back of Number 9. We have a neighbourhood watch here because there have been a lot of break-ins. We have to be careful about who we let into our homes."

Andrew and Gino showed their warrant cards. "We're checking around the houses before we knock at Number 9."

The man's behaviour softened. "Oh, that's alright then. I know Joan Murphy very well. I do some odd jobs for her and cut her grass. She's a lovely lady. I'm planning to do a few jobs for her this afternoon. She's a bit deaf, so give the door a hard knock. It might help if you have your warrant cards ready to show her when she answers the door.

By the way, I'm Bob Clarke. I live here at Number 18"

"Thank you, Bob," they both replied.

"Alright, Gino, let's make our way to Mrs Joan Murphy at number 9 and see what we can find out about Oliver Jones," he said with determination.

As they approached the front door, Gino gave it a firm knock. With their warrant cards ready, just as Bob had suggested, they waited. The door soon creaked open, and they introduced themselves as police detectives, showing their warrant cards. "Good afternoon, ma'am, are you Mrs Joan Murphy?"

"My, that was quick!" she exclaimed, a look of surprise on her face. "I only phoned the police station about one hour ago. Please, come in."

She led them through the hallway to the drawing room. "Please, take a seat," she offered.

Andrew, ever the concerned detective, got straight to the point. "Is there a problem, Mrs Murphy? Why did you call the Police?"

"Yes," she replied, her voice tinged with worry. "It's about my lodger, Oliver Jones. He's been missing for four days. I've tried calling him, but it goes straight to voicemail. That's not like him at all! He always lets me know if he has to work at another train station. I'm really worried something has happened to him. He hasn't been himself lately—very moody, it's not like him at all."

"Okay, Mrs Murphy, let's gather a few details about him. How long has he been staying with you, and how old is he?" "About 18 months," she replied. "I'd say he's around 29-30 years old."

"Mr Patel at the corner news shop mentioned he's very keen on model railways. He said he kept a magazine aside for him and had received some parcels for him recently, is that corect?"

"Yes, that's correct. He loved his model train set and frequently collected parcels from the shop."

"Could you show us to his room, Mrs Murphy?"

"Yes, of course. Be careful on the stairs they're much narrower than in modern houses. This place was built pre-war in 1937. I was born here and have lived here all my life."

Gino replied, "that's interesting. I like old houses; my family home is quite old. Andrew lives in a very modern place."

Mrs Murphy led them to Oliver's rooms. They donned plastic gloves before taking a closer look around. The room was fairly tidy, except for a pile of train magazines in one corner.

Andrew rifled through the drawers and unearthed a scrapbook filled with intricate notes and calculations on bomb-making technology. His heart raced as he carefully placed it back and whispered to Gino about the alarming find.

They moved to the bedroom, scanning the room for anything unusual, but everything seemed in order.

"Mrs Murphy," Andrew began, "we expected to see Oliver's model train set. Wasn't it supposed to be in one of his rooms? And we didn't notice a shed in your garden either."

"Oh, yes," Mrs Murphy replied. "He used to keep it up here, but it grew too large. I suggested he should move it to the Anderson Shelter."

Andrew and Gino exchanged puzzled glances. "What's an Anderson Shelter?" they asked.

Mrs Murphy chuckled. "Sorry, you both are too young to know. They were designed to protect UK households during air raids in World War II. Everyone on this road had one, but most have been removed. A few of us, including my husband, decided to keep ours.

When you go down into one, they're quite spacious. My husband, being a builder, stored his ladders and decorating equipment there. If you look out of this window, you can see a hump in the grass and the steps leading to the door."

Andrew and Gino peered out, spotting the subtle rise in the ground and the faint outline of steps. The mystery deepened as they realised there was more to discover beneath the surface.

Andrew and Gino gazed out once more and exclaimed, "Yes, we can see more of it now! From the back, it was completely hidden. Could you let us have a look inside and see Oliver's model railway?"

"Of course! Let me go downstairs first."

They followed Mrs Murphy down the stairs and out to the garden. "It's open," she said, "The door lock is broken, but my friend Bob is coming up this afternoon to fix it."

"Yes, we met him earlier," Gino said.

"While you're in there, I'll make some coffee. Be careful where you step, it's very dark inside." "Thanks," they replied

As they descended the steps and opened the door, they were enveloped in darkness. Gino felt along the wall for a switch, but Andrew suddenly shouted, "Stop, Gino! I have a bad feeling about this place. Forget the switch; let's use our phone torch-lights."

Gino wrinkled his nose in disgust. "I can't stand the smell down here. It's foul, putrid."

The model railway dominated the centre of the room. As they approached the far end, both men screamed in shock.

"Oh my god, it's Oliver! He's dead, and he's all wired up with electric cables on his arms and head. He must have electrocuted himself. What are we going to do, Andrew?" Gino asked, his voice trembling.

"We need to get out of here quickly," Andrew said, taking charge. "Gino, shut the door. Let's talk to Mrs Murphy, but don't tell her too much about Oliver yet. I'll call Simon and explain the situation."

As they exited, Andrew wiped the door handle, thinking ahead to when the forensics team would arrive. It was best if their fingerprints weren't involved.

Once inside the house, Mrs Murphy called out, "The coffee's ready!" But as she saw their pale faces, her expression changed. "Is something wrong? You both look like you've seen a ghost!"

Andrew helped her to a chair, his voice gentle yet serious. "Mrs Murphy, I'm sorry to tell you, but we found Oliver. He's dead."

"Oh no, oh no!" she cried, bursting into tears. "He was such a nice, quiet lad."

"Mrs Murphy, please listen," Andrew said gently but firmly. "We need to call the police and get an ambulance. It might be best for you to stay with a friend or a carer until the police give you the okay to return home. Do you have anyone nearby you can stay with?"

"I suppose I could go down the road and stay with Bob," Mrs Murphy replied, her voice trembling.

"That's a good idea," Andrew said. "Let Gino walk you there. He can explain the situation to Bob Clarke."

Still in tears, Mrs Murphy nodded. "I'll get my bag and keys. Andrew turned to Gino and whispered, "Don't tell Bob too much about how we found Oliver.

Gino nodded, helping Mrs Murphy to the footpath. They walked to Bob's house at number 18. Bob was surprised when he opened the door. "Can we come in?" Gino asked. Before Gino could explain, Bob ushered Mrs Murphy inside. "What's the matter, Joan? You look dreadful. Come, sit down. I'll get you a drink."

Gino followed Bob into the kitchen. "I need to tell you what happened, Bob, but you must keep this quiet. No one can know until the police finish their investigation.

When we stepped into the Anderson Shelter to inspect Oliver's model railway, we were met with a shocking sight: Oliver was inside, lifeless. It seemed he had been there for several days.

Mrs Murphy broke down in tears, so we asked if she would like to come and stay with you while the police and ambulance were here. She thought you wouldn't mind, so I walked down with her."

"Oh I 'm really sorry to hear that. It's very strange you should find him; I was planning to go up there this afternoon to fit a new lock on the door."

"Are you sure Mrs Murphy will be okay to stay with you, Bob? It may take a few hours. Is it alright to call you Bob?"

"Yes, of course, that's fine. I can look after her. It might be better if I'm with her when the police interview her, she might find it difficult to answer questions. She thought a lot of Oliver, though he had changed in the last few weeks—he was more pensive, something was deeply worrying him."

"Thank you, Bob. I can hear the sirens of the police cars and ambulance, so I need to head back to Mrs Murphy's house."

As Gino left, he saw two police cars and an ambulance parked outside. He approached Andrew and asked, "what did Simon say about all this?"

Andrew explained, "Simon was quick to make all the calls. We have a police car from Wood Green, another from Southgate, and an ambulance. We need to wait until the bomb squad arrives and clears the area for entry. I mentioned the exposed electrical cables, and both the police and medics agreed to wait. They should be here soon."

Gino glanced out and saw the bomb squad pulling into the driveway. The squad members jumped out and began putting on their protective gear.

One of the bomb squad engineers entered the house and asked, "who knows what the main problem is?"

Andrew stepped forward. "I'll show you to the Anderson World War II shelter. Oliver is inside with all the electrical wires everywhere, he might have been dead for a few days.

We didn't turn on the light switch we used our phone torches instead."

"Hey! Don't I know you two? Weren't you both at the Neasden Train Repair Depot when we were investigating the bomb on the tube train? You look different!"

Andrew replied, "Yes, you're right," and they showed him again their warrant cards.

The Chief Bomb Squad Engineer took one look at the light switch, his face turning pale. "Everyone, keep clear and get out of the house!" he shouted. "Police, please go and knock on all he neighbouring houses and tell all the residents to evacuate to the street." He pointed at the light switch. "This is wired to a large bomb!"

The police sprang into action, knocking on doors and urging residents to evacuate immediately. The ambulance medics returned to their vehicle, waiting for further instructions.

About 45 minutes later, the Chief Bomb Squad Engineer emerged, looking relieved. "It's all clear now," he announced. "Sorry for the delay, it took longer than expected to defuse the bomb. Medics, you can go in now and remove the body to take it to the hospital mortuary"

The police then went to find the residents to inform them it was all clear now and they could return to their houses.

A Police sergeant questioned Andrew and Gino about the whereabouts of the lady who owned the house. Gino responded, "I took her down to a friend, Mr. Bob Clarke, at number 18."

"Thanks, guys. We'll go down to have a word with her," the sergeant replied.

Meanwhile, the chief bomb squad engineer informed them that his team would remove all the copper wire, timers, and chemicals. He didn't share his name with anyone, which puzzled Gino. Andrew explained it was a security procedure as before.

Andrew then inquired if they needed to stay any longer.

"No, it's okay for you guys to go now. You were certainly spot on by not turning on that light switch. If you had, you wouldn't be here now—you'd be sky-high!" the chief bomb squad engineer said with a mix of relief and admiration.

"I know your boss, Simon Harris, well. As I told you when we were at Neasden, we've helped each other out on many occasions. I'll text him my report. Let's hope there won't be a third time we meet!'

Andrew and Gino nodded in agreement. "Yes, we hope so too."

As they left, they noticed the ambulance pulling away and the forensic team arrive.

Andrew made a quick call to Simon to update him on the latest developments. Simon replied. "I have spoken with the chief engineer of the bomb squad. He has sent over his report to me. You two were incredibly lucky—you could have been blown sky high!

I also called the police sergeant," Simon continued. "He provided a full report, which I'll forward to Zoe, for Val to upload to iCloud on our <u>Operation Live Wire</u> file. Let's see what Commander Matt has to say when he reads it."

As the day wore on, Simon noted the time. "It's getting late, and it's Friday. Let's all call it a day and you should go home now. We'll meet at our usual spot, City Hall, at 8:30 on Monday morning."

"Sounds good to us," Andrew replied. "By the way, how did Zoe get on in Lewisham?"

"I spoke with her," Simon said. "She interviewed the bus driver and checked out the disused building site and the skip. She couldn't access the mortuary yet, but she's hoping to get in early next week. The guy who reported the Express Removals van is on holiday for a few days, so she'll follow up with him when he's back. Val has uploaded all her reports to our <u>Operation Live Wire</u> file. Considering what happened to you two today, it's a suitable name.

Okay, guys, have a great weekend. See you Monday morning."

"Fine with us, Simon," they both agreed.

Gino glanced over at Andrew, his stomach growling. "Hey, can you keep an eye out for a McDonald's drive-through? I'm starving." Andrew nodded enthusiastically. "Good idea, Gino. I'm hungry too."

Not long after, a familiar large golden M appeared in the distance. They pulled in and Andrew chuckled. "We should take off these fake moustaches, We don't want ketchup and mustard all over them!"

They both laughed heartily, the tension of the day beginning to dissipate. Andrew sighed, "It's good to laugh, We were almost blown to pieces back there."

Gino nodded, his expression serious. "Yeah, Andrew, you saved both our lives. If we hadn't been there today it would've been Bob Clarke, when he went to put a new lock on the door."

"Christ, you're right," Andrew said, shaking his head in disbelief. "Why would Oliver want to make a bomb and set it to blow himself up?"

Gino shrugged, a sombre look on his face. I don't think we will ever know Andrew.

Andrew suggested that Gino drive to their lock-up at Borough Market so they could change back into their everyday clothes before heading to Hammersmith to lock the car in his garage and catch the bus back to their respective homes.

"No problem, Andrew," Gino replied. "Sounds good to me." "What are you doing over the weekend, Gino?" asked Andrew.

"Well, Sophia will be pleased we have the weekend off. We want to take our girls to the ice rink at Canary Wharf. They both love ice skating."

"Great, Gino. That sounds fun. It will be a few more years before our Dimitris can go skating. How about you, Gino, do you skate?" "No, Andrew. I tried, but I kept falling over.

What plans do you and Chloe have, Andrew?"

"I don't think we'll go far. We might take Dimitris for a walk down to Greenwich to see the Cutty Sark. He seems fascinated by its size. Maybe he'll join the Navy when he grows up."

They navigated through the busy traffic, swiftly, arriving at Borough Market with time to spare. After a quick change of clothes, they headed to

Hammersmith and caught the bus home. As they reached their stop, Gino got off first, calling back, "See you at 8 am on Monday, Andrew."

Andrew waved, replying, "It'll be interesting to see what Simon has planned for us next week." Gino grinned and shrugged. "Who knows?"

Andrew entered his house and called out, "Hi, I'm home, Chloe." From the lounge, Chloe's voice responded, "I'm in here! There's a news flash on LBC; you might want to see this."

Intrigued, Andrew joined Chloe, his eyes fixing on the television screen as the announcer relayed the latest news from British Rail. "A bomb exploded on a stationary train at the Neasden repair depot recently.

The Police have issued a statement. The suspect was found in an Anderson World War II bomb shelter in Wood Green, having electrocuted himself. The bomb squad was called in to defuse another bomb, and although the police had to evacuate the surrounding houses, no further explosions occurred."

"Well Andrew apparently the Anderson shelters were designed in 1938 and 1.5 million were distributed. A further 2.1 million were erected before the war ended in September 1945. Did you know that Andrew?"

"No Chloe I had never heard of them."

Chloe turned to Andrew, eyebrows raised. "What do you make of that news? "

Andrew exhaled slowly. "It sounds like the police did a very commendable job. I expect Simon will have a detailed report for our next meeting." He wished he could share the full story with Chloe, but some secrets had to remain hidden.

CHAPTER FIVE

As the clock struck 8 a.m., Andrew and Gino were already at City Hall early as usual.

"Hi Gino, how was your weekend?" Andrew asked, a curious glint in his eye.

Gino beamed. "It was fantastic, thanks! We went ice-skating at Canary Wharf. The girls dragged me onto the rink, and I only fell twice! It was a lot of fun."

"Glad to hear it, Gino! You'll be on TV in 'Dancing on Ice' next!" Andrew chuckled.

"I don't think so, Andrew," Gino laughed. "How about you? How was your weekend?"

"Pretty good," Andrew replied. "We took a walk along the Thames path to Greenwich. Dimitris loved it. When we got back, Chloe was on the phone with her mother, making arrangements for a Christmas holiday in Cyprus. Did Sophia mention the news about the guy who got electrocuted? He was a suspect in the underground train bombing."

"Yeah," Gino nodded, his expression serious. "She asked me about it, and it was hard not to mention we were there. "I know, Gino," Andrew said, his tone sombre. "I had the same problem."

Simon and Zoe arrived and they all went in and found a corner table. Gino ordered four coffees.

Simon was eager to get started. "Wow, guys! What a result! I never expected you would find the suspect so quickly and in such a dramatic fashion—electrocuted in a World War II bomb shelter. It's a good thing you were wise enough not to turn on that light switch. If you had, you would have been blown sky-high and wouldn't be here today. Your training at Hendon really paid off."

"Yes," Zoe said, agreeing. "I remember the electronics training. You did exactly what the training officers instructed—stay well away, use a mobile light, and never switch on the mains. Thank goodness you remembered. I have all your reports and the Chief Bomb Squad Engineer's notes ready for Val to put on file."

Simon continued."I've worked with him on many occasions related to defusing bombs. He's one of the best in the field."

Gino turned to Simon, a curious look in his eyes. "Simon, why didn't he share his name with anyone?"

Simon gave a wry smile. "It's part of the protocol. None of the Bomb Squad are allowed to disclose their identities."

Andrew nodded, leaning back in his chair. "I figured as much."

"Speaking of comments," Simon continued, "you two received quite a bit of praise. The forensics team is conducting a thorough search of Oliver's rooms and the World War II shelter now that it's secured. They uncovered a file on bomb-making, which Andrew found. They're sending me a copy for our records."

Simon paused, then added, "There are also three more small blue kit bags with those distinctive silver buckles, like the ones were found on the London underground train. He's got enough wire and chemicals to make two or three more bombs."

Gino sighed, running a hand through his hair. "Looks like we've got a lot more questions to answer and a mountain of investigating ahead of us."

"Yes" Simon said "take a note of the following.

1) What could have driven him to construct a bomb and place it on the Piccadilly line train, with a timer ominously set for 6 pm?

2) Why was 6 pm the chosen time? Was the intent for it to detonate then, as it eventually did the day after when the train was in the repair depot?

3) Did he stay on the train the entire journey, or did he slip off before it reached Holborn?

4) Who were the intended recipients of the additional two or three bombs he was planning to make?

5) Was he under pressure from a ruthless gang leader, who forced him into this deadly task?

6) What would drive him to such despair that he would take his own life, wiring a bomb to the World War II-era light switch.

We urgently need answers to all these questions to uncover the connection."

Simon's phone rang, interrupting the lively conversation. "Excuse me, guys, it's Matt. I'll take this outside," he said, stepping out of the room.

Moments later, Simon hurried back in, his face a mask of urgency. "I have to head back to the office for an urgent meeting. Have another coffee and stay here until I get back," he instructed.

Zoe raised an eyebrow as Simon left. "I wonder what that's all about. He made it sound serious."

About an hour later, Simon returned, looking visibly flustered. "Thanks for waiting, guys," he said, taking a deep breath. "Matt made a call to your retired S D I from Brighton. Andrew. He has uncovered a matter of critical importance to our country.

In the leather-bound book recovered from the imposter who was shot at Holborn underground station, three names were mentioned. These individuals are targeted for assassination. I can't reveal their names, but I can tell you one is a very prominent VI P, one is a member of Parliament and one is the British Ambassador currently representing our country in Iran.

He discovered that by locating four places where the letter 'S' appears in reverse, and three letters 'A ' they are upside down like a 'V' with a bar and he found two of the letter 'N' then a crucial clue was unveiled." Zoe, Gino, and Andrew exchanged alarmed glances. Zoe broke the silence. "Hence the word Assassination.

This is very serious, Simon. What's the next step?"

Simon, looking worried, replied, "It gets even worse, guys. Matt received a call from the forensic team at the Wood Green house. They found a small pad hidden in that World War II bomb shelter. It's confirmed to be the handwriting of Oliver Jones. The pad contains a list of three people—targets for assassination. The same three names are those in the book of the Jewish imposter who was shot in the back and fell in front of the train, right in front of you, Andrew."

They all looked flabbergasted. "How can that happen?" Andrew asked, bewildered.

"Well, it's a fact. Our Chief Matt and I had a crucial meeting with our Chief Metropolitan Commissioner. We had to lay out all the information we've gathered since day one. He agreed to speak with the three people involved and arrange 24-hour bodyguards for them.

While the threat level isn't considered high since the bomb maker took his own life, we still have to investigate who instructed him to make and plant the bombs.

Chief Matt Gibbons has proposed that you, Andrew and Gino, return to Wood Green to knock on a few more doors in Mrs Murphy's neighbourhood. You should also ask Mrs Murphy directly if she knows where Oliver Jones lived before moving in with her. If she provides any useful information, act immediately.

However, you need to tread lightly with Mrs Murphy. According to your report she's very upset, so a delicate approach is essential. As soon as you uncover anything that might help us identify who is behind the attempt to coerce Oliver Jones to assemble bombs, contact our Chief Matt Gibbons or myself immediately without delay.

Now we have uncovered a crucial connection—the same three names appearing, both in Oliver's notebook and in the records of the imposter Jewish man who was shot at London Holborn underground station. This discovery changes everything. Our immediate focus must be on this lead. I was about to assign you the task of tracking down the Express Removals van, but that will have to be put on hold.

I'm going to call Alan Edwards in Manchester to see if he can get his detectives, Dave Robinson and Asrov Khan, to assist us. I need them to comb through all the CCTV footage within a ten-mile radius of the house where our man, Ahmadi Levy, was staying. They owe us one after that post code mix-up led to the recovery of a stash of guns and bags of cocaine. This is our chance to take advantage of that favour.

Now, let's refocus on our discussion. Zoe, could you give us an update on the guy found in the Lewisham skip?"

Zoe double-checked her notes and began her report. "Okay, I headed over to Lewisham with Officer Brad Evans in an unmarked police car as instructed.

We thoroughly inspected the skip in the disused builder's yard. It still had our police blue tape around it, and the stench coming from the skip was horrendous.

I searched the area for any CCTV cameras and found three, all smashed to pieces. Next, we visited the house of the man who was almost hit by the Express Removals van while walking his dog. His wife informed us that he was away until Monday afternoon.

The forensic unit informed us that we wouldn't be able to see the body until later today. They did confirm that the victim was shot in the back.

I need to find out if it was the same calibre bullet from the same type of gun used at the London Holborn underground station.

When I asked about any identification on the victim, it was a surprise that there was none—no mobile phone, no wallet, exactly like the man who was shot at the London Holborn underground station."

"Alright, Zoe, I suggest you head over to Lewisham this afternoon. Take Brad Evans with you again and pick up another unmarked car. Keep us updated with your report."

Simon's phone buzzed urgently, cutting through the conversation. "Excuse me, I need to take this call," he said, stepping outside with a furrowed brow. When he returned moments later, his expression had darkened with concern.

"Let's move to that quiet corner," he whispered, his voice tense. "I have some very important news, and it needs to stay between us."

Once they were seated away from prying ears, Simon leaned in closer. "That was our Commander Matt on the line. He has received a call from the Prime Minister's Office—at 10 Downing Street. Matt's been urgently summoned to a security meeting this afternoon.

The Prime Minister, our Chief Metropolitan Commissioner, the head of Counter Terrorism and UK security, and the Chief of Parliament's security will all be there."

Simon paused, his eyes scanning the room. "The Prime Minister is seriously worried about the fact that a young man has used an old pre-war Anderson WW II shelter to build bombs. One of those bombs has already been planted on the London underground train. And now there's information that a VIP and a member of Parliament are under threat. The situation is critical, and the Prime Minister wants a full and thorough investigation—immediately."

"As a precaution, I need both of you to head to the armoury and pick up the body vests, the latest design pistols we have now in our armoury, and the clasps of ammunition we've set aside for you."

"Andrew, do you have a secure safe at your Hammersmith apartment?"

"Yes," Andrew confirmed. "It's a good size and well hidden."

"Perfect. Just make sure your guns and ammunition are locked up securely every night.

Right, I think we've covered everything. Zoe, go and collect your car and pick up Brad Evans, then go straight over to Lewisham. Andrew and Gino get to the armoury and then proceed to Wood Green. And remember—use your codex mobiles and keep me updated at all times. This is serious, and it could get dangerous."

Andrew, Gino, and Zoe all said "yes "in agreement, promising to stay cautious and keep him informed before they left the café. Tension was hanging in the air.

Gino and Andrew wasted no time, heading straight to the armoury to gear up. They quickly collected their firearms, ammunition, and bulletproof vests.

As they slipped on their old winter hooded coats, Gino remarked, "Glad we're sticking with these old coats. They're way more comfortable and less likely to draw attention."

Andrew nodded in agreement. "Definitely. But we should head over to the lock-up at London Borough Market and swap these hoodies for something a bit sharper. And don't forget the fake moustaches—we should blend in like we did before when we went to Wood Green. If Simon wants us heavily armed he must think there's a real chance of trouble."

"Yeah, I've been thinking the same,"Gino replied, his tone thoughtful. "Either he's heard something or just has a gut feeling something's kicking off."

As they finished up in the armoury Gino suggested, "let's buy a coffee and a sandwich to go, from the canteen before we head out." "Good idea," Andrew said. "What are you in the mood for?" "Ham and cheese works for me," Gino replied.

"Same here. I'll get two," Andrew said, already moving toward the canteen.

Later they caught a bus bound for the lock-up at Borough Market. Once there, they swapped their worn-out hoodies for something more presentable and slipped on their fake moustaches, blending in with the crowded city people.

"Gino, I've got an idea," Andrew said, his voice thoughtful. "We don't need to drive all the way to Wood Green. Let's take the Underground instead.

We can catch a train from London Bridge on the Piccadilly line. It'll give us a chance to check out Wood Green Station, figure out where Oliver Jones was working, and see what other stations he might've been assigned to."

"Brilliant thinking, Andrew," Gino replied, a grin spreading across his face. "It'll be a lot quicker too. Let's get moving."

After locking up the unit they headed straight for the station, as they were travelling by train. Gino was looking very curious. "Who do you reckon we should talk to once we get to Wood Green station?"

Andrew pondered for a moment before replying, "I'd suggest starting at the ticket office. We should ask for the works manager at the repair shop. They usually have a shed and a siding off the main line where they handle any necessary repairs. That's probably where we will get the info we need.

Then after that, Gino, if we don't get the answers we're looking for at the train station, I think our next move should be to check in with Bob Clarke at number 18. He might be able to shed some light on things. I mean, surely he would've noticed Oliver Jones having all that copper wire and those chemicals in that old Anderson WWII shelter. You'd think he'd have seen something when he was doing gardening work for Mrs. Joan Murphy, right?"

"Absolutely, Andrew. That seems highly likely. Who should we approach after that?"

"Let's talk to the neighbours, Gino—the ones at the back and the front of Mrs Murphy's house."

"Good plan, Andrew. We're just two stops away now, that was quick. What about Simon? Shouldn't we let him know we've arrived and took the train?"

"Of course, Gino. Send him the codex message and a text directly to his mobile."

"I'll do it as soon as we step off this train."

They arrived at Wood Green and Andrew immediately noticed the ticket office was still open. Seizing the opportunity, they approached the counter and requested to speak with someone privately. Showing their warrant cards, they explained that they needed to see the works manager in the repair shop.

The lady at the ticket office, eager to assist, said "of course," and led them through a side door. She guided them to a small, tucked-away room at the rear of the building. "If you don't mind waiting here, I'll call Mr Arthur Wilson. He'll be with you shortly," she offered with a polite smile.

"No problem at all," Andrew replied, appreciating her helpfulness. "Thank you."

After a few minutes the door creaked open and in walked a man clad in well-worn, greasy overalls. "Hello," he greeted, his voice rough but not unfriendly. "What can I do for you?"

Andrew and Gino simultaneously produced their warrant cards, the gravity of their visit evident.

"Mr Wilson," Andrew began, "we're hoping you can provide us with some information about Mr Oliver Jones. We understand he worked here under your supervision in maintenance.

I'm sure you've heard by now that he took his own life under tragic circumstances." "Yes" he said, his voice tinged with sorrow.

"It was deeply upsetting. He was so young—too young to feel that was his only option."

"We're trying to gather some information. Was he a good employee? How long had he been with you working at Wood Green station? Did he have many friends here? And do you know if anyone contacted him after his last shift?"

"I can answer all of that." Mr Wilson said, pausing to collect his thoughts. "He was a diligent worker, always committed to his duties. He'd been with us for about 18 months, mostly stationed here with me, though he was sometimes sent to other stations—a task he didn't much care for. He didn't have many friends here; he was something of a loner, really. A few colleagues might have spoken to him after his shift, but he kept to himself more often than not.

Now, about your last question—it's curious that you bring it up," he began, a hint of intrigue in his voice. "For the past six or seven weeks, there's been this man—dressed head-to-toe in black, riding a Harley Davidson motorcycle. He always wore a black helmet with a dark visor completely concealing his face. Every few days he'd be waiting for Oliver right outside the station entrance. They'd talk for quite a while, and I could tell it wasn't just small talk. The next day Oliver would be visibly on edge, not his usual self at all."

Andrew's eyes narrowed with interest. "Really? That's intriguing. Did you happen to overhear any of their conversations? Was the man on the motorcycle English?"

Mr Wilson hesitated, recalling the moment. "Well, last week, I was close enough to catch a bit of their exchange. To my surprise, the man wasn't English. If I had to guess, I'd say he was from Iran, Iraq, or somewhere in that region."

Andrew was very interested to hear this, sensing he might have more information. "Anything else come to mind that could help us track this guy down?"

"Yes, actually," he replied with certainty. "I'm almost positive he lives in the Ponders End area, in the borough of Enfield. I know that area well—my house isn't far from there. I've even seen him at a pub-restaurant by the River Lee. It's called The King's Head.

About two weeks ago, I saw him at the bar, having a drink, with his Harley Davidson motorcycle parked outside. He had chosen a seat by the window, and that's when a group of kids started messing with his H D jabbing it with sticks. I watched as he suddenly bolted out the door.

Whatever he said to those kids must have been terrifying because they scattered like leaves in a storm.

You wouldn't want to cross someone like him. If he's still around, he might be holed up in one of those four tower blocks, but with what happened to Oliver... who knows? He could have vanished into thin air by now. You'll have to ask around if you're keen to find him."

"Thanks for your help, Mr Wilson,"Andrew said gratefully. "Only one more question—do you happen to have a CCTV camera outside the front of the station? We need to check if it captured the number plate of the H D motorcycle he parked when he was talking to Oliver. We're in a bit of a hurry to get the details so we can run an ANPR—Automatic Number Plate Recognition."

Mr Wilson replied " Yes, we've got one out there. Speak to Sue Davies in the office; she should be able to help. If she's tied up and can't get to it today, tell her to give me a call. I'll sort things out and come down myself—though she won't let me near the place in these greasy overalls," he added with a wry smile.

With that, Mr Wilson headed back to his workshop.

Andrew turned to Gino with a sigh. "We've made a real mess of this by coming up here by train. Now we're stuck and can't even get over to Ponders End to track down this guy on his Harley Davidson motorcycle. Simon is going to give us hell for this!"

Andrew glanced at the train information screen. "There's a train arriving in a minute," he said quickly. "I'll catch it, change at Bank station, then go on the District line to Hammersmith. Once I get the car, I will get back here as fast as I can.

He turned, his mind already racing ahead. "While I'm doing that, could you check the CCTV footage with Sue Davies or Mr Wilson?

And if you can get a clear photo of the motorcycle's licence plate, have it run through the system. After that, go to Mrs Murphy's house. Actually, go to Bob Clarke first and ask how she is now."

"Got it, Andrew,"Gino replied. "I'll also pop into the corner shop and have another chat with Mr Patel. I'll ask if he knows where those parcels for Oliver Jones came from, and whether he ever noticed a guy on a Harley Davidson motorcycle talking to him, outside his shop."

"Good thinking, Gino! My train's pulling in now, so I'm off. Catch you later! And if anything comes up, don't hesitate to call me."

"Will do, Andrew. Take care, and I'll be in touch if I need anything," Gino replied as he watched Andrew disappear into the station platforms.

Gino then made his way to the station office, where he politely asked to speak with Sue Davies. A woman emerged, introducing herself as Sue, and asked how she could assist.

Showing his warrant card, Gino got straight to the point. "I need to review the CCTV footage from the front of the station. I'm looking for a man dressed in black on a Harley Davidson motorcycle He's been spotted here before."

Sue's eyes lit up with recognition. "Yes, I remember seeing him about 10 to 14 days ago. He was hanging around outside."

Gino was curious. "Was he waiting for someone?"

"Yes," Sue confirmed. "One of the guys from the repair shop was talking to him. I don't know him well but he's been working in the repair shop with Arthur Wilson.

Okay, let's get started rolling back for 10 -24, days it shouldn't take very long, we have new CCTV cameras on most stations now. We have had a lot of vandalism, we don't get any now," Before they started looking at the CCTV camera another lady bought in two mugs of tea. They both thanked her.

After about 30 minutes Sue shouted out."Yes,Yes, we have got him, look, sitting astride the motorcycle. I don't know much about motorcycles but that one looks very expensive." Gino said "It's a Harley Davidson they are top of the range, motorcycle. It probably cost a few thousand pounds.

Look that's the number plate AN 71 RAN. It's very clear. If I could take a photo of that on my mobile I can forward it to the ANPR Automatic Number Plate Recognition or it maybe IVRC International Vehicle Registration Code. It may not be a UK registration."

The atmosphere crackled with a mix of anticipation and excitement.

Gino expressed his gratitude to Sue Davies for her assistance with the CCTV, asking her to extend his thanks to Mr Wilson for the valuable information he provided. "I'm going to be busy now," Gino added with a hint of urgency, "but please also thank the kind lady who brought in the tea."

After he had put Mrs Joan Murphy of 9 Holly Road on his mobile location app, Gino quickly wrapped up the conversation and soon found himself strolling past the corner shop. As he glanced inside, he noticed Mr Patel very busy attending to a customer.

Patiently, Gino waited until Mr Patel finished the transaction. Once he had a moment, Gino approached and asked if he could spare a few minutes for a quick chat. Mr Patel, ever accommodating, called over one of his assistants to take his place.

"I hope you can help, Mr Patel. I have a few more questions to ask you about Oliver Jones,"

Mr Patel nodded, leaning back in his chair. "You mentioned in our previous call that you received some parcels for Oliver. Do you happen to remember who sent them?"

Again Mr Patel furrowed his brow in thought. "As far as I can recall, one of the packages was from Senza Group PLC."

"Senza Group, got it," Gino said, jotting down the name in his notebook.

Mr Patel continued, "there was a heavy box from Amazon. I remember it well because the box was damaged. I could see the contents inside—99.5% pure copper wire weight 4 kilo. When Oliver came to pick it up, I asked if he wanted me to return it since it was damaged, but he just smiled and said the wire was fine. He'd take it as it was."

Gino raised an eyebrow. "That's a lot of copper wire, for a model train set, isn't it?"

Mr Patel chuckled softly, recalling the moment. "I said the same thing to him, and he laughed. Told me he had a large train set."

Gino looked at his note, his curiosity aroused by what he'd heard. "One more question, Mr Patel—did you ever see a man outside your shop, dressed in black from head to toe? Black helmet, black visor, black leathers, sitting on an expensive motorcycle ?"

Mr Patel shook his head. "No, I can't say I've seen anyone like that."

Gino nodded. "Thank you, Mr Patel. You've been very helpful." His eyes wandered to the counter. "I see you have pasties and coffee. I'll take one of each, please."

Mr Patel smiled warmly. "Help yourself. No charge. Oh, and I still have Oliver's copy of *Model Railways Magazine.* Would you like to take it? It's paid for, and you can read it while you have your lunch."

Gino was pleasantly surprised by the offer. His stomach had been quietly reminding him it was lunchtime. He took a coffee, carefully selected a warm, flaky pasty, and picked up the magazine.

"Thanks again, Mr Patel," Gino said, genuinely grateful as he stepped out of the shop, the aroma of coffee and pastry mingling with the crisp air.

As Gino lounged on a bench outside the shop, he typed Senza Group PLC into Google. His eyes widened as the search results loaded—the company specialized in industrial polymers, chemicals, and even explosives. This wasn't the kind of business he had expected to stumble upon.

Without wasting a second, he dialled Andrew's number to check on his whereabouts.

Andrew picked up on the second ring. "Where are you?" Gino asked, cutting straight to the point.

"I'm about 20 minutes out," Andrew replied, a hint of frustration in his voice. "Got stuck in traffic. Honestly, I would've turned the blue lights on if I could."

Gino chuckled. "Yeah, you'd be here by now if you had. I managed to dig up quite a bit from Mr Patel," Gino continued, his tone more serious now. He quickly briefed Andrew on everything Mr Patel had revealed.

"Should I go ahead now and compile all this into a report for Zoe and Simon?" Gino asked.

"Definitely," Andrew responded. "Get it done and sent over in the next 15 minutes. I'll be closer to you by then. We can meet at Mrs Murphy's place afterward."

"Are you planning to drop in on Mr. Bob Clarke first?" Andrew added, "as I suggested."

"Yeah, I think it's a good idea." Gino replied, already considering his next move.

"Gino, make sure to ask him about Mrs Murphy, and see if he's noticed that guy on the Harley Davidson motorcycle. He might have more information that could help us."

"Got it, Andrew. I'm almost there. I'll check in with you in about 15 or 20 minutes."

Gino knocked on the door of Bob Clarke's house.

The door creaked open, and Bob's eyes widened in recognition. "Oh, you're one of the detectives. Please, come in."

"Hello, Mr Clarke. I hope you don't mind if I ask you a few more questions about Oliver—and I'm also curious about how Mrs Murphy is." "Of course, that's fine. Have a seat. I'll make us some coffee."

Moments later, Bob returned, setting down two steaming mugs. "So, how can I help you? And please, call me Bob."

"Thanks, Bob. I appreciate that," Gino replied.

"I was hoping you could tell me how Mrs Murphy is now. When did you last see her? And have you noticed a man dressed in black on a motorcycle hanging around outside her house?"

"Yes, I actually stopped by to check on her last night. She's still deeply shaken by Oliver's suicide. It really hit her hard—she thought of him as a son she never had.

We've been friends for about four years now, ever since my wife passed away. I took up part-time gardening to keep busy and look after several gardens in this street and the next.

I've noticed a motorcycle leaving Mrs Murphy's house a few times in the evening when I was out walking my dog. I assumed it belonged to one of Oliver's friends."

"Your dog's pretty quiet today Bob. Where is he? What's his name again? I can't quite remember," asked Gino.

Bob's face was etched with concern as he shared the news. "I used to call him Billy," he began, his voice heavy with emotion. "He passed away yesterday, and I can't help but miss him. We spent ten years together, you know. Every day, we'd go out for our walks, just the two of us." He paused, looking down. "I had him cremated, and his ashes now rest in the garden, where he loved to play."

"I'm really sorry to hear that, Bob," Gino said, trying to offer some comfort. "Thanks," Bob replied with a faint smile. "It's going to take some time to adjust, but I'll probably still go for my morning and evening walks. It just feels right."

"That makes sense, Bob. Speaking of the garden, it reminds me—what about that old Anderson WWII shelter in Mrs Murphy's garden? Do you or anyone else still have one?"

Bob shook his head. "No, I filled mine in years ago, like most folks around here. Turned it into a decent-sized shed instead. There aren't many houses that still have one of those shelters. Mr Murphy kept his, though. Said it was perfect for storing his paint and decorating gear. When Oliver asked Mrs Murphy if he could set up his model railway down there, I helped clear it out for her—moved all the old paint tins, brushes, and ladders. It's quite a space now.

The local police were pretty tight-lipped, but they did let it slip that Oliver could have been blown to bits. There was a bomb in the Anderson shelter.

They couldn't say much more, but they did mention you were smart not to flip that light switch. Leaving it for the Bomb Squad saved our skins. If either of us had touched it, we'd be nothing but a memory right now."

"Yeah, that was all Andrew's doing," Gino replied, still feeling the weight of what could've happened. "He remembered his training just in time."

"Thank God for that," Bob said, his voice tinged with relief. "Where's he now? You're not usually solo."

"We're on the same job today," Gino answered, glancing at his watch. "He's on his way—I'm meeting him at Mrs Murphy's in about five minutes.

I had better make my way up to Number 9 to see her, many thanks for the coffee and I will be careful what I say to Mrs Murphy, I don't want to upset her.

Gino said "Cheerio"to Bob Clarke and as he got to Mrs Murphy's house Andrew pulled up and parked up outside.

Gino was relieved and said "Hi Andrew, I 'm pleased to see you back, I 'm not used to working on my own. How was the journey?"

" It was okay Gino, we won't do that again. You have done well with getting the CCTV photo of this guy's number plate , how did you get on with Bob Clarke ?"

"Fine, he was very informative, he said Mrs Murphy is still very upset about Oliver as we expected, we will have to be careful speaking to her.

And yes, he has seen a motorcycle leaving her house a few times as he was walking his dog at nights , he wasn't close enough to him to describe what he was wearing, he only caught sight of him under the street light.

He spoke at length about the Anderson WW11 shelters, his voice tinged with both nostalgia and sorrow. But what really broke him was his dog—the poor little thing had passed away recently, and he was clearly still devastated.

I'll make sure everything is in my report for Zoe,"Gino said," but my thoughts are, how was she holding up after that gruesome discovery—the man found in the skip in Lewisham?"

"Yeah, we should definitely give Zoe and Simon a call once we leave here," Andrew added, "then head over to Ponders End."

When they finally reached Mrs Murphy's house they exchanged a glance before knocking. She opened the door cautiously, her eyes scanning them with suspicion.

"Hello, Mrs Murphy," Andrew said gently, "I'm Detective Andrew Brown, and this is Detective Gino Fernandez. We'd like to ask you a few more questions about Oliver."

"Oh... yes, of course I remember you both. Please, come in," she replied, her voice soft but tense.

"Thank you,"Andrew said as they stepped inside.

Gino said "thank you," his voice gentle yet probing. "How are you holding up, Mrs Murphy?"

She sank into the chair with a heavy sigh, her gaze distant. "I still can't get my head around it... what happened to Oliver." Her voice trembled. "He was always so good to me. Whether it was fetching groceries or helping with little things around the house, he was always there."

Andrew could see the strain etched on her face. Not wanting to push too hard, he decided to tread carefully, but there were questions that needed answers.

"Mrs Murphy," he began, his tone soft but serious, "did Oliver ever have visits from a man on a motorcycle dressed in black?"

Her brow furrowed in thought. "Yes, actually, he did. The first time I answered the door to that man... he was unsettling, all in black, and there was something aggressive about the way he spoke. He said he wanted to see Oliver. I didn't trust him, not one bit."

She paused for a moment, collecting her thoughts. "After that, Oliver must've arranged things over the phone because, during the other visits, Oliver was always outside, waiting for him. They would both disappear into the shelter."

Andrew exchanged a glance with Gino. "That's interesting," he said. "Did you get the sense this man was from around here? Was he English?" "No I would say he was from the Middle East maybe Iran or somewhere like that."

Andrew and Gino exchanged a knowing glance. Gino whispered, "Here we go again."

Suddenly remembering something, Andrew asked, "Oh, one more thing—did the forensic team take Oliver's phone?"

Mrs Murphy stood up from her chair, looking slightly surprised. "No, they didn't. It's still in my store cupboard. No one asked for it." She disappeared for a moment, then returned, holding the phone out to Andrew. "Here you are."

Andrew carefully wrapped it in his handkerchief, inspecting the device. It was a brand-new Samsung, the kind that needed a passcode to unlock.

"Do you happen to know if Oliver gave you the code?" he asked, though his voice lacked much hope.

Mrs Murphy gave a soft laugh and shook her head. "Sorry, I wouldn't know the first thing about it. I've never touched one of those gadgets in my life."

"That's quite alright, Mrs Murphy, thank you. You've been incredibly helpful," Andrew said, flashing a polite smile. "Before we go, would it be possible for us to take a look inside the World War II shelter? I noticed the blue police tape is still across the doorway."

Mrs Murphy nodded thoughtfully. "Of course, you're welcome to check it out. The lights aren't connected yet, but there's a large torch by the back door. Take that, and you should be able to see everything clearly. I'll pop the kettle on, so you can have a nice cup of tea when you're done. Oh, that reminds me. When you have looked in the shelter I have something more about Oliver to tell you."

Andrew picked up the torch and led the way, pushing open the creaky shelter door. The air inside was thick with an unsettling quiet.

Gino shuddered as they stepped in, his voice barely a whisper. "This place feels eerie, Andrew." Andrew nodded. "Yeah, it's got that vibe, hasn't it? Let's not linger too long. We'll check each side quickly and take a look at the model trains. "

As they moved deeper into the shelter their footsteps echoed faintly off the cold walls. Both men noted how the bomb squad had cleared out the copper wires, chemicals, and timers.

However, three small blue kit bags with silver buckles still lay in the corner—just as the Chief Bomb Squad Engineer had mentioned in his report.

Andrew stared at the model of the Flying Scotsman, his brow furrowed in curiosity. "Let's take a closer look at this model I'm really intrigued. Why is it backed up against the repair huts? And there's something about its number that's caught my eye. I wonder if it connects to Oliver's mobile phone."

Gino, tilting his head, asked, "What do you mean, Andrew?"

Andrew tapped his chin thoughtfully. "Well, I was thinking... maybe Oliver used the train's number as his phone passcode."

Gino's eyes widened. "Seriously? You think he'd do something like that?"

"Why not?" Andrew shrugged. "I know I'd probably use something like that if it meant a lot to me. The number on the train is 4472, let's give it a shot."

With a spark of excitement, Andrew pulled Oliver's phone from his pocket and punched in the code—4472. But the phone remained locked. "Hmm, no luck."

Then Andrew's eyes lit up with a sudden realisation. "Wait a minute! Since the train is in reverse, maybe we should reverse the number too."

Holding his breath, he entered 2744. The screen unlocked. Andrew punched the air triumphantly. "Hooray! We've cracked it! We'll take a look through his contacts before handing it to Simon. Of course, we'll explain how we figured out the code."

"Andrew, I never would've thought of that. Did you pick up this trick from your retired detective friend in Brighton?"

Andrew grinned. "Yeah, he always had a knack for solving the impossible."

As they emerged from the shelter, Mrs Murphy's voice echoed warmly through the evening air. "Come on in, I've got the tea ready for you!"

Andrew and Gino left the torch by the back door and made their way into the cosy lounge, where the scent of freshly brewed tea filled the room. Moments later, Mrs Murphy came in with a packet of chocolate-coated biscuits, a familiar glint in her eye.

"These are wonderful," Gino said, biting into one. "What are they?" Mrs Murphy chuckled softly. "Oh, haven't you ever tried these before?"

Gino shook his head, grinning. "Nope, never."

"They were Oliver's favourite. They're Wagon Wheels," she said, her voice tinged with fondness.

"Well, they're really good,"Gino said, licking a crumb off his thumb. "I'll have to buy some for my girls."

"I've got two packets left," Mrs Murphy offered generously. "Why don't you take them with you?"

Gino's face lit up. "That's very kind of you, Mrs Murphy, thank you!"

After a brief pause Mrs Murphy glanced at Andrew with curiosity. "So, what did you think of Oliver's model trains?"

Andrew's eyes gleamed. "Oh, the collection's amazing. I especially loved the Flying Scotsman—it's a real beauty."

"Yes, that was Oliver's favourite," Mrs Murphy said thoughtfully. "And it made sense—his passion for trains ran deep in the family.

His grandfather had been one of the train drivers, and his father too, an engine driver on the diesel goods trains. But his dad took early retirement after a traumatic incident... when a man jumped off a bridge, and no matter how hard he tried, he couldn't stop the train in time."

Gino glanced at Andrew, his eyes filled with concern.

"So, what are the plans for all the model trains in the shelter?" Andrew asked.

"It's all been arranged," Mrs Murphy replied. "Oliver's parents will be here in a couple of days. They live in Dunfermline, Scotland, so they won't be able to take everything back with them. They'll clear out his room, take some personal things, and the rest—the model trains—they're having an auctioneer come by to handle it.

Then all of it will be auctioned for charity, and the proceeds will go to the British Heart Foundation."

Andrew agreed. "That sounds like the right thing to do, considering how far away they live. I guess once forensics have finished, they'll return for Oliver's funeral."

Mrs Murphy sighed, her expression heavy with sadness.

"Yes, I asked if I could join them, and I told them Bob is coming here with a friend once the model trains are gone and the shelter is cleared out. They're going to fill it in and level it off, just like a lot of others have done."

"Thank you again, Mrs Murphy. We should get going now, and we really appreciate you remembering Oliver's mobile phone." Andrew and Gino both said goodbye.

"Yes, let's have a look at it before we leave here Gino." "I agree Andrew but let's not lose hope.Maybe we will find something buried in his messages." said Gino.

Andrew unlocked the mobile phone with ease, feeling a sense of triumph as the home screen lit up. Then scrolling through Oliver's contacts and emails he suddenly paused.

"Gino, take a look at this " Andrew muttered ,holding up the mobile. "He's received some pretty nasty threatening e-mails. Look, this is his name it's Azaad Olaar. This will help us when we get to Ponders End Tower Blocks and we track down the caretaker.

His name sounds Middle Eastern, Gino, as though he could be from Iran.We are still waiting for a verification on the Harley Davidson motorbike number plate you sent to IVRC International Vehicle Registration Code."

"That's right Andrew we should know soon. I will send all this information on to Zoe now and ask her to get an International security check on him."

Andrew and Gino were ready to leave. As Gino climbed into the car, he asked, "have you got the directions to Ponders End, Andrew?"

"Yeah, Gino," Andrew replied, buckling his seatbelt. "I spent some time checking it out on Google when I was on the tube heading back to my place. Got it saved on my phone—EN3 7ZQ. There are 4 Tower Blocks, each a different colour—yellow, red, blue, and green. We'll start with the one on the west side and try to track down one of the caretakers."

"Sounds like a plan," Gino said, revving the engine.

"It's not too far, about eight to ten miles," Andrew added, glancing out the window. "Once we arrive we should call Zoe and Simon to keep them in the loop."

Traffic flowed smoothly and before long they reached Ponders End. Gino had his eyes wide with excitement. "Look, Andrew! You can see the Tower Blocks from here."

"Yeah, I see them,"Andrew replied, scanning the area. "I'll pull into the first spot I find.

We'll need to call Zoe—ask her to get Simon's view on how to handle this guy. If we're lucky enough to figure out which flat he's hiding in, we still need to know which floor he's on. And more importantly, how Simon wants us to approach. No room for mistakes on this one."

He cut the engine and shot a glance at Gino. "Who knows how this guy will react when we show our warrant cards."

Andrew quickly dialled Zoe, setting the phone on the speaker. As the call connected, he filled her in on the situation. Gino chimed in, updating her again with the latest info from Wood Green.

"Got it," Zoe said after a moment. "Simon's in his office. I'll run this by him and get back to you ASAP. Oh, and one more thing—you've got a lot on your plate.

The Lewisham murder's getting messy, and there's plenty to untangle. And don't forget, we still have to track down that damn Express Removals van. It's like it vanished into thin air.

Take a breather for now. I'll give you a call when things are set. Simon said he wouldn't be surprised if you end up needing backup from the nearest police station."

Andrew glanced around and spotted a small coffee shop across the street. "Okay, Gino, let's stretch our legs and get a coffee," he said, leading the way.

They had barely settled in with their cups when Andrew's phone buzzed. He answered quickly.

"Hey guys, I just got off the phone with Simon. He now says you will need backup if this guy bolts. As you say he's got a Harley Davidson motorcycle and even though your Ford's engine is souped -up, he could still give you a run for your money. Simon mentioned he'd been in a similar chase years ago—back when he was in the thick of it, like you two are now.

Here's the plan: hold tight for a bit longer. Simon's talking to Edmonton Police right now. Once he gets clearance, I'll call back with the green light and backup.

So, take a few minutes, have another coffee, and think about how you're going to handle this guy. You'll need to be sharp when you get a chance to speak to him.

Oh, and nice work cracking Oliver's phone code. Val has uploaded your reports to our iCloud file; Simon and our Chief Matt will be reviewing them soon.

Give me five more minutes, guys, and I'll get back to you."

Andrew and Gino ordered another round of coffee, their minds swirling with the puzzle before them. They huddled over the table, eyes glinting with determination.

"I've been thinking," Gino said, tapping his fingers on the table. "We don't have much to work with—only that he is the guy who showed up in Wood Green to meet Oliver. That's it."

Andrew's phone buzzed, his expression hardening as he glanced at the screen. "It's from the IVRC—the International Vehicle Registration Code. His H D motorcycle is officially registered in Iran. Make sure you include that in a message to Zoe."

"Already on it," Gino muttered, fingers flying across his phone, "looks like we've got a good lead."

Andrew's attention shifted as he scrolled through his phone, searching for contact details for the Tower Block caretakers. "Got it, Gino. There are two caretakers—one works days, the other covers nights. They switch every two weeks." Andrew's first call came up short—the guy on the night shift said he didn't have the information he needed. Not discouraged, Andrew dialled the second number. This time, success.

"Roland Williams speaking, how can I help?"

Andrew straightened, his tone sharp but polite. "Mr Williams, this is Detective Andrew Brown from the Metropolitan Police. I'm inquiring about a resident—Mr Azaad Olaar, from Iran. Could you tell me which Tower Block he's in and the floor and room number?"

Mr Williams paused for a moment before responding, his tone firm. " I can't give out that information over the phone. It's company policy. If you want it, you'll need to come to Tower Block 1 and show me your warrant card."

Andrew agreed, even though Mr Williams couldn't see him. "That's fair," Andrew replied. "I appreciate the caution. We'll come over. Where exactly will we find you? I have my colleague detective Gino Fernandez with me."

"I'll be at my office, front entrance of the first block," Mr Williams answered briskly. " When you have parked your car walk over, and I'll meet you at the door."

Andrew ended the call and turned to Gino ,"it looks like we're going in."

Gino was adjusting his jacket. "Let's make it quick."

As they both stepped out of the vehicle, Andrew's phone buzzed in his hand. He glanced at the screen – it was Zoe, again.

"Hey, Zoe, what's up?" Andrew answered, stepping away from the car.

Zoe's voice crackled through the line, urgent but calm. "I've got an update from Simon. He's already dispatched a backup car from the Edmonton Police station. They're just a few streets away, watching you. If anything goes wrong, they'll be there in seconds. Got it?"

Andrew exchanged a glance with Gino, who raised an eyebrow. "Okay Zoe," they both replied.

"So, now that you've got the name of this man from Iran, what's the plan once you find out which block and flat he's hiding in?" "We're going over to the first Tower Block right now. The caretaker, a Mr Roland Williams, has his office near the front. He wouldn't give up any details about the residents over the phone — smart guy.

CHAPTER SIX

We will have to meet him in person, show our warrant cards, and see what we can pry out of him. Once we know the Tower Block and floor number, we'll have a little chat with our Iranian friend. I'll call you back once we've got something."

Andrew knocked on the office door, and after a few tense moments, it swung open. A stern-looking man stood in the doorway. "Come in, take a seat," he said gruffly. "Now, let's see those warrant cards."

"No problem." Andrew and Gino produced their warrant cards without hesitation.

The caretaker scrutinized them, his expression softening just slightly. "Alright, everything checks out. Like I mentioned before, we've got to be careful who we share information with. So, you're asking about Mr Azaad Olaar? The Iranian man, is that right?"

"Yes, Mr Williams, we'd like to know which block he's staying in, along with the floor and room number. Also, how long has he been living here? Have you interacted with him much? What's he like to talk to?"

Mr Williams began " He's in Tower Block 2 on the third floor, room 218. he's been living here for about seven months now. To be honest, I haven't had much to do with him—he can be a bit... aggressive at times. In fact, not too long ago, he had a heated argument with the guy in the flat next door. When I threatened to call the police, though, he quickly calmed down."

"Thank you, Mr Williams. Do you happen to know if he's in at the moment?"

"Yes, actually. He came in about an hour ago—you can't miss him. He always makes a grand entrance on that flashy motorcycle of his. Expensive-looking thing. He keeps it in the underground car park which you can only get into with a security code card and this is the same all the four Tower Blocks.

I will give you a code card but please make sure it doesn't get out to anyone, the company are very strict. The previous caretaker got the sack for being too sloppy with giving the front door and the underground car park numbers to the wrong people."

"Thank you, Mr Williams. That's all we need to know for now,"Andrew said.

As they walked away, Gino turned to Andrew. "So, should we head straight to Tower Block 2 and confront the guy? See how he reacts?"

Andrew hesitated. "I'm a bit uneasy about it. Maybe we should call Zoe first, don't you think?" "Yeah, I agree,"Gino replied.

Andrew pulled out his phone and dialled Zoe. She picked up almost immediately.

"Hey, guys! I was expecting your call. How did things go with the caretaker, Mr Williams?" she asked, her voice brisk and curious.

Andrew quickly filled her in on what they had learned. After listening, Zoe spoke up. "Simon has a suggestion: when you knock on this guy's door, don't show your warrant cards right away. First start by saying you're asking questions about Oliver Jones, the deceased. Mention that you believe he was a friend of his. But be on guard—if he gets aggressive, that's when you show the cards. Gauge his reaction carefully.

I've have come up with something that uses the latest tech on your codex phones," Zoe explained. "When you press 4, it triggers backup, and pressing 5 sends your postcode directly to the Edmonton Police station. You're immediately linked to the nearest patrol car, which is parked just a few streets away. Pretty cool, okay?"

"That's brilliant, Zoe," Andrew said, nodding in approval. "It's reassuring to have that in place. We'll get over to Tower Block 2 now."

"Great. Call me as soon as you've spoken to the guy," Zoe replied, her voice steady with a sense of urgency.

"We will," Andrew confirmed. Turning to Gino, he said, "Okay, let's go. Time to see what happens when we knock on his door."

The two men crossed the car park towards Tower Block. 2 Andrew glanced around as they walked, then suggested, "Let's check around the side first and see if we can find the underground car parking entrance."

"Good thinking," Gino, agreed. After a moment of scanning the area, he asked, "Do you reckon we should take the lift or stick to the stairs?"

Andrew considered it for a moment before replying, "The stairs might be safer. Oh, look, there it is—the entrance to the underground car park. Looks secure, probably only accessible for the tower's residents. Let's go in the front door"

As they approached, Andrew added, "We'll need the front door code Mr Williams gave us. You have it Gino?"

When they reached the front door, Gino swiftly punched in the security code, the soft beep echoing in the quiet hallway. The door clicked open and without a word they made their way towards the stairs. Gino's eyes darted around, taking in the surroundings. The place was immaculate--no garish graffiti plastered across the walls, nothing like the run—down Tower Blocks he'd been in before. It was a far cry from the chaotic scenes in Only Fools and Horses –no Del Boy antics here,only clean lines and *tasteful* décor.

"Hey, Andrew," Gino asked with a smirk. "Ever watched *Only Fools and Horses*? my girls couldn't stop laughing when Del Boy falls through the bar. Have you seen that one Andrew ?" "Yes Gino, it's great fun. We both like all the series.

Well, here we are on floor 3. It looks like we start here on the left with number 200 and work our way round to 218." They soon reached flat 218. Andrew looked at the door and said, "It hasn't got one of those door bell cameras like some we've passed, only a door bell and a spy hole. Give the bell a hard push Gino."

Gino glanced at Andrew and said, "alright, let's give it a go." As Gino pushed the bell switch a loud bell clanged from behind the door, echoing through the hallway, and the door cracked open just enough to reveal a glowering figure.

"Clear off!" the man barked, throwing in a string of colourful curses in both English and a language neither of them recognised. Before the door could slam shut, Andrew quickly wedged his foot in the gap, holding his ground.

With a calm, almost disarming tone, Andrew spoke up, "Sir, we're only here to check up on a Mr Oliver Jones.

I believe he was a friend of yours, could we come in and discuss this with you we are police detectives." They both tried to show their warrant cards.

Andrew kept his foot wedged in the door and said again "I told you we are police, and if you won't let us in to answer a few questions we will call for reinforcements from the local police and they will take you down to the police station for questioning."

Again, he was swearing in English and another language. He then gave Andrew's foot a heavy kick and slammed the door shut.

Gino looked at Andrew and said, "I expected that from when I was looking at his emails, they were all very nasty. What's our next move Andrew?"

Gino, I think we should go over to the car park and bring our car over to Block 2. Let's keep an eye on the underground garage too—if he sneaks out on his Harley Davidson, we'll need to tail him," Andrew said, glancing out of the window at the sheets of rain pounding down in relentless torrents.

"Looks like it's coming down hard out there," he added with a wry smile. "One of us will have to make a dash for it."

Gino gave a nod, pulling his jacket tighter around himself. "Your turn, Andrew. I'll get Zoe on the line, make sure she's keeping in touch."

Andrew took a deep breath, bracing himself for the dash through the downpour. "Alright, keep her posted—I'll bring the car around." With a final nod, he bolted out of the door, his footsteps quickly lost in the roar of the rain as Gino dialled Zoe, ready for whatever came next.

Andrew darted toward the car, adrenaline kicking in as he got into the driver's seat.

He circled around to Tower Block 2, where Gino was already waiting. They moved with purpose, navigating to the rear of the building.

Spotting a secluded area shielded by dense green hedges and tall trees. Andrew eased the car into a hidden nook, safely tucked out of sight from anyone emerging from the underground car parking. Their car was now a silent shadow, concealed and ready for whatever was coming next.

"What did Zoe have to say, Gino?"Andrew asked, his tone laced with anticipation. Gino glanced over. "Well, she wasn't exactly surprised. Said she had a hunch this might happen. She wants us to stay put, keep an eye on him if he makes any moves. She'll have the police tailing us for backup.

And here's where it gets interesting—she thinks this Iranian guy might be on an international watchlist. She's already contacted International Security and is waiting for confirmation. If he's who she suspects, we might be in deeper than we thought." "So, this isn't a routine surveillance?" "Not by a long shot," Gino replied.

"Alright, Gino," Andrew said, peering through the thick hedge, "she might be onto something, so stay sharp,"

About fifteen minutes later, the garage door creaked open, and the man they'd been waiting for—an Iranian with a fierce expression dressed in black came out on his roaring Harley Davidson.

With a smooth move, he swung onto the main road, oblivious to the eyes tracking his every move. Andrew fired up the engine and eased into the road, keeping a cautious distance as they tailed him.

Gino, tension clear on his face, kept one hand hovering over his codex mobile, ready to call in backup with a quick press of 4 and 5 if things got messy. They weren't alone either—a police car lurked in the distance, prepared to close in if needed.

The rain hammered down in relentless sheets, the windscreen wipers thrashing at full speed to keep Andrew's view clear. Ahead, the motorcyclist cut through traffic with nimble, unpredictable movements, darting between cars like a shadow. But Andrew was right on his tail, his focus razor-sharp as he manoeuvred to keep up.

Gino squinted at a road map on his phone "Looks like he's heading toward Epping Forest," he muttered, glancing up as the bike disappeared around a bend.

Andrew tightened his grip on the wheel. "Call Zoe. Let her know where we're headed. Ask if she thinks we should put the blue lights on if he really takes off and we need to push through traffic."

Andrew kept pace, hanging back several cars to avoid drawing attention. He didn't want the man to suspect he was being tailed. Gino squinted at the satnav, muttering, "looks like I was right Andrew, we're on the B1393, headed straight for Epping Forest! Zoe said to only use the blue lights if we thought it was absolutely necessary."

"Yeah, Gino, I think he knows we're onto him," Andrew replied. "He's weaving, and checking his mirrors... and now he's slowing down."

The tension in the car was thick. Any moment, the target could pull off, make a break for it—or worse. Andrew's grip tightened on the wheel as they prepared for whatever was coming next.

"Christ, Andrew, look out! Shouted Gino. He's stopped dead in front of us and has a gun aimed right at us!"

Andrew's foot slammed the brakes, but he barely had a second to think before two shots cracked through the night. The first bullet ripped into the front left tyre, which burst apart in an ear-splitting blast, and the second shattered the right headlight, spraying glass like shrapnel into the dark, rain-soaked air.

The car spun, teetering on the slick road as Andrew wrestled with the wheel, heart hammering. The tyres screamed against the wet asphalt, skidding dangerously close to the steep drop-off on the side. With a brutal jolt, the front end crashed down into a muddy ditch, the car shuddering to a halt. Rain hammered against the roof, the two of them trapped in a dead silence—exposed, vulnerable.

Andrew stepped out of the car, hazard lights flashing against the darkening sky, casting a faint, rhythmic glow onto the roadside.

Gino dialled Zoe immediately, and pressed 4 and 5 on his codex his voice steady but tense as he recounted the unexpected mishap. Zoe gasped on the other end of the line, her concern evident. "You two are incredibly lucky," she said, her voice filled with relief. "It could have been so much worse."

Thinking quickly, Zoe promised to arrange for help. "I'll get Tony Edwards, the transport manager, to go out with his truck. He'll probably bring someone along to help him get the car out of the ditch and back safely." She paused, calculating the options.

"In the meantime, if you need to get moving, you could call a taxi to take you to the nearest station. Or, if a police car is in the area, they might be able to give you a lift." Her efficiency reassured them both.

Andrew replied. "We will have to wait until Tony arrives and has our car loaded on the breakdown truck before we can make our way home."

"Oh, and I' m awaiting a call from the Head of Counter Terrorism and UK Security to see what they can uncover about Azaad Olaar. Meanwhile, Simon mentioned that our Chief Matt Gibbons has made contact with the British embassy in Tehran, Iran, to follow up from their end.

And then once I have any updates from Edmonton Police H Q I'll get back to you with everything I know."

The Police car that had been following them pulled up, sirens blaring and lights flashing like a scene out of a movie. An officer stepped out, his breath visible in the cold wet air, and looked at Andrew and Gino with concern. "We heard two shots fired. We got a call from the station asking us to check in on you," he said, scanning their faces. "Are you guys all right? Do you need help arranging a tow to get the car out of the ditch?"

Andrew stepped forward, managing a grin despite the mishap. "Thanks, Officer! We're all good. Already got a pickup truck on the way. Don't worry about us, chase after him fast and watch out, he may stop and take a shot at you!"

The officer gave a quick nod, tipping his hat slightly. "Alright then, but you guys be careful out here.

"You need to get to Epping Forest—fast!" Andrew shouted, his voice sharp with urgency, and catch the guy."

The Police car roared to life, tearing down the road and leaving a swirling cloud+ in its wake. About 25 minutes later, the wailing scream of an ambulance filled the air as it raced past them, blue lights flashing like wild beacons.

Above them the rhythmic whirl of a helicopter broke through the havoc. Both men craned their necks to see the bright red air ambulance slicing through the sky.

"Hey, Gino," Andrew said, his voice tinged with tension. "What do you think is going on? Do you think they've finally caught up with Azaad Olaar?"

Gino said "I hope so. That guy's dangerous—he could've shot either of us. Might not hesitate to do it again. I'm sure Zoe will fill us in soon." After a while Zoe rang again. "Okay guys I have received a call from the Edmonton Police H Q with the latest news update

As the first police car, hot on your heels, finally caught up with him, the scene turned chaotic. In a swift, calculated move, he spun around, fired a shot straight through the windscreen, shattering it into a shower of jagged fragments. The bullet narrowly missed both the police officers, embedding itself deep into the rear seat.

The torrential rain and the myriad of fast-flowing streams made the chase even more treacherous. Forced to brake hard, the driver spun the car in a desperate manoeuvre.

The violent jolt triggered both airbags to explode with a deafening *whoosh*. Miraculously, despite the impact, the officers emerged unscathed.

Meanwhile, the escalating drama might have caught your attention: a second police car racing by and the thundering rotors of an air ambulance slicing through the stormy skies."

"Yes, we witnessed the other police car and ambulance speeding past, sirens blaring, followed by the unmistakable whirl of the air ambulance overhead. It was clear that something serious had occurred."

"Hang on, I have now received an update directly from Edmonton Police Headquarters with more information.

The second police car swiftly closed the distance, tracking him into a dense wooded area, scattered with the freshly felled remains of towering trees. As they closed in, the roar of his motorcycle suddenly faltered; the bike lost traction on a slick, rain-soaked patch of forest floor. The tyres skidded wildly, throwing him off balance. Swerving out of control, he collided with a tree, the impact hurling him through the air like a rag doll.

His flight ended abruptly and gruesomely as he landed on a jagged spike protruding from a felled tree, the wood piercing deep into his chest. Blood poured from the wound, pooling beneath him in a grim testament to the violence of the crash.

The police officers wasted no time, leaping from their vehicle and racing to his side. Their boots crunched through the wet undergrowth as they approached, the scene before them confirming their worst fears.

He lay motionless, his face pale and ghostlike, his breaths shallow and ragged. The blood loss was obvious and he looked close to death.

They were soon on their mobile calling for reinforcements and were quickly assured that an ambulance was en route and would arrive shortly.

One of the police officers on the scene, drawing on his past experience with a similar incident, assessed the grim situation. After examining the size, shape, and trajectory of the wooden spike, he concluded that its removal would require the precision of a trauma surgeon in a fully equipped operating room. Realising the urgency and complexity of the case, he promptly contacted headquarters in Edmonton H Q and strongly recommended dispatching an air ambulance for faster, specialised assistance.

You mentioned an ambulance racing past, its siren wailing, followed by the unmistakable thrum of helicopter rotors overhead.

From the sound of it, they might need to leave the impaled object in place until the patient reaches the hospital—it's often the safest course of action in such cases. If you listen closely, you might even catch the ambulance making its return trip; they're impressively swift when it comes to rushing urgent cases to the nearest emergency hospital.

I'll keep you updated as soon as I hear more from the Edmonton H Q.

Let's hope Tony Edwards gets to you soon to pull your car out of that ditch. I've got a mountain of reports for Val to upload to our iCloud file, <u>Operation Live Wire</u> and Simon's scheduled a meeting for 9 a.m. tomorrow at our usual spot. Let me know if you run into any trouble getting home."

Gino leaned back with a curious expression, fixing his gaze on Andrew. "Well, Andrew, what do you make of all that?" he asked, his tone laced with intrigue.

"It's not looking good, Gino," Andrew said, shaking his head. "We've been lucky one too many times. First, that bullet aimed at you back in Manchester—now this. If his first shot had gone through the windscreen, it would've been on your side. Instead he nailed our front left wheel with enough force to send us careering off the road. I couldn't hold the steering, and we ended up in that deep ditch. I just hope Tony can fix the damage—otherwise, he will have to find us another car."

"Look, Andrew! The air ambulance is flying past!" Gino exclaimed pointing skyward with wide eyes.

Andrew barely glanced up, his focus on their predicament. Nearly an hour crawled by before the hum of an approaching engine finally broke the monotony. A breakdown truck rumbled to a halt near the ditch, and Andrew's face lit up.

"Tony! You're a sight for sore eyes." Andrew called out "we are pleased to see you"

Tony jumped out of his cab accompanied by one of his mechanics. "Well guys, what happened here?"

Andrew briefly explained the situation with chasing an Iranian guy on a Harley Davidson motorcycle and having two shots fired at them.

"Blimey, guys! Sounds like you had a close call. How on earth did you end up in the ditch?"

"Well, Tony, after the tyre was shot out I tried my best to steer away from the bank, but the wheel had a mind of its own. I couldn't keep control and before I knew it the car veered right over the edge."

"That must've been terrifying! Sounds like the steering gave up on you. And what's the story with the smashed-offside headlight?" "Yeah, he shot out the light! I'm pretty sure that bullet was meant to go straight through our windscreen."

"Okay, listen up. I need to get the chains secured around the axle and get my truck across the road. In the back of the truck you'll find two yellow high-vis jackets—take them. You both look soaked to the bone, and by the looks of it, the rain isn't letting up anytime soon. I'll get this sorted once everything's secured, I need you to stop traffic in both directions. Okay guys?"

"Yes, no problem at all," Andrew and Gino replied in unison, stepping aside to flank the breakdown truck. They positioned themselves strategically, creating enough space for Tony to back out and manoeuvre the vehicle around.

They had been managing the traffic jam for barely ten minutes when the shrill screech of tyres cut through the air. A police car skidded to a stop, it's blue lights were flashing scanning the scene. One of the police officers gestured briskly toward Andrew and Gino signalling them to approach their Police car.

"Alright, listen up, guys!" barked the officer, his voice firm and commanding. "This is straight from HQ—we were sent here in a hurry to hold up the traffic while the tow truck gets your car out of that ditch."

He paused, scanning the scene with a sharp eye before the other police officer stepped forward and asked, "which one of you is Detective Andrew Brown?"

"That's me," Andrew replied, pulling out his warrant card. The officer scrutinized it carefully, nodded, and then turned to Gino. "And you must be Detective Gino Fernandez?"

The tension in the air crackled for a moment as everyone waited for Gino's response.

"Yes," Gino replied, flipping open his warrant card. The other officer said. "Okay guys why don't you both get in the back of our patrol car and dry off a bit? We'll take care of everything here. Once your car is loaded onto the tow truck and on its way we'll drive you to Edmonton Green train station so you can catch a train home."

It wasn't long before Tony managed to free the stranded car from the ditch. The winch of the cable signalled the end of the vehicle's brief, unintended off-road adventure. With the car securely loaded onto the breakdown truck, Tony dusted off his hands and gave the car a final almost triumphant glance. Andrew stepped out of the police car, and handed back the high-vis- jackets. "Thanks for the quick work Tony," he said, his tone half-professional half-relieved.

Tony, ever the model of efficiency nodded and gave a quick thumbs-up. "Part of the job," he said with a grin, already climbing back into the driver's seat of the truck.

The vehicle rumbled to life and as he pulled onto the road back to the police compound. He rolled down the window and called out, "I'll keep Simon updated on the repairs, shouldn't take too long!"With that Tony was gone, the orange beacon on his truck casting rhythmic flashes. The sound of his engine faded into the distance leaving Andrew standing on the roadside, the faint smell of diesel hanging in the air. Another job done.

Andrew climbed back into the police car, the tension thick in the air. As the vehicle sped toward the train station, one of the officers glanced over his shoulder, his expression carefully neutral but his words carrying weight.

"I've been instructed to update you." The Police officer said, his tone clipped and formal. "Our Chief Constable at HQ has spoken directly with your Assistant Commander, Simon Harris. He confirmed that both you and he are operating under Special Branch directives." The words hung in the air like a revelation, shifting the atmosphere inside the car. Andrew felt the weight of this new layer of the situation, the implications settling into place as they raced onward.

"Our report strictly documents your car skidding into the ditch—no mention of the tyre being shot or the headlamp shot to pieces. We're not authorised to include those details. A copy of this report will be forwarded to your boss Simon Harris by our HQ. This is the official account we've provided. During our investigation of the accident on the B1393, it became clear how treacherous the conditions were that day. A Ford Mondeo struck a large pothole, skidded sideways and plunged into a deep roadside ditch. The torrential rain was relentless with windscreen wipers working overtime as visibility was severely reduced. Remarkably, no other vehicles were involved, and both the driver and passenger escaped unharmed—a lucky outcome given the hazardous circumstances. What do you think of that guys?"

"That's fine thanks, it's a great relief for us."

"Okay, we will report back to our H Q that you both are accepting our version of the accident. Here we are guys, this is Edmonton Green rail station, have a good journey home."

Andrew said , "thanks for the lift," and they didn't have to wait long before the train arrived.

On his way home, Andrew dialled Zoe to share an update. He detailed the Road Traffic Police report and mentioned that Tony was on his way back with their car. Then with a tone of curiosity he asked, "any new developments on the Iranian guy, Azaad Olaar?"

"Well," Zoe began, her voice trembling slightly. "The latest update isn't good. He's on life support at the Epping Hospital. They're not saying much but it doesn't sound hopeful. They've told us there's barely any chance he'll pull through. The Air Ambulance arrived fast—they did everything they could. But they had to transport him with that jagged spike still lodged deep in his chest. It's... it's awful."

Zoe took a steadying breath before continuing, "I'll keep you posted. Are you on your way back yet?"

"Yes, Zoe, we're on the train from Edmonton Green now." Andrew said, a note of relief in his voice. "The Road Traffic Police were surprisingly eager to drop us off at the train station."

"Don't forget, we've got that meeting in the morning you two," Zoe reminded them her tone sharp but familiar.

"Got it," they chorused in unison, exchanging a knowing glance. It was clear they had no intention of letting the meeting slip their minds—or of letting Zoe down.

As they drew closer to the heart of London, Andrew turned to Gino with a reminder. "Don't forget, we need to stop by our lock-up at Borough Market," he said. "We'll swap over these overcoats there, then catch a bus or the underground to my place in Hammersmith. Once we're at the apartment, we'll stash the guns ammunition and bulletproof vests in the safe." His tone was calm but the weight of their cargo hinted at the gravity of their mission.

"Crikey, Andrew, it had slipped my mind—I need to text Sophia and let her know we're held up and won't make it home on time." "Good call, Gino, same here. I reckon it'll be quicker if we stick to the underground straight to Hammersmith once we're done at London Borough Market."

"Do you think so Andrew?"

"Yes, if we take the Hammersmith and City line, we'll pass through Holborn Station. Everything's running smoothly now," Andrew said, glancing at the map.

Gino hesitated, his voice tinged with unease. "I know, but I can't stop thinking about what we saw when we there. It's like it's burned into my mind."

Andrew agreed. "I get it, Gino. But sometimes the best way to deal with it is to keep moving forward. Passing through again might help—it's better than trying to bury it."

As the train screeched to a halt at Holborn Station the duo exchanged glances, the metallic hiss of the opening doors filling the carriage. Gino's voice broke the moment tinged with unease. "It feels strange," he murmured, his eyes scanning the endless length of the train. "You can almost picture it—people falling over each other when the train stopped too suddenly." The thought lingered in the air like a shadow, making them both shiver. Relief washed over them as the doors closed and the train rattled back to life, carrying them away from the unsettling stillness of the station.

They soon reached Hammersmith Station and made their way to Andrew's apartment, weaving through the large evening crowds. Once inside, Andrew carefully secured their guns and ammunition and the bulletproof vests, locking them away with precision. He turned to Gino with a wry smile.

"Well, Gino," he said, his voice carrying a mix of fatigue and intrigue, "it's been a strange day hasn't it? Let's make our way home and get some rest. Tomorrow, we'll hear what Simon has to say at the meeting—and see if Tony's made any progress with the car."

"Yes, Andrew, I've been thinking about that. He'll likely fit the spare wheel and sort out another one to keep as a backup. Replacing the front headlight might take some time, but I'm sure he's got a few good contacts to speed things up. The real concern, though, is the steering mechanism—that could prove to be a bigger challenge."

"You sure know a lot about cars, Gino," Andrew remarked, raising an eyebrow. Gino grinned. "Of course! My father runs a garage back in our home town in Italy. Whenever we visit during the holidays he lets me work with him. It's like a family tradition."

"Well, let's hope Tony can get our car fixed." Andrew said. " If he can't, we'll have to settle for a silver BMW like Simon's. What do you think of that Gino?"

I'm sure he'll fix it," Gino said with a hint of scepticism. "Simon won't let us have a BMW. He's determined to send us into those unwelcome areas no matter what."

Andrew glanced at his companion, adjusting the collar on his overcoat. "Before we catch the bus have you figured out what you'll say to Sophia? You know she's going to ask if we had a good day."

"Yeah," Gino replied with a dry chuckle. "Probably best if we stick to the same story as the police report." "I agree Gino. I will see you in the morning at the usual time." They both caught their buses home.

As Andrew stepped through the door, Chloe's cheerful voice rang out from the kitchen. "Hi, Andrew! Could you pop upstairs and see Dimitris first? He hasn't quite settled yet. I know it's late but he really wanted to say goodnight to you."

"Of course, Chloe," Andrew replied, taking off his coat. Moments later he descended the stairs with a soft smile.

"He's fast asleep now. Looks like he just needed a little reassurance. So, what's on the menu tonight?"

Chloe beamed as she stirred a pot on the stove. "We're going Italian tonight! Spaghetti Bolognese, paired with home made ciabatta bread—cooked to perfection in my brand-new air fryer."

Andrew took a deep breath, letting the rich aroma fill his senses. "It smells incredible, Chloe, I can't wait. I will pour you a glass of your favourite wine"

As they enjoyed their meal, Chloe turned to Andrew, her eyes alight with a mix of intrigue and disbelief. "Have you heard the news this afternoon?" she began, lowering her voice slightly as if to heighten the drama.

"Apparently, there was a high-speed chase through Epping Forest—a police car pursuing a man on a motorcycle in the pouring rain. It sounds like something out of a movie! Then out of nowhere the motorcyclist stopped and fired a shot straight through the police car's windscreen!"

Andrew raised his eyebrows, clearly caught off guard by the intensity of the story.

"Thankfully," Chloe continued, "neither the driver or the other police officer in the car was hurt. But get this—the newsreader said another police car managed to catch up with the gunman. That's when things got even crazier. There was some kind of accident, and they had to call in an air ambulance to rush him to the hospital. Can you imagine?"

She shook her head in amazement as the rain outside their window pattered softly, a faint echo of the chaos she'd just described.

"Yes, Chloe we did hear about that. I'm sure we'll get more details during our morning meeting."

"Oh, that's good to know! And I'm so relieved you're not speeding around in a police car every day in this awful weather. How was your day?"

"Well, Chloe, let's say today wasn't without its challenges. We ran into a bit of trouble on a wet windy road during the torrential downpour."

"Oh no, Andrew! What happened? I hope it wasn't anything too serious!"

"Well our journey took a dramatic turn when we hit a nasty pothole hidden in the shadows of the roadside. Driving through the relentless downpour our visibility was terrible, and I didn't see it in time. The left tyre exploded with a loud bang and before I could react, the car swerved wildly sliding straight into a deep ditch.

Attempts to reverse out were futile—the car was well and truly stuck. With no other choice we called Tony Edwards, our trusted breakdown manager. He braved the storm, arriving with his recovery truck to haul the car out of the soggy trap. Tony managed to pull it free and took it straight to the Police Compound for repairs.

As for Tony? Always the professional, we got a lift to the nearest rail station and caught the train home leaving us grateful for his help and a story to tell."

"Thank goodness you weren't hurt! The government really needs to fix all these potholes. Far too many of our roads are downright dangerous," Chloe exclaimed with a mix of concern and frustration.

Andrew chuckled, masking his unease. "Sounds like you should be in Parliament, Chloe!" he quipped, though he had his fingers crossed behind his back betraying his silent hope she wouldn't dig too deeply into the subject.

Then, Andrew's phone buzzed in his pocket, breaking the tension. Glancing at the screen, he frowned slightly. "Excuse me, Chloe—it's Simon. I'll take this in the lounge," he said quickly, slipping out of the room before she could utter a word.

"Hi Simon what's the latest?" asked Andrew.

"I had a call Andrew, from at the Epping Forest Police HQ. As we suspected the Iranian guy has passed away in hospital. With that in mind I'm cancelling our morning meeting. Instead, I'll arrange a search warrant for you to check out his flat in Ponders End first thing tomorrow.

Also, while Tony is still working on your Mondeo, you can use my BMW to get around. Once you've wrapped up the search at his flat, head up to Epping Forest to follow up on things there. Let me know how it goes. Could you snap a few photos of the incident and send them to Zoe for her records?

It's the weekend already, so we'll tackle everything when we can get together for a morning meeting. Next week's going to be full-on as we dig into tracking down that Express Removals van. It's got to be found, this has been going on for far too long.

By the way, do you have space in your garage for my BMW? Is it long enough for the car to fit in?"

'Yes, Simon, that's no problem."

"Great! Just take good care of it?

Meet me at the police compound tomorrow morning at 9 a.m." Simon instructed firmly. "I should have the search warrant by then. Is that clear, Andrew?"

"Got it," Andrew replied without hesitation. "I'll text Gino and let him know, I'll pick him up in the morning."

Then Simon ended the call.

Chloe, who had been quietly observing tilted her head with concern. "Is everything alright?" she asked softly.

"Don't worry, Chloe," Andrew said with a sly grin. "Tomorrow morning, we're getting a search warrant for a flat in a Tower Block. And you'll never guess—Simon's actually letting us borrow his BMW for a few days!"

Chloe raised an eyebrow, "promise me you won't go driving it into a ditch, Andrew!"

Andrew chuckled, shaking his head. "Believe me, Chloe, that's *not* on my to-do list."

"I'll text Gino to let him know I'll pick him up in the morning. Then, we can settle in for a cosy evening, and you can fill me in on everything you've been up to on this dreary, rain-soaked day." After updating Gino about the change of plans, Andrew felt a sense of relief as he sank onto the sofa beside Chloe, ready to enjoy her company.

Chloe approached Andrew with a curious look. "Did you hear about the weather today? Some areas in England and Wales got an entire month's worth of rain in just one day!"

Andrew agreed, his expression a mix of concern and relief. "Oh, we did more than hear about it—we drove through it! Thank goodness our house is on a hill. How about you? Were you able to brave the storm and get Dimitris to his playgroup?"

"Yes, I wrapped him up warmly, and we spent the morning soaking in the magic of one of his favourite pastimes. He was absolutely thrilled, his joy contagious as we enjoyed every moment together. Later in the day, I caught up with my mother in Cyprus. She's been eagerly hinting at how much she'd love for us to visit, and now she's making plans for us to go for a few days over Christmas. The thought of going adds a layer of excitement to the season—so many special moments to look forward to!"

The next morning, Andrew arrived at the Police compound bright and early, his eyes immediately drawn to the Ford Mondeo suspended on the ramp. The vehicle looked weary but salvageable, and Andrew felt a flicker of hope as he approached Tony who was busy inspecting the car.

Tony glanced up and gave a reassuring nod. "Good news," he said, wiping his hands on a rag. "I've got a replacement wheel ready to go on, and the headlight will be here in a few days. All that's left is a thorough check of the steering mechanism and you'll be back on the road in no time."

Andrew couldn't help but smile. The prospect of having the Mondeo running again was a bright spot in what had been a challenging few days. "Don't rush it Tony, Simon is letting us have his BMW, for a few days." "Really Andrew." "Yes, here he is now."

Simon strode in, waving a crisp envelope in the air. "Morning, folks!" he called out, his voice carrying an air of excitement. He turned to Andrew with a grin. "I've got the search warrant right here, so you're all set. By the way, have you let Tony know I said you could borrow my BMW, for a few days?"

"Yes," and in a playful tone, "I told him to take his time with the repair. "He'd better not." said Simon. "I'm only letting you borrow my car for a few days. Here are the keys—drive safely. It's much drier today, so you should have a smooth ride."

"Don't worry, Simon, we'll take good care of it," Andrew reassured him with a grin as he pocketed the keys and headed out to pick up Gino.

Traffic crawled along, turning the short drive to Gino's house into a gruelling 30-minute ordeal. By the time Andrew pulled up, Gino was already waiting, his excitement spilling over as he got into the car

"This is amazing, Andrew! So much better than that old Mondeo," Gino exclaimed, his grin stretching from ear to ear.

Andrew chuckled, gripping the wheel with a sense of satisfaction. "I know, I was just as shocked when he handed me the keys. Maybe he figured we earned it after what we went through yesterday. And at least today's shaping up—no rain to dampen our plans."

The air between them buzzed with anticipation, the frustrations of traffic already fading as they sped off into a much brighter day.

After nearly an hour on the road, Andrew finally steered the car into Ponders End. The streets seemed quiet with only the occasional flicker of light in the windows of the towering apartment blocks. "I'll pull up in front of Tower Block One," Andrew said, glancing at Gino. "Let's see if Mr Roland Williams, the caretaker, is around."

The car eased to a stop. Gino was soon out and they approached a door marked by years of wear. He knocked firmly.

A gruff but welcoming voice called out from the other side. "Come in!"

As they stepped into the entrance, a lively chocolate-and-white dog bounded out to greet them. The furry ball of energy leaped excitedly, tail wagging like a propeller. Gino laughed and stooped to ruffle the dog's soft ears, revelling in the enthusiastic welcome. Andrew, on the other hand, edged away cautiously—dogs weren't exactly his favourite.

Gino beamed as he turned to Mr Williams. "He's a Springer Spaniel, isn't he? We didn't see him around yesterday. What's his name?"

Mr Williams laughed, nodding toward the wriggling pup. "Yes, he is. This is my dog, Doodle. Quite the character isn't he?

He spent the entire day at the vet," Mr Williams explained, his tone tinged with frustration. "He bolted into the wooded area near where you were parked, waiting for Mr Olaar to come out on his motorbike. And guess what? He dashed straight into a thorn bush and ended up cutting his paws."

Andrew's eyes narrowed slightly as he continued, "You remember us? We're the detectives who called yesterday, asking about Mr Azaad Olaar—the guy from Tower Block 2"

"Of course, if you were hoping to catch him today you're out of luck. For some reason he didn't come back last night," he said, his voice edged with unease.

"We're aware he didn't return." Andrew replied sharply holding up a document. "We have a search warrant for his room. You'll need to accompany us to Tower Block 2."

"I will, but there's nothing left to see. It's all been cleared out," came the unexpected reply.

"What?!" Gino exclaimed, his voice tinged with disbelief. "When did this happen?"

"Earlier today," Mr Williams said. "As a matter of fact. around eight this morning."

Gino's eyebrows shot up in alarm. "Who was it who cleared out his flat? Do you know?"

"Yes," Mr Williams said. "Two men in a van. They showed me a letter authorising them to empty his flat. They even offered to settle any outstanding rent arrears."

"Can you describe what the men looked like and the kind of van they were driving? Were there any distinctive markings on the back of the van? Also, do you have a functional CCTV camera covering the entrance to Tower Blocks 1 and 2?"

"Yes, the CCTV cameras at Tower Blocks 1 and 2 are operational now so you'll be able to review the footage. The van was white, with the words Express Removals printed on the back. As for the men, they appeared to be of Middle Eastern descent and spoke broken English."

"Oh, here we go again Andrew."

Gino and Andrew followed Mr Williams over to Tower Block 2 and up the stairs to floor 3 room 218.

As they entered Andrew snapped on a pair of white cotton gloves. Gino followed suit, his expression tense. Mr Williams raised an eyebrow.

"Is that really necessary?" he asked, his tone teetering between curiosity and doubt.

Andrew gave a wry smile. "Absolutely," he said. "The local police will probably want to send over a fingerprint team for process of elimination."

Gino nodded grimly. "Makes sense."

They pulled open every drawer in the kitchen, rifling through the drawers few remaining contents with relentless determination. Gino dragged the units away from the walls his breath quickening as dust swirled in the air. "Nothing yet," he muttered, frustration creeping into his voice.

Andrew wasn't ready to give up. "Keep looking, Gino," he urged, his tone sharp with urgency. "Something has to turn up—check behind the furniture if you have to." Gino nodded, his resolve hardening as he pushed a heavy cabinet aside revealing a shadowy space behind it.

They were both in the dimly lit bedroom. Andrew's gaze swept across the room his eyes landing on the sturdy bed in the corner. He ran a hand over the mattress and whistled softly. "This is a hefty mattress," he said raising an eyebrow at Gino. "Grab the other side, will you? Let's flip this thing and see what we're dealing with."

After struggling for what felt like forever, they finally managed to pull the mattress up from the other side. Andrew's eyes widened as he caught a glimpse of it. "Look, Gino! We've found something!" he shouted, his voice tinged with excitement and relief.

In his hands was a small, flat leather case worn and mysterious. Andrew unfastened the clasp carefully, as if the contents might hold secrets long buried. Inside, he found Azaad Olaar's passport, its edges slightly frayed, and two credit cards. One was embossed in crisp English but the other bore unfamiliar symbols—perhaps from a distant country or an organisation he couldn't immediately recognize.

"Gino, take a look at this," Andrew said, holding up the foreign credit card with a mix of curiosity and unease. "We need to get this to Zoe right away. She'll know what to do."

Gino nodded, his expression sombre as the weight of their discovery began to sink in. What had they stumbled upon and why did it feel like the start of something much bigger? Gino shouted out as he peered under the bed. "What's Doodle up to? He's under there, scratching the carpet and growling!"

Andrew crouched beside him gripping the bed frame. "Yeah, grab that side Gino. Let's pull the bed out and see what's going on."

With a grunt, the two of them heaved the bed away from the wall. As it moved the sight beneath made them pause. The carpet was frayed and loose where Doodle had been clawing at it, exposing a gap along the edge.

"Look at this," Andrew muttered, pointing. Together, they lifted the carpet back and uncovered something unusual—a floorboard that didn't quite fit with the others, its edges unevenly raised.

Gino glanced at Andrew, his eyes widening. "You think there's something under there?"

Andrew's eyes darted to the dusty floorboard beneath their feet. "Gino," he whispered, his voice tinged with urgency, "we need to get this floorboard up. What tools do we have on hand?"

Gino smirked, reaching into his pocket. "You know me, Andrew," he said with a glint in his eye, pulling out a trusty penknife. "I never go anywhere unprepared. Let's see what this little blade can do."

Andrew nodded, a mixture of determination and nervous energy showing across his face. "Alright, let's give it a go," he said, his hands hovering, ready to assist.

The small blade gleamed under the dim light as Gino crouched down his movements precise yet forceful. The air seemed to hold its breath as the two men worked in tandem, intent on revealing whatever secrets lay hidden beneath the floorboards.

Gino crouched low, sweat beading on his forehead as he wrestled with the stubborn floorboard. As his fingers found the right angle, with a click—the board sprang up with surprising ease.

"Hold on!" Andrew said quickly flicking on his phone's torch. The beam cut through the dark, illuminating a hidden compartment beneath the floor. His eyes widened. "You're not going to believe this," he muttered, reaching in with cautious hands.

One by one, he pulled out five tightly-packed cotton bags each weighing about 4 or 5 kilos. The weight of the discovery hung heavy in the air.

"This has got to be drugs," Andrew said, his voice low but urgent. "We need to get these back to our HQ, ASAP."

Mr Williams watched with wide eyes, his astonishment evident. "I can't believe it, "he exclaimed. "I never expected we would find anything, especially not like this. We owe it all to my dog Doodle."

Turning to Andrew, he added with a curious smirk, "I thought you didn't like dogs." Andrew grinned, his tone light but sincere. "Well, I do now!

Please remember, Mr Williams, discretion is not only requested—it is required." Mr Williams replied, "yes, I completely understand and accept that this is your procedure."

"Mr Williams, what you have witnessed in this flat today is not something to be taken lightly. It is a highly sensitive Police matter and I must stress that any disclosure of today's events—be it to newspapers, television stations, or online platforms—will result in legal consequences. Do I make myself clear? We will need your full address as well as your mobile and home phone numbers before we leave."

"That's fine with me." Mr Williams replied.

"I've seen what happens to people who leak classified information. One man I knew faced a crushing fine. He lost his job and struggled for years to find anyone willing to hire him again. I can't let that be my fate."

"Thank you, Mr Williams," Gino replied his tone firm but with a hint of warmth. "And that applies to you as well Doodle," he added, reaching down to give the dog an affectionate pat on the head.

"Could you please now, Mr Williams, take Gino with you to review this morning's CCTV footage? See if we can capture a clear image of the van's licence plate and get a good photo of the two men—it would be incredibly helpful. Oh, and don't forget to provide Gino with all your personal details."

As Gino departed with Mr Williams and Doodle in tow, Andrew called Zoe. Speaking in a hushed yet urgent tone, he recounted the whirlwind of events: the startling discovery of Azaad Olaar's missing passport and credit cards, and the jaw-dropping find of five cotton bags brimming with illicit drugs. He emphasised how he had firmly warned Mr Williams to keep his lips sealed, stressing the gravity of the situation—a matter steeped in police confidentiality.

"Honestly, Andrew, I'm amazed at how you and Gino always manage it. You never fail to uncover something intriguing! I can't wait to find out what drugs are involved this time. Once Gino retrieves the CCTV photos have him send them over to me immediately. I'll look into analysing them. Oh, and well done on giving Mr Williams that warning about maintaining confidentiality—it was a smart and professional move.

What are your plans now? Are you coming straight back?" Zoe asked. "Not yet," Andrew replied. "Simon suggested it might be a good idea to go up to Epping Forest and take a few photos of the scene of the accident."

"That sounds like a sensible plan," Zoe agreed. "While you're at it, it might be worth noting the time it takes to get from the spot where you went into the ditch to the forest entrance. Could help us piece together the timeline.

Don't forget to let me know when you're on your way back," Zoe said, her voice steady but eager. "And make sure to give me a call when you're close. I'll meet you at our Police compound, and then you can check on Tony to see how he's coming along with your old Mondeo."

"Okay I've got it, Zoe," Andrew replied confidently. "As soon as Gino has the CCTV photos we'll be out on the way." "Perfect, keep me in the loop," Zoe said, "and have a safe journey in Simon's BMW."

Gino and Mr Williams returned after about thirty minutes, both looking rather pleased. Gino was quick to approach Andrew, a triumphant grin on his face.

"I've got some great photos of the Express Removals van," he announced, holding up his mobile phone. The number plate's crystal clear and I managed to get decent shots of the two men as well."

"Brilliant work, Gino!" Andrew exclaimed, visibly relieved. "Send those over to Zoe right away." "Already on it Andrew," Gino replied, typing on his phone.

Andrew looked up and said, "While you were away I double-checked everything. That's it—no more loose carpets, all sorted." He turned to Mr Williams, his tone shifting to a more serious note. "Now, if you could give us a hand with these bags to our car and lock the flat door after us. I'm afraid you won't be able to rent this flat out for a while—the fingerprint team will need access as soon as possible."

"Oh, is that really necessary?" asked Mr Williams. "Yes I'm afraid so Mr Williams it's standard procedure and it will eliminate yourself."

After Mr Williams had locked the flat door Andrew said "I have been thinking we should go down and have a look where he parked his Harley Davidson motorcycle in the underground parking."

"That's okay, we can go down after we get these bags in your car," replied Mr Williams.

Simon's BMW car boot was loaded and firmly locked and they followed Mr Williams round the side to the parking entrance. He used his pass key and as they went in the lights all switched on automatically. "Over here is where you need to look. This is where he parked his motorcycle."

Andrew went straight to a fairly large metal trunk. "I would like to have a look in this trunk Mr Williams please. It has a large 5 code padlock. Would you have a hacksaw and a large hammer we could use to break it open?"

"Yes, " he replied, "I will have to go over to the workshop in Tower Block 4. I won't be long."

Andrew was looking at the padlock and said to Gino, "I wonder if we could work out the code to open this padlock. What is his Harley Davidson number plate?"

"Good thinking Andrew, it's AN 71 RAN." "Okay," said Andrew, "let me think about it, we need 5 numbers. It's no good, that wouldn't work out, Gino. What about the Number plate on the elusive white Express Removals van? "

"Yes, I got a good photo from the CCTV and I have forwarded it to Zoe. It's AC 57 IZ."

After a few minutes thought Andrew exclaimed "yes, Gino let's try this, I think I've got it, try 13579." "Right I will" said Gino, as he punched the numbers into the padlock. "No luck Andrew, it won't budge." "Okay Gino, have a try at the reverse method, 97531. Gino did and the padlock sprang open. "Great,"shouted Gino, "How did you work that out Andrew? "

"Well that was how my ex SDI at Brighton taught me, Gino."

Then, as they opened the trunk, Mr Williams walked in carrying a large hammer and a hacksaw. He noticed straight away the trunk lid was open and looked in astonishment. "How did you manage that, guys?" He asked.

"Well, we need to keep our little secrets Mr Williams, let's have a look in the trunk, Gino."

Gino lifted the lid and passed out a tool set, a grease gun, an oil can, a tyre pressure gauge, oily rags and fresh clean cloths, then he exclaimed, "look at this, Andrew, two guns and a case of ammunition.!" Andrew took the guns and ammunition! Then he wrapped them in the fresh clean cloths. "Okay Gino, put everything back and close the lid and scramble the padlock code."

Mr Williams looked on in amazement at them. Andrew warned him, as he did when they were in the flat, that everything he had seen there was to be kept confidential and was not to be disclosed to anyone or to any media. "Is that clear Mr Williams?" he said. "Yes, certainly." he replied.

Andrew and Gino took the guns and the ammunition out to Simon's car and locked them safely in the boot with the five cotton bags.

"We need to be on our way now Mr Williams, thanks for your help. This is my card. If you think of anything else or have any problems following what happened today please give me a call."

"Okay, thanks, I will keep your card handy."

Andrew and Gino embarked on their journey to Epping Forest, a sense of purpose driving them forward. "Don't forget to log the mileage, Gino," Andrew reminded him, "Zoe's waiting for the update." Their mission? To investigate and report back on a startling discovery—two firearms and a case brimming with ammunition. Once their task was complete the plan was clear: secure the haul and deliver it safely into the armoury upon their return.

"I wonder what Simon will say about all that has happened today, Gino," Andrew muttered, a hint of unease in his voice.

Gino smirked. "Oh, you know Simon—he'll be breathing down our necks until his BMW is back where it belongs."

"Yeah, well, one crisis at a time," Andrew replied, straightening his jacket. "First, we head to Epping Forest, photo the incident site, and then get those bags of drugs, guns, and ammunition back to HQ. Let's move."

Andrew gripped the wheel, his face tense with concentration, as he drove through the winding country roads.

About 25 minutes later, he eased the car to a stop at the side of the road, right where the ditch awaited like a scar in the landscape. Switching on the hazard lights, the rhythmic blinking cast an amber glow.

Both Andrew and Gino climbed out of the car, the crunch of gravel under their shoes breaking the silence. Gino took one look at the gaping ditch and let out a low whistle. "Blimey Andrew I didn't realize it was that deep as it was full of water when our Mondeo went in head first."

"Yeah Gino, we were very lucky again. Right, let's move on."

Andrew's knuckles whitened as he gripped the steering wheel, his eyes scanning the winding country roads with laser focus. The hum of the engine was the only sound, a steady backdrop to the tension crackling in the car. After about 25 minutes of navigating the by-roads he pulled over with precision, the vehicle coming to a stop just shy of a cleared area that carved through the woods like an old wound. The hazard lights were switched on, their amber flashes painting the scene in a staccato rhythm.

The silence of the countryside was broken as Andrew and Gino stepped out of the car. Gino's gaze travelled to the gaping area of the incident and he let out a slow, appreciative whistle. "Well," he drawled, "this is where he skidded." The Police blue tape was still tied to the trees and fluttering in the wind.

Andrew turned to Gino, his voice steady but laced with urgency. "Take a few photos and then we'll get moving," he said, his gaze lingering on the grim scene before them. The image of what had happened was hard to shake—a man, thrown from his motorcycle and impaled on a jagged tree branch among the chaos of fallen trees. It was a scene out of a nightmare, chilling enough to make the air feel heavier.

Andrew glanced at Gino again. "As soon as you've got what you need, let's get back." The unease hung between them like the dense forest shadows, urging them to finish quickly.

Andrew paced around nervously, glancing at Gino, his voice tinged with impatience. "Come on, Gino! Have you got enough photos yet?"

Gino adjusted his camera one last time, a satisfied smirk on his face. "Yeah, I'm good. Let's go."

They hurried back to Simon's sleek silver BMW, the soft hum of the engine a stark contrast to the unease settling over Andrew. As he was about to close the door, his phone buzzed sharply in his pocket.

He took it out, answering briskly. "Detective Brown speaking."

A voice crackled on the other end, frantic and breathless. "Detective Brown? It's Roland Williams! I need help—quickly! Please, send someone here immediately!"

Andrew straightened from the urgency in Mr Williams tone, tightening his grip on the phone. "Calm down, Mr Williams. What's the problem?"

"I'm terrified! The white van with Express Removals on the back was here but this time with a different man." Mr Williams's voice trembled as he continued. "He parked right outside my office, stormed in, slammed the door open with a bang, and demanded the room passcode key to Mr Olaar's flat. I told him I couldn't give it to him, but—" his voice cracked, "he pulled out a gun and said he'd shoot me!"

Andrew's grip tightened on the phone. He could hear the panic in Mr Williams's voice, raw and urgent.

"Where is he now, Mr Williams?" Andrew demanded, his voice tight and cutting, though his chest felt like a coiled spring ready to snap. "I... I gave him the room passcode key," Mr Williams stammered, a bead of sweat tracing his temple. "He's in Block 2 now. What should I do? Should I call 999?"

"Listen closely—there's no time to lose. Lock your office door this instant. Then, call 999 and make it crystal clear: you're under threat, and there's a gun involved. Stress the urgency. We're racing to you at full throttle, and I'll have

HQ mobilize Police units immediately to your location. Help is on the way—just hold tight.

"Alright, Gino, let's move. I'm switching on the blue lights—let's see if we can make it back to Tower Block 1 faster than the 45 minutes it took to get here," Andrew said, his tone sharp with urgency. "Call Zoe now, Gino. Make it clear to her just how critical it is to get the Edmonton Police to Ponders End immediately. Tell her the suspect has a gun. I'm seriously worried about Mr Williams safety."

"I'm on it, Andrew," Gino replied, already ringing her number. "Zoe needs to hear this loud and clear."

Andrew floored the accelerator, leaving the shadowy forest behind in a blur. His car surged onto the road, the blue police lights slicing through the air like a beacon. Weaving deftly through the traffic, he pushed the limits of control as drivers scrambled to clear a path, yielding to the authority of his flashing pursuit.

Zoe called back, her voice steady but tinged with urgency, to confirm that Edmonton Police were dispatching a unit immediately, with another en route as backup. She pressed for details, asking how far away they were and urging them to carefully consider their approach to the armed suspect. The tension in the air was palpable as every moment counted.

Andrew's mobile was always on hands free when they were driving and he stated they still had about another 20 minutes to get back to Ponders End. Gino said, " we are going to be very careful when we arrive. If he is still there, we have our bullet proof vests on and we are armed. I hope the Edmonton Police will soon arrive. We are very concerned for the safety of Mr Williams."

"Yeah, that's really concerning, guys, please drive carefully—speeding through traffic is no joke. Let me know when you arrive and update me on the situation," Zoe added with a tone of urgency. "Got it," Gino replied with a nod, his voice steady. "Will do."

Andrew pressed the accelerator, the sleek BMW slicing through the traffic with precision. "We're making great time," Andrew said, a grin spreading across his face as they sped forward.

Gino leaned forward, pointing enthusiastically out of the window. "Look over there—you can see the Tower Blocks! We're nearly there!"

"Perfect," Andrew replied, his eyes flicking briefly toward the skyline before focusing back on the road. "Simon's BMW handles like a dream. This car is fast, it's a masterpiece on wheels."

The hum of the engine underscored the excitement as the Tower Blocks came into sharper view, drawing them closer to their destination.

"We've arrived, Gino!" Andrew exclaimed, his foot slamming on the brakes as their car shot into the maze of towering buildings. The vehicle came to a screeching halt in front of Tower Block 1, tyres screaming in protest.

Their blue flashing lights painted the scene in an almost surreal chaos— one police car stood guard outside the entrance, its sirens blaring like an urgent cry for attention. But of the van they were looking for? Not a trace!

Andrew and Gino leapt from the car and sprinted towards a police officer peering intently through the shattered office window. Their movements were sharp and purposeful, drawing the officer's attention immediately.

"We're with the London Metropolitan Special Branch," Andrew began, his voice steady but urgent. They both showed their warrant cards. Gino was flashing a quick glance over his shoulder as if to emphasise the gravity of their presence. "We've been working here undercover."

Their words hung in the air, charged with the weight of unspoken danger and the tension of a covert mission suddenly brought to light.

Andrew recounted how they had been there with Mr Williams, the caretaker, about an hour earlier. His brow furrowed as he turned to the police officers. "What's going on?" he asked.

"Well, said one of the police officers, his voice steady but laced with urgency, "we only arrived a short while ago. We received a report that a man in a van threatened the caretaker—your Mr Williams—with a gun. Through the cracked window we could make out a jagged hole in the glass, something that resembles the aftermath of a bullet's impact. The caretaker is lying motionless on the floor, his body slumped in a way that suggests unconsciousness—or worse."

A sense of urgency lingered in the air as the door remained stubbornly locked from the inside, as if whatever happened here was meant to stay hidden.

"I've called for an ambulance urgently, but time is slipping away. We're considering using a ram to break down the door, but there's a major issue: he's lying on the floor, just inches away from the door. You can see him clearly through the window, vulnerable and motionless. Every second counts."

"Yes," said Andrew, "Let's hope the bullet didn't hit him and maybe he has fallen and hit his head, we need to get in there fast."

Gino flashed a grin at Andrew. "Come on, let's check out this door lock." He pulled out his penknife again, but this time it looked different—its blade had been replaced with a set of tiny, precise, pointed pieces, almost like a miniature tool kit in one hand. With a swift motion, Gino set to work on the lock, his fingers working with practised precision.

In just a few seconds, there was a satisfying *click*, and the door swung open. Gino paused, he didn't want to push the door hard against Mr Williams, ensuring he didn't harm him. He eased the door open, the quiet creak barely audible in the still room.

As the wail of sirens grew louder the ambulance screeched to a halt, its blue lights flashing in the chaos. One of the police officers, scanning the scene, caught sight of the small penknife in Gino's hand that he used to open the door lock. With a raised eyebrow, he moved toward Gino and remarked, " that's quite the handy little tool you've got there."

Gino, without missing a beat, gave a small grin and shrugged. "Yeah, just part of the job," he replied, as the blade had saved him from trouble more times than he cared to count.

The paramedics moved swiftly, carefully avoiding any force against the door as they entered. Their focus was entirely on Mr Williams as they worked to stabilize him. Meanwhile, Andrew turned to the police officers."When you arrived, did you see the van?" he asked.

One of the officers shook his head. "No sign of any van," he said, a thoughtful look crossing his face. "But I'd wager he heard our sirens and bolted—probably figured he didn't have much time before we'd be hot on his heels."

Andrew frowned, imagining the scene unfolding just moments before they arrived. It seemed like the suspect had planned his escape.

"Yeah, that's how it goes," said Andrew. We've been chasing that van for ages, " He admitted with a sigh.

"Well, you're in luck, guys! We've got some top-notch, state-of-the-art CCTV cameras covering every road in this area. I'll contact the Road Traffic Police right away. If you can give me your contact number I promise I will call you the moment we trace him."

"Fantastic! Here's my contact card," Andrew replied with a grin. "By the way, the van's registration is AC 57 1Z. Gino managed to pull it from the CCTV footage this morning."

"That sounds about right," Andrew muttered, "I had suspected as much. I thought he would have gone before we arrived." But before he could dwell on it, one of the paramedics emerged from the ambulance. "The caretaker, Mr Williams, is conscious now," he reported. "He's got a nasty bump on his head, though, so we'll need to take him to the hospital in Edmonton for further care.

Which one of you is Detective Brown?" The paramedics sharp voice cut through the tension, "he'd like a word with you before we take him."

Andrew swallowed hard, stepping forward. "That's me," he said, his voice steady despite the weight of uncertainty pressing down on him.

Without hesitation, he followed the paramedic's into Mr. Williams's office, the door closing behind them with a quiet but firm click, leaving the others to wonder what lay ahead.

Still groggy, Mr Williams mustered enough strength to speak, his voice a little shaky but determined. "Andrew," he said, "could you do me a favour? Please call Jane—my wife. You've got our home phone number. Let her know I had a fall, bumped my head, and I'm being taken to Edmonton Hospital for a check-up. Keep it brief—I don't want her worrying too much.

Here's my boss's mobile number. His name is Rob Jackson. Call him right away and ask him to get over here—fast. I need him to cover for me." "Of course no problem at all," Andrew replied, with a confident grin.

Andrew glanced around the room before adding, "mind if we take a look at your CCTV? Gino knows where it is, he was with you earlier. And I'm guessing this guy was after those bags we found stashed under the floorboards in Mr Olaar's flat."

Mr Williams glanced up at Andrew, his brow furrowed slightly, and said "yes, that's no problem."

Andrew leaned in to hear more clearly, a spark of curiosity in his eyes. "Thanks. Just two quick questions—was he English? And did he mention what he was looking for?" Mr Williams paused, his gaze unfocused as if searching for a memory lost in the haze. "English? No, definitely not. If I had to guess, I'd say he was from Iraq... or maybe Iran" he murmured, his tone uncertain yet intrigued. "He stormed up to the office door and threw a vicious kick at it, a loud sound echoing. When the door didn't budge, he turned to the window, fists hammering against the glass, his voice raw with rage. Where are the bags of cocaine? What did you do with them? he screamed, each word sharp and jagged.

Before I could even process what was happening, he raised a gun. My heart stopped. There was the deafening crack of the shot through the window and I felt the world tilt as I stumbled backward, everything going dark. The next thing I knew the paramedics were trying to wake me, their voices distant, as if pulling me back into life."

The paramedics returned to the office, their expressions calm yet focused, and gently asked Andrew to move. "We'll need to bring in a wheelchair," they explained, preparing to transfer Mr Williams to the waiting ambulance. Within moments, the wheelchair was manoeuvred into the office, its quiet wheels sliding across the floor.

Before long the paramedic team were wheeling him out, the cool air brushing past as they moved swiftly toward the ambulance. The vehicle's doors swung open with purpose and in no time they were on their way, the sound of the siren piercing the stillness of the day.

Andrew relayed Mr Williams message to Gino, his voice steady but urgent. "I need you to call Jane, his wife," he said, glancing toward the shattered office window. "Explain what happened here. Keep it brief, no need to tell her the full story, and let her know the ambulance is taking him to Edmonton Hospital."

"Got it," Gino replied, already reaching for his phone. "I'll call her right away, I have his home number from the details Mr Williams gave us this morning."

"Good," Andrew said with a nod. "In the meantime, I'll call the number Mr Williams gave me. It's his boss, Rob Jackson the caretaker's supervisor. He needs to get down here fast, to arrange for a glazier to replace this window, and sort out cover for Mr Williams while he's out of action"

As Gino dialled Mr Williams wife, Jane's, number, the weight of the situation settled heavily on both men. Time was of the essence, and there was no room for delay.

"We'll need to wait for Mr Williams boss to arrive so we can issue a strong warning. He cannot, under any circumstances, disclose anything about today's events—whether to newspapers, TV stations, or online platforms. As I've already explained to Mr Williams I'll make sure these two police officers are also brought up to speed on what we've uncovered here."

As Andrew finished explaining the sensitivity of this case, another police car screeched in and pulled up beside Simon's BMW. Two police officers jumped out and ran over to the Tower Block office.

They came to a sudden halt, their eyes locking onto Andrew and Gino with a spark of recognition. "Wait a second," they blurted out, their voices tinged with both surprise and amusement. "Aren't you the two who went flying head first into that ditch on that ridiculously rainy day? We picked you up and drove you to the train station, didn't we?"

"Yes, that's us," Andrew replied with a knowing nod. The Police officer continued. "You know, it struck me as odd when our Chief called us into his office before we left. He gave us strict instructions. No sensitive information in the report until he's reviewed it himself. He said it was critical. He also mentioned the possibility of two undercover detectives from London's Special Branch showing up. We didn't think it'd be you two again. Guess fate likes to play games!

Alright, if you could give us a quick rundown of today's events you're free to head back to your HQ," the first police officer said, his gaze drifting to the sleek silver BMW parked nearby. "I'm guessing that beauty belongs to you?"

"Yes, but it's just a temporary replacement," Andrew replied with a slight shrug. "Our Mondeo might be ready by tomorrow."

"Well, good luck with that," the police officer said with a smirk. "By the way, our Chief Constable wanted me to let you know he's in touch with your Simon Harris. He'll be sending him a copy of our report like last time." "Thanks for that," Andrew replied calmly. Before he could elaborate, one of the first police officers approached, his expression tense. "We've been called back to HQ," the officer announced briskly. His partner nodded in agreement. "That's fine with us," the second one added. "We can handle things from here."

Andrew provided them with all the critical details he could, his tone sharp with urgency.

"When Mr Williams' supervisor, Rob Jackson, arrives, ensure he understands—this incident must remain confidential. No leaks to newspapers, TV stations, or streaming platforms," he emphasized, his gaze firm and unyielding.

The Police officer agreed, his response measured. "Understood. We're regularly briefed on disclosure protocols and will handle this accordingly." "Before we set off," said Andrew, "let's review the CCTV footage to get a clear photo of the guy in the van. Gino will guide you through it, showing you exactly where the recordings are stored. You'll need those images for your reports."

"Follow me," Gino said, his voice low and urgent, as he led the way through the front office. He navigated confidently, weaving past desks and filing cabinets until they reached a smaller dimly lit room tucked away at the back.

"This is it," Gino announced, his tone carrying a hint of triumph. Within moments, he pulled up the time logs and CCTV footage. The grainy images revealed a man stepping out of a van, his movements sharp and impatient. The audio caught his angry shout: "I need a room passkey for Mr Olaar in Block 2!" he demanded, his eyes fixed on Mr Williams who looked startled but compliant.

The same white Express Removals van, with its unmistakable registration AC 57 1Z, had rolled up early that morning. Two men had swiftly emptied his flat without raising suspicion. Now, the image was clear—one of them stood out. The driver was dark-skinned, with a thick black beard, dressed head-to-toe in black: a hoodie, trousers, and scuffed trainers. "Hey, look." Gino exclaimed, his voice cutting through the tension. "Here's a great shot of him— waving a gun!" Gino and the police officer took several clear photos from the CCTV.

After capturing enough photos, the police officer assured Gino that he would immediately dispatch them to all police divisions, urging swift action to apprehend the suspect. Gino nodded, adding that he would send his copies straight to Metropolitan HQ for rapid distribution.

"We should try to locate the bullet fired through the window," he suggested. With urgency and determination Gino pulled a sleek, compact magnifying glass from his pocket, its polished metal glinting in the light. He stepped closer to the shattered window, crouching slightly to inspect the bullet hole in the fractured glass. His gaze sharpened as he tilted his head studying the minute details with meticulous care.

"What are you looking for?" asked the police officer, curiosity mingled with impatience in his tone. Without glancing away from the glass Gino replied, his voice calm but purposeful. "During a special branch technical observation course this was something we learnt. I will show you that what we need to know is the trajectory of the bullet.

I'm carefully inspecting the hole, trying to pinpoint the radius. Ah, there it is—right at the top! That means the bullet landed below four feet. Quick, give me a hand to push these filing cabinets further apart so we can get a clearer view. Perfect—there it is, lodged right in the wall plaster like a frozen moment in time.

With a swift flick of his wrist, Gino produced his trusty penknife once more. His movements were deliberate but steady, each cut precise as he worked around the embedded bullet. Beads of sweat formed on his brow but he didn't falter. At last, he prised the bullet free and carefully wrapped it in his handkerchief, his hands steady despite the tension in the air.

The Police officer standing nearby could only look in astonishment, his expression a mix of awe and disbelief. Gino turned to Andrew, his voice low but firm. "The CCTV photos are really clear Andrew. "

Gino then said he remembered the technical observation course he went on. It showed him exactly how to retrieve a bullet. "That's how I knew where to look for this." He held up his handkerchief and showed Andrew the extracted bullet, now a pivotal clue in the unfolding mystery.

The police officer leaned back with a thoughtful smile. "Well guys, I've got to say, I've learned a lot from you two. So, what's next?"

One of the other police officers chimed in, "what about the flat? You know, the one occupied by the guy on the Harley Davidson—Mr Olaar. We'll need to check it out to gather some details for our report."

Andrew mentioned, that during their earlier visit, Mr Williams had provided them with a key card for the coded door, which they returned to him when leaving. "When Rob Jackson arrives, he'll be able to provide you with a key card as well. The flat is located in Tower Block 2, on the third floor, room 218. We also requested Mr Williams ensures the door remains locked, as a police fingerprint team is scheduled to visit the premises.

But the real shock came when we prised up the floorboards under his bed. That's where we found the goods—bags of cocaine, tucked away. If you're interested, I can take one of you over to Tower Block 2's underground parking. That's where he kept his Harley Davidson, gleaming like a trophy. The place is locked down with tight security, but who knows? If we time it right, we might catch someone leaving and slip inside. What do you think?

"Okay let's give it a try," one of the police officers said, his voice tinged with determination. He gestured for Andrew to follow as they made their way towards the parking garage doors. As they approached the garage doors, the faint hum of an engine grew louder—a car was pulling out.

"Hold it!" the police officer barked, breaking into a quick stride. He darted towards the door managing to wedge himself in just before it swung shut. Andrew hurried to catch up, and together they slipped inside the brightly lit garage. Andrew said, "he parked his Harley Davidson over here. There is a large trunk against the wall. "

The Police officer looked closer at the trunk squinting at the padlock. "This is a five-digit coded lock. How on earth did you manage to get it open and find the guns and ammunition you reported?"

Andrew shrugged, trying to downplay the effort. "After a few tries I cracked the combination," said Andrew.

Then the police officer raised an eyebrow, clearly impressed. "Seriously? You guys never cease to amaze me. Show me the number—I want to take a look for myself." Andrew said "okay" and recited, "Nine-seven-five-three-one."

Andrew gestured toward the trunk, explaining that the guns and ammunition were at the bottom of it. " Now they are all locked in the boot of the BMW and ready for the police armoury," he added with a touch of relief. The officer looked in, carefully rummaging through the contents before snapping the trunk shut with a decisive click. Twisting the padlock they scrambled the code ensuring everything was secure. Without a word, they turned, pushed open the garage door, and headed back toward Tower Block 1, their shoes echoing faintly against the pavement.

As they returned, a sleek new car had pulled up in their absence. Stepping out, a sharp-dressed man introduced himself as Rob Jackson, his tone laced with curiosity and concern. "What happened here? And how is Roland Williams?" he asked, his eyes scanning the scene.

Andrew, ever quick to act, turned to the police officers. "Perhaps you could give Mr Jackson the details of what happened here?"

The Police officers exchanged glances and said yes of course in agreement. "That works for us, we'll take it over from you," one of the police officers replied, gesturing towards Rob Jackson. "Would you show us to room 218 in Tower Block 2? We'll coordinate with the fingerprint team to process the scene." Rob Jackson hesitated for a moment, then straightened his jacket. "Yes please follow me," he said, his voice steady, though the flicker of unease in his eyes was hard to miss.

Andrew and Gino thanked him, and as they were leaving one of the officers called out, "Good luck guys in finding the Express Removals van, we will keep you informed of any sightings from our road Traffic Police and will check our Chief Constable sends our report to your office for the attention of Simon Harris."

As they left Ponders End behind, Gino called Zoe to give her the update: they were on their way back to the police compound. The journey was smooth and uneventful, filled with the quiet satisfaction of a job well done.

When they finally arrived, Andrew skilfully steered Simon's BMW into the compound. The sleek car glided to a stop its engine purring like a contented cat. Waiting for them under the dim glow of the compound's security lights were Simon and Zoe, their faces a mix of anticipation and relief.

Simon gave his car a once-over, running his hand along the dusty exterior. "Well," he said with a faint smile, "I'm glad everything seems fine—just a bit on the dirty side."

Tony, the Transport Repair Manager, strolled over, wiping his hands on a grease-stained rag. "Don't worry about that," he assured him. "Once we're done we'll have it sparkling like new. I'm aiming to have the Mondeo ready by tomorrow—fingers crossed. Let me know if you'd like further refinements!"

Andrew opened the boot, revealing the cache inside. Simon wasted no time time in wanting to take the guns and ammunition, "I'll get these to the armoury," he said. Then before heading off he called out, "we'll reconvene tomorrow morning—same place same time," I think we're finally making progress. Now we just need to get our hands on that bloody Express Removals van."

Zoe beamed, a spark of admiration lighting up her face. "You guys never fail to deliver. Seriously, it's amazing." She eyed the bags of cocaine. "I'll take these, but I could use a hand."

Without hesitation, Gino stepped forward. "I've got two of them," he offered, lifting the bags. Andrew and Gino exchanged knowing glances; they might be a motley crew but when it came down to it they always found a way to get the job done.

Andrew approached Tony, curiosity etched on his face. "How's the Mondeo coming along?" he asked.

Tony wiped his hands on a rag and motioned for Andrew to follow. "Come and take a look while you're waiting for Gino," he said. Leading the way to the workshop he pointed at the Mondeo still perched on the ramp. "I'm just waiting on a small part for the steering control," Tony explained. "It's supposed to arrive tomorrow morning. As soon as it's sorted and ready for the road, I'll let Simon know." Andrew replied eyeing the car thoughtfully.

"Thanks, Tony, it's reassuring to know everything's in safe hands." Tony leaned against the car and asked, "How did you get on with Simon's BMW?"

Andrew grinned. "It's a beast of a car. Very fast." Tony chuckled knowingly. "Yeah, thought so."

"Got to test the blue lights too," Andrew added with a hint of mischief. "Speeding through traffic was..exhilarating."

Then Gino returned, with a tired but satisfied expression. "Right, let's get moving," Andrew said. "I'll drop you off. Leave your body vest, gun, and ammunition with me—I'll lock them up in my safe."

"Thanks, Andrew," Gino replied, handing over the gear. He stretched, clearly feeling the weight of the day. "What a day it's been. Honestly I'm just glad to be heading home at a decent hour."

As Andrew pulled up outside Gino's house, Gino hopped out of the car with a grin. "Cheerio! See you in the morning!" he called out, giving a quick wave before disappearing through the front door.

Andrew wasted no time heading back to his sleek Hammersmith apartment, weaving efficiently through the quiet streets. He pulled Simon's pristine BMW into the garage, the engine purring softly before falling silent. With meticulous care, he secured the vests, guns and ammunition inside his steel-reinforced safe, its door closing with a satisfying click.

After double-checking every lock and ensuring the alarm was armed, Andrew glanced at his watch. "Now I can catch the bus back home," he thought as he stepped out into the cool night, his mind already calculating tomorrow's plans as the city's dim glow painted the horizon.

Chloe's face lit up with relief as Andrew walked through the door. "I'm so glad you're home," she said, her voice trembling slightly. "I've been worried sick. There was a report on the news about a shooting at a tower block in North London. Last night when Simon called you, he mentioned you had a search warrant for a flat in one of those buildings."

Andrew was pulling off his jacket. "You're right, Chloe. We were there but the shooting had already happened before we arrived. It was just one shot fired through a window. Honestly, I'm surprised it made the news—it wasn't as dramatic as they probably made it sound."

Andrew shifted the conversation with a warm smile. "How's our little Dimitris today?"

"Oh, he was such a delight!" Chloe replied, her eyes lighting up. "He's been full of energy, running around all afternoon at play school. He's fast asleep now, completely worn out."

"That's great to hear," Andrew said, rising from his seat. "I'll go up and say goodnight to him."

A few moments later, Andrew returned, a soft smile lingering on his face. "He looks so peaceful when he's asleep," he remarked, his voice tinged with affection.

Chloe brought their evening meal to the table, and Andrew felt a wave of gratitude. After an eventful day the quiet warmth of home was what he needed.

CHAPTER SEVEN

The next morning, Andrew and Gino met outside their usual meeting spot, the City Hall Coffee House. Gino's brow furrowed with concern as he asked Andrew, "what's our next move?" His voice was tinged with urgency. They had been tossing around ideas about how to finally corner that elusive Express Removals van when Simon and Zoe arrived.

"Morning, everyone," Simon greeted, his tone brisk yet warm. Zoe added a quick, "let's find a spot," scanning the café for a quiet corner.

Gino nodded, already stepping towards the counter. "I'll get the coffees today," he said.

Minutes later, the four of them were huddled together, steaming mugs in hand. Simon glanced around the table his expression serious."Alright, listen up. We've got a lot to go over.

1) We now know the name of the guy who was shot at the Holborn underground station, Ahmadi Levy. We know he was an imposter and is from Northern Kurdistan. What's the latest on him, Zoe?" "Well, I have had my team checking him out with fingerprints and DNA and we have contacted the British Consulate General in Erbil, who represent the UK government in the Kurdistan Region in Northern Iran. They have not requested we repatriate the body, as they have no interest."

2) "So what's the next move with him Zoe?" Zoe replied, "I have checked with the local authority and the body can be cremated within 72 hours from release by forensics team." "Okay Zoe, we should authorise the forensics to release the body to the local authority. I will double check this with Matt and get back to you.

3) Now about the young guy who planted the bomb on the London underground train and committed suicide. We know his name is Oliver Jones. I have received a letter from his parents and they were very complimentary about you two guys when you were at the house where he lodged with Mrs

Murphy, and they said, thank God you didn't turn on that light switch. They had his body sent up to Scotland and they had a family funeral.

4) Okay, next is the guy who was found in a skip at Lewisham. What's the latest Zoe ?" "Yes, again we have a body but as yet we haven't got his name. My team have tried all avenues like we did with Ahmadi Levy. We again contacted the British Consulate General in Erbil. We are certain he is from Northern Kurdistan. The consular officer was helpful and he tried to find out about him. We sent him photos and a full description, but still to no avail."

5) "Zoe, I will discuss this case with Matt. We may have to get both guys cremated. I will check who pays for the cremation?" Zoe said "I think it's the local authority. I also checked with Border control and they have no records of either one so we have to conclude they are both illegal immigrants."

6) "So now to 'Azaad Olaar,' the guy who forced 'Oliver Jones' to make bombs and plant one on a London underground train, and when you guys discovered where his flat was, you chased after him. He fired two shots at you and another police car and it was very unfortunate his life ended by an accident in Epping Forest.

7) What's the latest with him Zoe?" "Right. This has happened yesterday. The Iran embassy in London have requested we repatriate his body and his Harley Davidson motorcycle to Iran. This will be at their cost. I don't know what the next step is Simon." "Okay, Zoe, I will get this sorted with Matt. I think it will have to be agreed with the Prime Minister in Parliament.

8) And now we have another case, the guy who turns up at Ponders End Tower Blocks expecting to recover 5 x 4.5 kilo bags of top class cocaine, the estimated value is £2.5 million, two guns and a box of ammunition. Then when he finds it's gone he takes a shot at the caretaker. Fortunately the Edmonton Police were there then you guys arrived and he had raced away. All we have are photos of him and the van from the CCTV.

9) Have you checked out the Express Removals van registration Zoe?" "Yes, it is registered as a horse box in Mid Wales! I sent the van registration to Manchester for the attention of Alan Edwards and he has confirmed they have picked up the van on the Road Traffic Police CCTV leaving Manchester and heading for the M 60 after picking up 'Ahmadi Levy.'"

10) "We must engage all our resources to catching this guy in the bloody Express Removals van before someone else gets shot. Zoe, keep chasing all

Road Traffic Police and check out with the Edmonton Police. They promised to help us find him and keep us all informed.

11) Okay. Andrew and Gino listen up. I need you to get over to your Hammersmith office and start digging into this Express Removals van. Contact every removal company in East London and any small firm that might need a van for quick moves. There has to be a connection somewhere. I suspect the van is stolen, so start by asking around.

12) And we still have to continue with a follow up on the smart lady and man who were on the underground train. We have recently received more information from the Eurostar Police, this needs to be to discussed, it may involve you going on the Eurostar to Paris.

Andrew and Gino both left City Hall and soon arrived at Andrew's Hammersmith apartment. As they got started Gino said, "This looks like it's going to be very time-consuming, Andrew." "Yes, Gino but we have to keep calling as many firms as we can. Someone, somewhere knows about the Express Removals van. Simon needs us to find an answer."

After a couple of hours of fruitless calls, they were growing frustrated. "Let's take a little break, Gino,"Andrew suggested. "There's the Greek deli around the corner which I love, we have been before."

"Great idea," Gino replied, stretching. "I could use a break."

Switching off their computer screens, they stepped out of the office and into the busy street. The aroma of freshly baked bread and brewed coffee greeted them as they entered the cosy deli, a welcome contrast to their tedious morning. The deli's warm ambiance and cheerful chatter instantly lifted their spirits. They enjoyed their lunch and discussed the mystery of the missing Express Removals van.

As they dined, Andrew said "I've had a thought. In one of Zoe's reports I'm certain she mentioned her team was tracking all the CCTV cameras on the underground. They followed the Express Removals guy out to Shoreditch, but then lost him.

Maybe we should drive over that way and check out a few firms. We should let Simon and Zoe know our plans before we go."

"Sounds sensible to me, Andrew," replied Gino. "It'll be better than making loads of phone calls. Some of the people I've spoken to clearly don't believe who we are and are reluctant to give any information over the phone about their transport.

I can't shake the feeling that some of these managers are lining their pockets with a little something extra from the drivers," Andrew said, his voice low and edged with suspicion. His hand hovered over his phone, ready to call Simon, when it buzzed unexpectedly against his palm. A wry smile tugged at the corner of his lips. "Perfect timing," he muttered under his breath, answering the call.

"I was about to phone you with an update and a suggestion," Andrew began. "I think we should go over to the Shoreditch area." Simon paused briefly, then responded, "Good idea. By the way, Tony has informed me your Mondeo is ready—it's fully repaired." Andrew said, with a grin to Gino, "looks like the Mondeo is back in action, let's get moving."

Simon said, "if you can drive over now Andrew, I will be pleased to finally get my BMW back. While you're out that way to Shoreditch it might be worth checking out Hackney, Stepney and Poplar too. I have received a call from Edmonton Police HQ—they've been combing through all the road traffic CCTV footage leading into Central London. The van has been spotted along the embankment."

Simon greeted them at the police compound with a satisfied grin as he laid eyes on his freshly returned BMW. The tension of the day seemed to ease in his expression. Meanwhile, Andrew and Gino climbed into their now-repaired Mondeo, the engine purring like new. "Be careful out there," Simon cautioned, "the weather is changing and snow is forecast," his tone serious despite his earlier smile. "The moment you sense trouble, don't hesitate—use the Codex Mobile, and don't forget, if you feel you are in any trouble please call Zoe or myself immediately."

As they drove off, Andrew focused on the road while Gino tested the comfort of the passenger seat. "Feels good," Gino said. Andrew agreed with a nod of approval. "Tony's done a top-notch job on the repairs, Andrew, It actually reminds me of my dad—he could fix up any car like it was second nature."

Andrew chuckled. "Must run in the family, then. Let's hope we don't need another repair anytime soon."

When they arrived in Shoreditch they found a spot to park and set off on foot, determined to make some progress. They visited both large and small removal companies, along with carpet and furniture outlets, but their efforts yielded nothing. Still, there was something about speaking to people face-to-face that felt more promising, even if the results weren't there yet.

"Alright, Gino," Andrew said with a sigh, brushing off the slight sting of disappointment. "Let's head to Hackney, Stepney and Poplar."

Once again, they parked and walked the streets, stopping by potential leads. Yet luck continued to elude them. Finally, Andrew glanced up at the darkening sky. The first traces of sleet were falling, cold and biting.

"Come on, Gino," he said, rubbing his hands together. "Let's find a coffee bar. We need a break—and something to warm us up before we freeze out here."

They stumbled upon a cosy coffee bar not far from where they'd parked. Settling in, they ordered their usual coffees and dived into a discussion about their next call. The gentle hum of conversation and the scent of freshly brewed espresso filled the air—until Andrew suddenly leapt from his seat. "Look Look! Gino, it's him!" he exclaimed, pointing out through the window.

Gino turned to see what had sparked Andrew's outburst. Sure enough, right outside the window, stuck in traffic, was the wanted white van with 'Express Removals' emblazoned on the back.

"Come on, hurry!" Andrew shouted, his voice tinged with urgency. They bolted out of the coffee bar, the chill of the outside air hitting them like a slap. The car doors hissed open automatically, and they jumped in slamming the doors shut in unison.

Gino's fingers were soon on the codex phone, his breath shallow as he punched the keys—4, then 5—triggering an urgent backup request. The engine roared to life as they edged into the traffic.

"Where is he?" Andrew asked, scanning the line of vehicles ahead. "There," Gino said, "in front of that dark Volvo only a few cars away." Only seven or eight vehicles separated them from their target.

Without looking up, Gino called Zoe again. Her sharp intake of breath was audible over the line. "You're sure it's him? I don't believe it?"

"Positive." Gino replied.

"Okay, listen," she said, her voice firm but quick. "Don't lose him, but don't let him suspect anything. Keep your distance. I'll call Simon. As soon as backup is close, light up—blue lights, sirens the works. But keep in contact with me, Gino. Don't let him get away!"

The line went dead as Andrew accelerated, his pulse pounding in time with the car's engine.

After about ten minutes, Andrew caught sight of the first police car in his rear-view mirror. It was only a few vehicles behind him, its blue lights flashing and siren wailing. The cacophony of sound cut through the evening air causing cars and lorries ahead to move over, creating a clear area to allow both cars to get through quickly. Andrew caught site of the van making a sharp left turn, his wheels skidding in the snow.

Gino said, "I can hear another police car in the distance Andrew." "That's good," replied Andrew, "we could do with another car in front to stop him." "Yes, I agree," said Gino. Zoe rang again and asked what was happening. Gino gave her the latest update and said that two police cars were behind them. She said to keep the line open.

Andrew squinted at the satnav, his knuckles white against the steering wheel as he tried to make sense of the flickering directions. The embankment loomed closer with each passing second, the van hurtling forward at a terrifying pace. Snow was coming down fast, a swirling, blinding white that turned the area into chaos.

The tyres screeched on the icy road, and suddenly, everything tilted. With a gut-wrenching skid, the van careered over the pavement's edge. Time seemed to slow as the vehicle launched forward—then plunged straight into the icy embrace of the River Thames.

On the other end of the phone, Zoe's voice was sharp, incredulous. "Bloody hell!" she shouted. "Has he actually gone into the Thames?"

Andrew and Gino exchanged stunned glances, their disbelief growing as they had watched him manoeuvre through such treacherous conditions at breakneck speed.

Moments later, the wail of sirens faded as two police cars pulled up behind them. Andrew turned to Gino, gesturing toward the approaching police officers. Andrew said, "we are both from Special Branch." One of the officers stepped forward, with a wry smile. "Yeah," he said dryly, "we guessed you were."

Andrew stared in disbelief at the van bobbing in the currents of the Thames. "What happens now? The van's floating away fast!" he exclaimed.

The water surged, carrying the vehicle further down river at an alarming pace. "Are you contacting the River Police?" asked Andrew." "Yes," came the swift reply. "We're already on it. They need to move quickly—if it drifts much further, it could collide with the Thames Barrier."

Tension hung in the air as they watched the van's precarious journey. Emergency teams were mobilising; soon, someone would be sent into the water to attempt a daring rescue of whoever might still be inside.

"Can you confirm who was in the van? Was it one person or two?" one of the police officers asked sharply.

Andrew replied firmly. "It was only one man, he was tall and dark-skinned, dressed head-to-toe in black—black trousers, black shoes, black coat. We've got photos of him and the van. He was armed, carrying a gun, and he fired a shot at a caretaker in a tower block yesterday."

"Oh, and what nationality is he?"

"We suspect he's Iranian. We've already been tracking two from Kurdistan, and when we pursued another target from Northern Iran, well... let's just say he met an unfortunate end. His body is currently about to be extradited back to Iran."

The police officer paused, a shadow of grim satisfaction crossing his face. "As for this one? When they fish him out of the River Thames, I imagine it'll follow the same story."

Gino's phone rang, his voice trembling as he fought back tears while hearing the news. His wife Sophia had received a call from his mother in Italy—his father had been rushed to the hospital after suffering a massive heart attack. The situation was dire, the doctors didn't hold out much hope for his survival. Sophia told him his mother's plea was urgent. She said to tell Gino to catch the next flight to Italy before it was too late.

Gino's voice carried a mix of relief and urgency. "Sophia's been in touch with Heathrow," he said. "She managed to get me a seat on the 8 pm flight to Malpensa Airport, Milan, tonight. She's also arranged for a car to pick me up and drive straight to Ospedale Maggiore Policlinico di Milano."

"Alright, Gino," came Andrews calm reply. "Don't stress. I'll make a quick call to Zoe and sort everything out."

Andrew's hands trembled as he called Zoe, urgency thick in his voice. "Zoe, it's about Gino's father—it's serious."

Zoe didn't hesitate. "Alright, Andrew, let's not waste a second. Find a police officer and pass him your mobile phone. We need to act now!" Without a moment to lose, Andrew scanned the area, went to a nearby police officer, and quickly explained. "Zoe, from our Metropolitan HQ needs to speak to you. She has critical information about Gino and me."

He handed over his phone, and Zoe's sharp, commanding tone came through the line. She wasted no time relaying everything she knew, her words carrying the weight of urgency and precision.

Zoe firmly instructed the police officer to ensure that their report excluded any mention of the car chase following the van. With a professional air, she provided her Metropolitan Police HQ email address and requested a direct copy of the finalised report.

The police officer was in agreement, assuring her that the task would be handled without issue. Pleased with his cooperation, Zoe offered a polite thanks before the police officer handed Andrew's phone back to him.

Alright Andrew," Zoe instructed, her tone calm but commanding. "Head straight to Gino's house, then take him to Heathrow. Use the blue lights—if you move quickly you should make it on time. Once you get to Heathrow Terminal 5 take the left turn and enter through the emergency and VIP access point. I'll call the control centre and arrange clearance for you and Gino."

"Okay, Gino, let's get going," Andrew said, his tone firm as they both got into their Mondeo. The snow had eased, leaving behind a slick, slushy mess that sprayed up as the tyres churned through it. Once they were clear of the embankment, Andrew switched on the blue lights, their glow cutting through the dim evening gloom.

"Don't need the police officers thinking we're in trouble," Andrew muttered to himself, gripping the wheel tightly.

Gino stared out of the window, his face tense, his breath fogging the glass. Andrew glanced at him, his voice softening. "I really hope your dad pulls through, Gino. I know it's a lot for you and Sophia to deal with." "Yeah," Gino said quietly, his voice thick with worry. "Thanks, Andrew. I can't stop thinking about him. It's... it's hard."

The flash of blue lights transformed everything. It was amazing to see how traffic parted, clearing the way.

"Right, Gino, we're making good time now," Andrew called out, his eyes scanning the road as they cruised past the iconic Westminster Bridge. "When we get closer to your place we'll pull over somewhere discreet. We'll stash the bulletproof vests, guns and ammunition in the car boot.

Once I'm back at my Hammersmith apartment, I'll secure everything in the safe." He glanced at Gino with a knowing look. "You don't want Sophia seeing you geared up when she says goodbye, do you?"

"You're absolutely right, Andrew. Like you said, I have to tread carefully when talking to Sophia about our daily activities. It's a real challenge sometimes—keeping myself from accidentally spilling something I shouldn't."

Gino pointed ahead. "There's a lane coming up on the left, pull in now."

Andrew replied, "okay, that looks fine," as he was parking in the lane. Andrew pulled out his phone. While we are here, Gino, I will send Chloe a quick text to let her know I'll be home later."

They quickly stripped off their bulletproof vests, holstered their guns and stashed the ammunition safely in the boot of the car. "Alright, Gino," Andrew said, getting into the driver's seat. "Next stop—your house."

When they arrived, the warm glow of the porch light revealed Sophia and Gino's two daughters waiting eagerly by the door. The moment Gino stepped out Sophia rushed to him, wrapping her arms tightly around his neck as if she hadn't seen him in years.

As they turned to go inside, Sophia glanced back with a welcoming smile. "Come in, Andrew! Don't worry, we won't keep him long. I really appreciate you taking him to Heathrow."

"That's perfectly fine, Sophia. If there's anything we can do to help don't hesitate to give us a call. I'll keep Chloe updated—she'll definitely be on the phone tomorrow," Andrew assured her.

As Gino was double-checking his passport and the holdall Sophia had thoughtfully packed for him, Gino said his goodbyes to his two girls and Sophia. Moments later Gino and Andrew were on their way, the anticipation of the journey ahead for Gino beginning to set in.

Gino glanced at the satnav, the soft glow of the screen reflecting on his face. "Heathrow's about 45 minutes from here," he said, checking the time. "It's 6.15 pm now. Andrew are you keeping the blue lights on?" Andrew said "yes," his hands steady on the wheel as the siren wailed. "Absolutely, Gino. We'll save some time and get you there with enough to spare for check-in before the gate closes."

True to Andrew's word, they drove through the streets weaving expertly through traffic. The distinctive blue lights cleared the way and they pulled into Heathrow's emergency entrance. Gino, still amazed by the speed, found himself with time to spare, ready to face the next stage of his journey.

As Gino stepped out of the car, Andrew leaned out of the window with a heartfelt smile. "All the best, Gino. I hope your dad's feeling better by the time you get to the hospital," he said, his voice tinged with genuine concern. Then, as Gino walked away, Andrew called out one last time, "Don't forget to keep in touch! We'll miss you."

With a final wave, Andrew eased the car back onto the road heading towards Hammersmith. Once there he parked the Mondeo in his garage, its engine's low rumble echoing in the quiet.

When inside his apartment he moved swiftly but methodically—first securing both sets of bulletproof vests, then carefully locking away the guns and ammunition in his safe. Satisfied everything was in its proper place he double-checked the locks on every window and door. The apartment was a fortress, now silent and secure, with the alarms primed.

Andrew exhaled, picked up his coat and stepped into the cool night. The bus ride home a stark contrast to the tension-laden tasks he'd just completed.

Andrew felt a wave of relief as he stepped through his front door after one of the strangest days he'd ever experienced. The chaotic pursuit of the Express Removals van—which had somehow concluded with it plunging into the River Thames—still played on his mind. How lucky they'd been to spot the van from their seats at the coffee bar! But the day's bizarre twists hadn't ended there. The news about Gino's dad weighed heavily, casting a shadow over an already surreal chain of events.

Chloe's voice carried a warm, curious note as she called out, "Hi, darling! I'm so glad you're back. Have you had a busy day? You mentioned you had to go to Heathrow, but you didn't say why. What's going on?"

Andrew sat down on the sofa beside her, his expression unreadable. Chloe's brow furrowed as she studied his face. "You look troubled, is everything okay?"

"Well, it's been quite a hectic day," Andrew began, his tone weary but tinged with concern. "Gino had some upsetting news this afternoon." Chloe looked up, her face clouding with worry. "What happened?"

Andrew sighed and launched into the story. "It's his dad. He has been rushed to hospital after suffering a massive heart attack and taken a turn for the worse. Sophia didn't waste a second—she got Gino a seat on the 8 pm flight to Italy. I drove him to Heathrow myself."

"Oh no, that's awful news!" Chloe said, her voice full of sympathy. "They must both be so anxious. Poor Gino... and Sophia too. I'll call her first thing in the morning to check how he is."

Andrew nodded, a small reassuring smile breaking through his sombre expression. "She'll appreciate that. I told her you'd phone her soon—it'll mean a lot to her."

Chloe looked up with a smile. "I expect you're hungry, Andrew. Have you had lunch today?"

"Yes, we have," Andrew replied settling into the chair. "We were in Hammersmith this morning and couldn't resist stopping at our favourite deli for a snack."

"Oh, that's good to hear," Chloe said warmly. "I've got the slow cooker going with a Greek Stifado—perfect for weather like this. It's the one you like best isn't it?" She glanced towards the window where the snow was still falling gently. "How was the drive in all this snow?"

"It wasn't easy at times, Chloe," Andrew admitted with a wry smile. "But the good news is we've got our Mondeo back now and Simon's over the moon to have his BMW again." He paused, glancing out at the dreary weather. "We had to drive cautiously though. Visibility is terrible in these conditions."

Later, after they'd finished their evening meal, Andrew's phone buzzed insistently on the table. "It's Simon, Chloe, I'll take it in the hall."

Simon apologised for interrupting his evening but assured him that Zoe had kept him fully informed about everything that had unfolded throughout the day. He expressed his heartfelt sorrow over the sad news about Gino's father.

"I suggest you take a day off tomorrow," Simon said. "I have a meeting with Matt in the morning, and we need to discuss finding a replacement for Gino. Meanwhile, I'm still awaiting the latest update from the River Thames Police about the van."

"What did Simon say, Andrew? Was it about Gino?"

"Yes, Chloe. He's planning to discuss it with Matt in the morning. Oh, and good news—he's given me the day off! If it's still snowing we can build a snowman for Dimitris!"

"That's wonderful, Andrew! Dimitris will love that. And if the paths aren't too icy we could take a walk along the River Thames or maybe climb the hill to the park. What do you think?" "That sounds good, Chloe, let's see what the weather is like in the morning."

"Andrew, did you catch the 10 o'clock news? A van was speeding through the snow. It lost control, and smashed straight through the barrier into the River Thames! The River Police sent a diver down to investigate, but when they opened the van, it was completely empty. Now they're scouring the embankment, searching for a body. What do you think of that, Andrew? Is something like this even possible?"

"Well, Chloe, I suppose it's possible. Maybe he threw the door open in a hurry to make his escape. Simon will probably have more answers once he gets the report from the River Police. I've heard of cases where someone managed to survive, even fully clothed, if they were a strong swimmer. It's rare, but not impossible.

Let's see what's on the other channels," Andrew muttered, his finger hovering over the remote. But his thoughts were miles away. If only Chloe knew the truth—that it was him chasing the van. A chill crept up his spine as another thought hit him like a punch. "What if he's alive? What if he scrambled up the embankment and escaped?"

Next morning, as sunlight streamed through the kitchen window, Andrew sipped his coffee and glanced at Chloe, who was busy buttering toast. "You know," he began, "I've got the day off today."

Dimitris, their energetic little whirlwind, was darting around the table, giggling and chasing his toy truck. Without missing a beat, Andrew scooped him up into his arms. "How about we go out today, buddy? Maybe there's still enough snow left to build a snowman!"

Chloe looked up with a thoughtful expression. "Where could we go, though? There's hardly any snow left around here."

Andrew walked to the window and pulled back the curtain, surveying the thin patches of melting snow outside. "You're right," he admitted, rubbing his chin. Then his face lit up with an idea. "Chloe, what if we catch a bus to Richmond? We could take a walk up Richmond Hill—it's always beautiful there, snow or not."

Chloe smiled, her eyes sparkling. "Now that sounds like a plan, Andrew."

Dimitris squealed with excitement, and the promise of a day's adventure filled the room with energy.

They caught the bus and shared pushing Dimitris in the push chair when he didn't want to walk. They found enough snow for a snowman and as fast as they built it young Dimitris knocked it over. They found a nice restaurant and had lunch. Chloe managed to have a look in a few shops while Andrew looked after Dimitris.

As the bus rumbled along the familiar route home, Andrew's phone buzzed in his pocket. He glanced at the screen—Simon. With a quick look at Chloe, who was gazing out of the window he answered, keeping his voice low.

"Hello Simon," Andrew said quietly, "We're having a family day out and we're on the bus heading back. I don't want Chloe overhearing anything she shouldn't."

Simon's voice came through the line, calm and efficient as always. "Got it, Andrew. I'll keep it brief. I wanted to let you know—I've spoken to Matt, and we've agreed on a replacement for Gino. We'll meet at the usual spot tomorrow morning at 9:30. Is that okay with you?"

Andrew nodded instinctively, even though Simon couldn't see him. "Yeah, that's fine. I'll be there on time."

"Great," Simon replied. His tone softened a touch. "Enjoy the rest of your day, Andrew. And give my regards to Chloe."

"Will do. Thanks, Simon." Andrew disconnected the phone then put it back in his pocket. Chloe turned to him then, her face bright with curiosity, but Andrew smiled. "Did you catch any of that, Chloe?" Andrew asked leaning back in his seat. "Simon and Matt have found a replacement for Gino. I'll find out who it is at the morning meeting."

"Yes, Andrew," Chloe replied, glancing up from her book. "I caught bits and pieces. He sends his regards, as always—so thoughtful of him."

Andrew nodded, a faint smile tugging at the corner of his mouth. "That's Simon for you. I'm sure he'll arrange for Gino to take compassionate leave—with full pay, of course."

Later, when they returned home, Andrew took charge of Dimitris, gently feeding him his supper before tucking him into bed. Meanwhile, Chloe busied herself in the kitchen, preparing two steaming mugs of hot chocolate. She set them on the coffee table, along with the cream cakes she had purchased from the Richmond cake shop earlier that day. They settled into the quiet warmth of the evening, enjoying the rich sweetness of the delicious cakes. Andrew said. "This is fine Chloe, we had quite a large lunch today."

The next morning Andrew was up early ready to get down to the City Hall coffee bar. His thoughts lingered on one question: who would replace Gino? It felt odd walking in without his usual companion, the place seeming quieter somehow.

Andrew didn't have to wait long. Simon appeared first, striding confidently around the corner. He looked sharp in a light blue coat, a neatly perched trilby hat and a tweed scarf that added a touch of flair. Close behind him came Zoe, with her high boots clicking against the pavement, a fawn coat cinched at the waist, a cheerful striped woolly hat, and a black pear shaped shoulder bag.

But it was the third person, the woman walking with them, who immediately caught Andrew's attention. She was someone he hadn't seen before. Her look was unpolished but striking: a dark green boiler suit rolled at the cuffs, sturdy brown shoes, short cropped hair and a dark green bobble hat that sat slightly askew. She had an air of quiet confidence that made Andrew wonder who she was—and why she was here.

Simon found a quite corner and Zoe ordered the drinks, three coffees and one lime tea. Andrew looked at Zoe and was thinking it was usually four coffees when Gino was there.

"Okay, let's get started, said Simon. "First, let me introduce you to Ravidid Bhatir - she likes to be called Ravi. Following the meeting I had with Matt we decided to ask Zoe to take over from Gino straight away as he could be away for some weeks.

Right, Ravi, could you give Andrew and Zoe details of your background?"

"Yes, Simon. Though I have an Indian name I was born in England, in Slough. My father is a surgeon and works at Charing Cross Hospital. My mother is English and is an estate agent in Brentford, where my parents live now. My partner and I live in Kew which isn't far away.

My partner is Tom. He works in the Kew Leisure Centre and is a qualified personal instructor. We haven't started a family yet, maybe one day! We both go out running together though he is faster than me, but he is good and will wait for me to catch up.

I have passed all my police exams and I'm a qualified Detective. I have a first class marksman badge in shooting." "That's good Ravi, the same as Andrew, Gino and me." said Zoe, "And I'm very pleased to be accepted to work with Special Branch after working with the UK Security and Protection, checking out illegal immigrants.

Oh, Simon! Yesterday afternoon and evening, Zoe walked me through all the files on iCloud <u>Operation Live Wire</u>, and I have to say, I was thoroughly impressed. She's done an absolutely excellent job with Val our team secretary I'll do my best to keep everything updated and will stay in close contact with Zoe and Andrew, ready to step in and provide backup whenever they're out and need support."

"Yes, Ravi, I'm confident you will. As Zoe mentioned, feel free to call me anytime or stop by my office if you sense Zoe and Andrew might be walking into trouble. It's quite possible you'll hear from other officers about any unusual activities in the areas they're heading to, so it's crucial to keep them in the loop and up to date."

"Simon, there's one more thing. Would it be possible for me to visit the mortuary? I need to see Ahmadi Levy—the man shot in the back at Holborn Underground—and the other victim, the one found dead in the skip at Lewisham, also shot in the back. We don't have a name for him yet. I want to go soon, before they're cremated. I need to inspect their clothing. You see, I spent months with my father when he was volunteering to treat the sick in Iran and Iraq. I'm sure something about these cases feels familiar. I'm convinced there's more to uncover about both of them."

"Yes, that's fine with me. You could head out this afternoon," he said, his tone brisk. "Zoe, could you arrange for Police Constable Brad Evans to escort Ravi in an unmarked car? You've got the postcodes? The bodies are in two separate mortuaries, I believe?"

"Okay, I'll give him a call," Zoe replied, already reaching for her phone. "I have the two postcodes. I've been to the Lewisham mortuary with Brad—that's where the guy from the skip is. But I haven't been to the Fulham one yet, where Ahmadi Levy is."

Simon leaned forward, his voice low and deliberate. "I'm sure you've already heard—the body of a man was pulled from the river last night. A group of walkers on the Thames Path spotted him floating face down near the Thames Barrier. Gruesome sight no doubt."

He paused. 'I'm waiting on the River Police to send over their report, but the moment it lands I need you—Zoe and Andrew—to get on it. Find out everything you can about him. What details did he have on him? And more importantly, track down the garage where they have taken that bloody Express Removals van, I want you to take a good look inside.'

"If I could make a quick comment about that Express Removals van, Simon," Ravi interjected, her tone serious. "I've been working on a string of investigations involving vans entering the UK, and a lot of them are tied to cocaine smuggling. When you get a chance to check out the van, Zoe, see if you can take a look at the spare wheel, and have the tyre removed—there's a good chance you might find something. We've uncovered bags of cocaine stuffed inside the spare wheels before."

Simon raised an eyebrow, glancing between Zoe and Andrew. "Well, folks, Ravi hasn't been with us long, but it seems like she's already handed us something worth looking into.

Okay, Andrew and Zoe, you've got your hands full. First, follow up on the van and the driver, then dig into the mystery of that man and woman who left a case full of nothing but three bullets in a small leather case on the train. What's your first move, Zoe?"

Zoe straightened up. "Well, Simon, first things first—I need to head over to Hammersmith with Andrew. After that, we'll visit his lock-up at Borough Market. And if Gino's bulletproof vest doesn't fit me," she added with a smile, "I'll need to exchange it. Andrew, can we do this now?"

"Absolutely, Zoe. Based on what Ravi has shared, let's get the Mondeo and track down the garage where the van is now. That'll be our top priority," Andrew said decisively.

"Good call, Andrew," Zoe replied, nodding in agreement.

Simon turned to Ravi, his tone firm but calm. "Alright, team let's get moving. Ravi, keep me updated on any progress. Our Chief, Matt, is under a lot of pressure to wrap this case up, and we need answers—fast."

As they stepped out of the coffee bar, Zoe turned to Ravi with a determined look. "I'll call Brad Evans now," she said. "I'll give him your number—he'll do his best to get to you quickly. He's a good guy and he's fascinated by our detective work, especially how we always seem to get results."

Zoe paused for a moment, then added, "I'll text you and Brad the postcodes and full addresses for both mortuaries. Brad's already taken me to the one in Lewisham twice, so he should have no trouble finding it."

After Zoe explained everything to Brad Evans, his initial concern quickly faded. "No problem," he said, already planning his next move. He assured her he'd get down to the police compound, track down Tony, and sign out an unmarked car. "I'll pick up Ravi soon," Brad added with confidence.

Meanwhile, Andrew and Zoe made their way to the nearest stop, ready to hop on the number 23 bus to Hammersmith. Back at Metropolitan HQ, Ravi strolled alongside Simon, the two making their way through the busy streets towards the office, where more pieces of the puzzle awaited.

As Simon and Ravi stepped out of the lift onto the fourth floor of the office block, Ravi's phone buzzed in her pocket, She pulled it out and glanced at the screen. It was Brad Evans.

"Hi, Ravi. It's Brad. I've got the car and I'm ready to take you. Can you meet me by the West Gate in about five minutes?"

"That's perfect Brad, thanks," Ravi replied. "Did Zoe give you the postcodes and the full addresses?"

"She did," Brad confirmed. "And she mentioned I had taken her to the Lewisham location a couple of times before."

"Yes, she mentioned that to me," Ravi said, with a smile even though Brad couldn't see her. "Could you take me to the Lewisham one first?" "Of course, no problem. See you at the West Gate," Brad assured her.

"Great. See you there." Ravi ended the call and slipped the phone back into her pocket, already running through her mental checklist for the day.

Ravi got into the unmarked police car waiting at the West Gate, where Brad greeted her with an easy grin and a flood of questions. As they set off for Lewisham, Brad's curiosity made the ride lively. He seemed genuinely fascinated by Ravi's background, and Ravi found herself happily sharing her story. The traffic, thankfully, was light, allowing them to make excellent time. Brad, having parked there twice before navigated the parking, pulling into the perfect spot like it was second nature.

Ravi walked confidently into the reception area, her heart racing with a mix of nerves and pride. For the first time, she would show her brand-new Special Branch warrant card. Holding it up for the receptionist to see, she was met with a polite yet curious glance.

"Can I help you?" the receptionist asked, her tone was professional but slightly wary.

"Yes," Ravi replied firmly. "I'm here to examine the belongings of a man currently listed as unidentified in your mortuary. I've been informed by my superiors that he may soon be cremated. He was found in a skip in Lewisham."

"You're absolutely correct," the attendant confirmed with a polite nod. "We have him in Bay 41. I'll call for one of our pathologists to escort you. I need to tell you it's freezing down there."

Minutes later a young man appeared, his presence crisp and clinical. He was dressed in a pristine white coat over neatly pressed slacks and a button-up shirt, exuding an air of quiet efficiency.

"Hello," he greeted, with a professional yet friendly tone. "If you'll follow me, I'll take you to Bay 41."

Ravi inclined her head politely. "Thank you," she replied. "I'd like to focus on inspecting his clothing, if that's alright?"

"That's fine, we have his clothing stored in a cabinet nearby. I'll show you," the pathologist said, leading Ravi to Bay 41. He retrieved a large, sealed bag containing the clothes and handed it to her. Then, gesturing toward a sturdy wooden bench, he added, "you can use this bench to lay everything out. Please make sure to put on the white cotton gloves before touching anything."

"Of course," Ravi replied, her tone calm but focused. She slipped on the gloves, and Brad followed suit.

"Alright, Brad," Ravi continued, her gaze steady. "I need your help. Let's spread out every piece of clothing—I want a thorough look at all of it."

Together they carefully began unpacking the items, methodically arranging them on the bench for inspection.

The pathologist watched intently, curiosity etched on his face as Ravi methodically examined the items before her. She began with a meticulous inspection of the victim's clothing—his shirt, vest, underpants, black trousers and long coat. Her movements were precise and deliberate as though she were searching for a clue hidden in plain sight.

Then she paused, her gaze locking on a small item resting among the others. Picking up the skullcap—the kippah—she turned it over carefully in her hands. "This," she murmured, "is something I need to look at closely."

Holding it up to the light, she rotated it slowly, her eyes narrowing. "There!" Ravi exclaimed, pointing to a faint white line running through the fabric, from the top of the skullcap—the kippah---down to its back. She glanced at Brad, her voice tinged with triumph. "Can you see it? That's what we've been missing."

"Yes, Ravi, I can see it. But what's the significance?"

"Well," Ravi leaned in, her voice lowering as if the weight of her words demanded secrecy, "it means he's from North Kurdistan. He's a Kurdish separatist—a member of a tribal, religious and racial group."

"Seriously? Should someone like that even have been allowed into the UK?"

"Absolutely not," Ravi replied with conviction. "I've been working with UK security, tracking illegal immigrants. It's incredibly challenging to keep tabs on everyone coming into the country."

"Alright, Brad, now let's take a look at his sandals. Where are they?" Ravi asked, her eyes narrowing with focus.

Brad rummaged through the canvas bag at his feet, muttering under his breath. "Ah, here they are!" he exclaimed, pulling out the worn sandals and setting them on the bench with a clatter.

"Thanks, Brad," Ravi said, already reaching into the side pocket of her green boiler suit. With a triumphant flourish, she produced a magnifying glass. "Okay, let's have a closer look."

She angled the glass over the heel, her voice calm but laced with intrigue. "Check out the stitching here. These sandals have quite deep heels. See how the spacing of the stitches is wider on the right foot than on the left? Take a look at both sides. Brad squinted, leaning over her shoulder. "You're right! The stitches don't match at all. But... how did you know that?"

I've seen this before," Ravi muttered, but Brad barely heard her. She turned sharply, her focus elsewhere. "Let me have a word with the pathologist," she said, striding purposefully across the room.

Catching his attention, Ravi gestured him over. "Could you get me a small paring knife I can use?" she asked, her voice calm but firm.

The pathologist said, "yes sure, give me a moment." True to his word, he returned in less than two minutes, setting a sleek paring knife on the bench in front of her. The metal gleamed under the light. "Be careful," he warned. "It's razor-sharp."

Ravi picked it up with deliberate care, her expression unreadable but her intent unmistakable.

"Okay, Brad, hand me the one with the slightly spaced-out stitches," Ravi instructed, her voice sharp with determination.

Brad handed over the sandal, his curiosity piqued. Ravi adjusted her gloves, her focus razor-sharp as she picked up the paring knife. Slowly and deliberately she began cutting through the carefully stitched fabric. She could see something unusual beneath the layers.

"Yes... yes!" she exclaimed, her voice rising in excitement. She carefully pulled out a folded $100 bill, crisp despite its concealment. But that wasn't all. Alongside it was a card. Her eyes scanned the surface. It was a phone number.

She flipped the card over, her brow furrowing in intrigue as she read the name: Azwer Kalhol. Brad's mouth fell open, and even the pathologist, usually unshaken by the oddities of their work, froze mid-step.

"Who is he?" Brad whispered.

Ravi smiled, her mind already buzzing with possibilities. "That's what we're about to find out."

Ravi turned to the pathologist and said firmly, "I'll need to confiscate the sandals with the $100 bill and the card bearing a name and phone number. These need to be sent back to our Metropolitan HQ as evidence in a missing person case. Before I take them, could you photograph the name for your records? Now that we've uncovered this, it may delay the cremation, so your superiors will need to be informed."

The pathologist looked in surprise. "Of course, I'll take care of it right away. Honestly, I'm astonished you even thought to check there—we completely missed it. This will certainly change how we handle things in the future. Let me grab a plastic bag for you."

"Thanks," Ravi said with a smile. "If you could show us out now we can finally get warm." Ravi and Brad peeled off their white cotton gloves, the chill of the room still clinging to their fingers, and gave their thanks to the receptionist before heading back to their unmarked police car.

As they got in the seats, Ravi rubbed her hands together briskly. "Alright," she said, turning to Brad, "on to the next one. Zoe said it's at the Fulham Public Mortuary."

Brad gave a curt nod, tapping the postcode into the car's navigation system. "Got it," he muttered.

The drive wasn't kind to their schedule. Traffic crawled, and the hour stretched long as they inched toward Fulham. By the time they arrived the late afternoon sky was heavy with low-hanging clouds. Brad pulled the car around to the back of the mortuary, cutting the engine with a sigh.

He glanced at Ravi. "Do you think this one will be the same as the last?"

Ravi hesitated, staring out at the building before them, its silhouette stark and unwelcoming. "I expect it will," she said, keeping her voice low.

" Lets find out Brad, the only difference this time is that we actually know his name—assuming it's real."

They went up to the reception desk, Ravi showing her new warrant card She gestured toward Brad. "This is Constable Brad Evans. We're here on official business."

Her tone was firm but polite as she continued, "We need to carry out a check on all Ahmadi Levys clothing. We were informed his body is here awaiting cremation"

The receptionist picked up the phone and called for a pathologist. Moments later, a woman entered the reception area, her expression calm but curious.

"Can I help you?" she asked.

Ravi stepped forward. "You have the body here of Ahmadi Levy," she explained. "We need to inspect his clothing before he's cremated."

She gave a look, unfazed by the request. "Of course. Follow me—he's in bay 29."

Without further questions, she led Ravi and Brad down the quiet sterile corridor. Ravi had expected her to ask why they needed to see the clothing, but she didn't. The silence felt heavy as they arrived at bay 29.

Ravi hesitated before speaking. "Would it be possible to lay out his clothing?"

The pathologist handed out a pair of white cotton gloves each. "You'll need these." As Ravi pulled the gloves on, the weight of the moment settled over her. They both exchanged a glance before turning to the garments knowing that whatever they found could change everything.

Please, use this bench right here," she said, lugging a large plastic bag over to it. The weight of the bag made it crinkle and slip in her grip before she set it down with a thud.

Ravi and Brad wasted no time spreading the clothes out neatly across the bench, as they had done back in the Lewisham mortuary. Brad glanced at Ravi. "Are you going to check for the same details?"

Ravi replied, "Yes, Brad. Let's start with the skullcap—kippah." She picked it up turned it sideways, and examined the fabric closely through her magnifying glass. Her eyes sharpened as she traced a nearly invisible imperfection. "There it is," she murmured, running her finger along the small white line woven into the texture. It ran from the top to the back—exactly like the other one. Ravi looked up at Brad, his expression confirmed. "Yes you are right, it is exactly like the other one," he agreed. Ravi reached out. "Now Brad, pass me the sandals please"

The pathologist stepped closer, curiosity etched across her face as she peered over their shoulders. Ravi glanced up.

"Do you have a small paring knife I could use?" Ravi asked.

The pathologist said. "Yes, one moment." She disappeared briefly then returned, placing a sharp paring knife in Ravi's outstretched hand. "Careful," she warned. "It's very sharp."

Brad handed Ravi the right sandal, and she carefully began slicing through the stitches, the paring knife gliding through the worn leather with precision. Silence hung in the air as they watched her work, tension mounting with each careful cut.

Then, Ravi's eyes widened. "Yes," she said out loud, "We've got something."

She lifted the flap of material, revealing a crisp $100 bill and a small card tucked neatly inside. She flipped the card over—and there it was. His name, 'Ahmadi Levy.'

The pathologist's couldn't believe it, She stared in astonishment. "How could you possibly know that?"

"Ravi gave a wry smile. 'It's all part of security training," she said. "If you can find me a plastic bag, I'm afraid we'll have to confiscate the skullcap, the sandals the name card, and the $100 bill."

The pathologist quickly retrieved a suitable bag, handing it over with a slight furrow of her brow. As she led them to the exit they exchanged polite thanks with both her and the receptionist. Then with a quiet sense of finality, they slipped off their pristine white cotton gloves and stepped outside leaving behind an air of unanswered questions."

Ravi flashed a grateful smile at Brad as they made their way back to Metropolitan HQ. "Thanks for taking me today," she said. Brad returned the smile. "It was my pleasure. Honestly, I learned so much from you."

Ravi chuckled. "Well, I hope you remember it all—it might come in handy one day."

"I'll do my best," Brad assured her.

Before long, they reached the Metropolitan HQ. Ravi bid Brad farewell before heading straight to the fourth floor. Bursting into Simon's office with an excited energy, she declared, "Simon, we have had an incredibly successful day."

Simon was taken aback by everything Ravi had revealed about the two mortuary visits. He took a deep breath, processing the details before speaking.

"Alright, first things first—leave both bags with me. Our Commander will definitely want to examine them, especially the $100 bills and those small cards. Also, make sure Val updates the report on our Operation Live Wire file in iCloud, just as Zoe showed you. That will be crucial."

Simon paused, then gave Ravi an approving look. "You've done an outstanding job, Ravi. I'm seriously impressed."

Meanwhile, Andrew and Zoe had been keeping themselves busy. As soon as they arrived at Andrew's apartment in Hammersmith Zoe wasted no time trying on Gino's bulletproof vest—only to find it was too small.

Andrew, ever practical, suggested they take the Mondeo and drive to HQ for an exchange. But as he was about to go to the garage, Zoe's phone buzzed. It was the River Thames Police, calling with the crucial information she had requested.

One of the River Police officers said. "The van driver we pulled from the River Thames has been identified as Akbar Jafari. When we examined his body, we found a wallet containing credit cards, a mobile phone—and more disturbingly, a gun with several rounds of ammunition. Given the evidence, it's highly likely he was from Iran. You might want to collect everything from our office and take it back to Metropolitan HQ for further investigation."

Zoe's phone was on speaker, so Andrew caught every word. She responded eagerly, "thanks, we'll come over right away. Oh, and would it be possible to take a look inside the van?"

"Of course," came the reply. "I'll send you the postcode now." Andrew gave Zoe a nod, ready to get moving. "Let's go. I'll lock up, and we can call in our compound on the way. I'll wait while you swap the bulletproof vest."

Zoe wasted no time returning to HQ. As soon as she arrived she swapped her bulletproof vest, barely catching her breath before a message came on her phone. It was from the Woolwich Police station—not far from Poplar, where the van had plunged into the River Thames.

The officer on the line didn't only confirm the location; he also provided the exact address and postcode for the garage holding the recovered vehicle— G-M Garage Repairs, in Greenwich. Whatever secrets the van held, they were waiting there.

They arrived at the Woolwich Police station, showing their warrant cards at the front desk. One of the officers raised an eyebrow. "We thought you two were from Special Branch," he said, intrigued.

A tense discussion followed about the Express Removals van that had plunged into the Thames—and the grim discovery of the driver's lifeless body, face down in the river. The room buzzed with unease as the implications sank in.

Finally, one of the officers turned to Zoe, handing her a wallet, a mobile phone, a gun and a pack of ammunition. "These all belonged to him. As I said on the phone, we thought you might need to get them back to your HQ."

Zoe pulled out the credit card from the wallet, inspecting the name embossed on it. She glanced at Andrew and said, "the officer was right—his name is Akbar Jafari. Now, let's see what Ravi thinks. Is he from Iran or Northern Kurdistan?"

Andrew and Zoe exchanged a quick look before turning to the Police officer. "Thanks for your help,"Andrew said.

Zoe added, "a copy of the report will be sent to your Senior Officer. This incident needs to stay confidential."

With that, she turned to Andrew. "Alright, let's check out this G-M garage."

After almost 40 minutes of busy traffic, they finally spotted the garage and pulled up outside. Stepping inside, they were met with a cluttered scene—cars and vans packed into every available space. The air smelled of oil and rubber, and the hum of distant machinery filled the room. Andrew's eyes scanned the area until he found the van they were looking for: the Express Removals van, tucked away in a dimly lit corner.

Without hesitation, they both showed their warrant cards. A nearby staff member, wiping his hands on a grease-stained rag, glanced at them with mild curiosity. "Can I help you?" he asked.

"Yes," Andrew said, eyeing the battered Express Removals van parked in the corner. "We'd like to take a look at it. Did you fish it out of the River Thames?"

The mechanic let out a dry chuckle. "Pretty much, it took some serious effort to get the high-lift cables underneath, but we managed. Hauled it up and brought it here on the pickup truck. It wasn't exactly a smooth ride though.

Why do you need to check the van? There's nothing inside." "We're interested in the spare wheel. Does it have one?"

"Yes, of course. Let me grab my adjustable spanner. The wheel is stored in the floor well. When we got the van back, I noticed a threaded rod and a large nut securing it. I'll open it up for you and we can lift the spare wheel out."

After a few minutes, he appeared with his adjustable spanner, swung open the rear door, and got to work. The stubborn nut resisted at first, but with a grunt and a determined twist, he finally managed to loosen it. As he reached in to lift the wheel out of the well, he let out a surprised huff.

"Crikey, this is heavy! They're not usually this bad!"

Andrew stepped forward. "Hold on, I'll give you a hand."

Together, they heaved the wheel onto the ground with a dull thud. The mechanic wiped his hands on his overalls and glanced at Andrew.

"Alright then... now what do you want to do with it?"

Zoe examined the tyre with a curious frown. "Can we deflate it and take the tyre off the wheel?" she asked.

"Okay," the mechanic said reaching for the valve. As the air hissed out, he raised an eyebrow. "Didn't have much in it to begin with," he muttered before disappearing to fetch a pair of tyre levers.

The tyre removal was no easy task. The mechanic wrestled with the stubborn rubber tyre, gritting his teeth as he tried to free it. Andrew stepped in to help, and after a tense struggle, the tyre finally gave way. But as they pulled it off, the mechanic's jaw dropped.

Nestled inside were eight tightly packed cotton bags, each hefty—probably two and a half kilos apiece. A thick silence hung in the air before the mechanic spoke, his voice low with suspicion.

"What the hell is this? Do you think it's drugs?"

"It's possible," Zoe replied, her brow furrowing in thought. "We'll need to take all the bags to our lab for testing. Do you have a bag or a box we could use?"

"No problem," the mechanic said, disappearing into the garage. Moments later, he returned with two sturdy boxes, and dropped them down with a thud.

"Perfect, thanks," Andrew said, wasting no time. "We'll pack these up and be on our way."

Zoe's voice was firm, her gaze unwavering. "Listen carefully—what you witnessed today is a highly sensitive police matter. Under no circumstances can you share this with newspapers, TV stations, or any news outlets. If you do, there will be serious legal consequences. Do I make myself clear?"

"Yes, I fully understand, I won't even tell my mates," he replied.

Oh, and before we leave, we'll need your mobile number and home address," Zoe added with a friendly smile.

"Of course, no problem," he replied, quickly rattling off the details. Zoe jotted them down as Andrew gave her his approval.

"Great, that's all sorted!" Andrew said. "Thanks again."

After that, they packed the cotton bags into their car boot, and exchanged a final wave as they drove off, leaving the hum of the garage repair shop behind them.

"Well, said Andrew! Who would have thought it? Ravi was spot on—if all eight bags do contain cocaine they would be worth a fortune to the drug barons."

"I'm calling Simon now," Zoe said, already dialling. "We need to arrange a meeting in the police compound."

Simon picked up the call almost instantly. His reaction was immediate and explosive.

"What?!" he shouted. "Cotton bags in the spare wheel tyre may be full of cocaine? How the hell did the border control miss that?" His voice was thick with disbelief. "This needs to be discussed with Ravi.

Give me a call when you're close to the compound, and I'll come down to meet you," Simon instructed.

"Yeah, will do," Andrew replied casually.

"He sounds a bit on edge, Zoe," Andrew added after a pause.

Zoe exhaled, glancing out the window. "I imagine he's under a lot of pressure. He really wants this case closed so he can move on."

Andrew replied, "I get that. Honestly, I'll be relieved when this is all behind us. We've dealt with enough—guns, ammunition, cocaine... it's been a hell of a journey."

The traffic was lighter than expected. As they neared their destination, Zoe called Simon to let him know they were almost there. They made good time, pulling up smoothly at the Metropolitan compound, where Simon and Ravi were already waiting.

Andrew unlocked the car boot and they took out the eight cotton bags, the gun, rounds of ammunition and Akbar Jafari's wallet, complete with credit cards and his mobile phone.

"Alright, Andrew—Zoe and Ravi, I'll need your help carrying everything inside. Zoe, can you also double-check that Val has recorded everything correctly in our iCloud file for Operation Live Wire? Chief Matt wants us all to meet with him tomorrow morning at 9am in City Hall. But don't go in to the coffee bar—his secretary will book one of the office rooms on the first floor. Is that okay for everyone?" "Yes "they all replied in unison.

Andrew turned to Zoe with a suggestion. "Why don't you meet me between 8:30 and 8:45? I always met Gino at that time to catch up before our meetings—we went over the previous day's events." "That's fine for me," Zoe agreed, as she went off with Ravi.

Simon, who had been listening intently, asked, "any updates on Gino's father, Andrew?"

Andrew replied that he hadn't heard the latest update but promised to call as soon as he got back to his apartment and secured the Mondeo for the night. Hours later, true to his word, he picked up the phone and called Gino's number.

When Gino answered, his voice was heavy with emotion. He was still at the hospital, and the news wasn't good. In a trembling voice, he confided that the doctors didn't expect him to make it through the night.

A wave of sadness washed over Andrew. "I'm so sorry, Gino," he said softly, struggling to find the right words. "I'll let Chloe and the others know."

After the call, Andrew secured the office for the night and hurried to catch a bus home. For once, he was home earlier than usual, and Chloe's face lit up in surprise.

Before she could even ask about his day, Andrew told her the news about Gino's dad. Chloe's expression moved to concern. "I'll call Sophia in the morning," she said. "She always likes to speak to me."

As for his day, Andrew could only sum it up in one word—interesting. There had been some promising developments, and just as things were winding down, Chief Matt had dropped a bombshell: a mandatory meeting for the entire team at 9 a.m sharp. Whatever was coming, it was bound to be important.

"That's great to hear, Andrew! He's truly exceptional at what he does, and as you've mentioned before, he always looks out for his team. But don't worry about that right now—Dimitris is in his playroom, calling for you!"

Andrew didn't hesitate. With a smile, he dashed upstairs, where his little boy was already waiting, excitement shining in his eyes. Within moments, laughter and the sounds of playful competition filled the room.

The next morning Andrew stood outside City Hall, the crisp air carrying the sounds of a city already in motion. It wasn't long before Zoe arrived, her pace brisk, eyes sharp. As they exchanged quick greetings, their conversation naturally turned to the previous day's events.

"I wonder what Chief Matt has to say this morning," Andrew said glancing toward the building.

Zoe folded her arms, her expression thoughtful. "I've been thinking about that," she said. "I have a feeling he wants to finally close out the cases we've been working on for sometime.

And more importantly—" she shot Andrew a knowing look, "he'll probably want us back on the trail of that man and woman you and Gino were looking out for on the underground train."

"Well, Zoe, we're about to find out—here they come now."

Simon was the first to greet them with a bright "good morning!" before motioning for the group to follow him. He moved with confidence, exchanging a few words with a staff member who led them to a reserved meeting room on the first floor.

Once inside, Chief Matt took a moment to scan the room before offering a firm nod. "Good morning, everyone," he said, his voice steady and authoritative. "Let's get straight to the point. Here's why I called this meeting for this morning.

Right, let's get started. We now have it confirmed we have 4 dead men to deal with.

CHAPTER EIGHT

The first one. This involves Ahmadi Levy, who was gunned down on the platform at Holborn underground station. After extensive investigation, we can now say with certainty that he was a member of a North Kurdistan rebel unit—a fact definitively confirmed after Ravi's visit to the mortuary yesterday. I understand that the Kurdish authorities have no interest in extraditing him, so his body will have to be cremated here.

The second one. He was also shot in the back and he was dumped in a skip. Until yesterday we had no clue who he was or where he came from. Now we know—he was also a rebel from Northern Kurdistan. His name is Azwer Kalhol.

Ravi, can you check with the embassy? If they confirm there's no request for extradition we'll proceed with cremation, just like the first one.

Now number three. We know his name—Azaad Olaar. An unfortunate accident ended his life, but not before he left chaos in his wake. Originally from Iran, he was the mastermind behind the London railway employee who built the bomb and ultimately took his own life. The discovery of a chilling assassination list sent shock waves through the ranks, forcing me to bring it to the attention of the Prime Minister himself.

The Iranian embassy has officially requested his body to be returned—along with his prized Harley Davidson motorbike. Simon and Ravi, would you please organise it. But not before we confirm the payment has been received with no exceptions.

And finally, number four—Akbar Jafari. His name has now been confirmed. We pulled him out of the River Thames after he tried—and failed—to escape during a high-speed police chase. We recovered his wallet and credit cards, confirming he's also from Iran. Simon and Ravi, please contact the Iranian embassy once again to see if they want his body extradited. My bet? they will. But, as always, make sure we receive payment first, with no exceptions.

On another note, I want to acknowledge the hard work all of you have put into these cases. You've all gone above and beyond. And let's not forget— Andrew and Gino have been damn lucky to dodge a few bullets along the way.

In three of these cases a substantial quantity of cocaine has been seized— one in Manchester, another in Ponders End, and now, hidden in the spare wheel of that bloody Express Removals van. And, I must say, I'm quite pleased to hear it finally sank! Altogether, the haul has a staggering street value of £6.5 million.

I'm now officially closing all three cases. But before that, I want Andrew and Zoe to pick up where we started—with the man and the woman on the train.

Zoe shot Andrew a knowing glance, a silent exchange passing between them.

I've just received fresh information from the Eurostar Railway Police. Two sets of names—one English, one French. I will request my secretary, to forward them to you, with the latest CCTV photo's.

Does anyone have any questions?"

Simon started to speak, his expression tense.

"Ravi, I need some clarity on a few things that have been bothering me." His voice carried an edge of urgency.

"First question," he continued. "Your report confirms that both Ahmadi Levy and Azwer Kalhol are tied to this rebel unit in Northern Kurdistan. Do we have any follow-up intelligence? How many members of this group are reported to be in the UK? And more importantly—are they still operating under the disguise of being Jewish?

Second question, smuggling cocaine inside spare tyres—is that a new trick or an old one? I've never heard of drugs being hidden in tyres before. Wouldn't border control's X-ray scanners easily catch that?"

"Simon, I can tell you what I know. This group is a Northern Kurdish militant organization—an armed guerrilla force driven by separatist ambitions. Ruthless and relentless, they've been known to kill for control of the heroin and cocaine trade, using drug trafficking to fuel their operations. Tourists? They see them as little more than currency, kidnapping for ransom without hesitation.

There are rumours that they've stopped operating in the UK under the guise of Jewish identities, but the real question remains—how many of them are still here? That, we don't yet know. We do know they have taken a more lucrative option in concentration of the supply of the black dinghies and outboard motors for the illegal immigrants from Turkey to Greece who are mostly from Afghanistan and Syria. They charge up to $15,000. they also supply dinghies to France for illegal immigrants to the UK.

Great question number 2, Simon. While all ports are equipped with high-quality X-ray scanners, the sheer volume of drugs being smuggled into the UK remains a serious issue. Interestingly, this year has seen a higher number of drug consignments hidden in shipments of fruit and even inside new cars— many of which have been intercepted, leading to arrests and convictions.

I'll be looking into this further with the Port Authorities, particularly the possibility of drugs being concealed in spare wheels. As of now, I don't recall any cases of this happening, but if smugglers are using small vans for distribution within the UK, and the police aren't actively watching for it, those vehicles could be slipping through unchecked. I'll make sure this gets investigated.

I hope that answers your questions Simon."

"Thank you Ravi that's appreciated." Simon replied.

Andrew said, "you know what, Ravi,? I think you're right. That wheel was large —so heavy it took two of us to lift it out. It didn't even fit the van properly! But honestly, if you just looked at it, you'd never guess it was the wrong size."

Matt was thoroughly impressed by Ravi's sharp and insightful responses to Simon's questions. As the discussion unfolded, he remarked, "given what we've just heard from Ravi about the rebels from Northern Kurdistan, and considering the escalating situation in Israel and Gaza, I will draft another letter to all three Chief Rabbis with the latest updates. I have no doubt this news will bring a great sense of relief to the Jewish community.

Oh, and once again, a huge thanks to Andrew Zoe and Gino—because of the way they handled everything, we got the result we needed. I think that just about wraps it up, so let's keep moving forward."

As they were about to leave the office, Andrew's phone buzzed. He glanced at the screen.

"Excuse me," Andrew said. "It's Chloe—I should take this."

He stepped out to answer the call, his voice fading as he moved away. When he returned, his expression was sombre.

"That was Chloe," Andrew said, his tone more serious now. "She has heard from Gino—his father passed away this morning. Sophia and the girls are flying out to Italy, and it looks like Gino will have to take over his father's garage." He exhaled, processing the news. "I'll update you when I know more, but for now... looks like it's just you and me on the road, Zoe.

As the group parted ways, each heading in a different direction, Ravi called out, "don't forget to keep in touch!"

Simon grinned, adding, "and keep using your Codex mobile!"

"We will! " Andrew and Zoe responded in unison.

Zoe turned to Andrew. "Andrew, what's our first move?"

"Okay, Zoe, here's the plan. First, we'll catch a bus to the Borough Market, where I've got a lock-up filled with disguises—plenty for you to choose from.

Then, we'll take the Underground to my apartment-office in Hammersmith, where we can dig into everything we have on the man and the woman. With the CCTV footage from Holborn station and the Eurostar departure at St Pancras International, we should be able to piece together their movements."

If we can speak with the French Railway Police at the Gare du Nord departures and request access to their CCTV footage, we might need to catch a train first thing tomorrow morning.

They quickly caught a bus and arrived at Borough Market, where the usual lively crowd bustled around food stalls and boutique shops.

"Stay close," Andrew said over his shoulder. "The unit is right at the far end."

Navigating through the throng of shoppers, Andrew pressed forward with Zoe right behind him. At last, they reached the unit. He swiftly unlocked the door and stepped inside, Zoe following closely.

As Zoe glanced around, her eyes widened in surprise. The space was packed with clothing, an overwhelming collection of garments.

Andrew chuckled as he glanced over his collection. "I didn't actually buy most of this myself," he admitted. "Other stallholders just offloaded their old stock on me."

Zoe sifted through the assortment with amusement. "I see a few ladies' headscarves... some wigs... Oh! Look at this!" She held up a set of dreadlocks. "Aren't these the ones Gino was wearing when he was sitting on the station platform?" She grinned mischievously. "Maybe I could wear them next time we need to go out in disguise, Andrew!"

Andrew burst out laughing. "You know what, Zoe? I think you'd actually pull it off!"

Zoe was deep in thought. "You know, I could go through my wardrobe and set aside the clothes I barely wear. I could store them in your lock-up unit. Would that be alright with you, Andrew?"

Andrew hesitated for just a second before agreeing. "Yeah, that's fine, Zoe. But listen... no one knows I have this unit. Not even my wife, Chloe." He exhaled, running a hand through his hair. "She doesn't know the full extent of my work as a detective. I think she has a pretty good idea, but she chooses to stay quiet about it."

"That's okay for me, Andrew. Now that I know, I think it's a fantastic idea—certainly something we never would have guessed back at the office."

As Zoe spoke, something on the bench caught her eye. She let out a sudden laugh and held up a black-and-ginger fake moustache. "Well, I won't be putting one of these on!" she declared, grinning.

Andrew chuckled. "I don't think they'd suit you, Zoe!"

Again Andrew glanced at his watch. "Come on, let's lock up. We'll go out the back exit and catch the underground from London Bridge station and take the Northern line to Bank station, then switch to the Central Line to Hammersmith. We can get off at Holborn station."

They stepped out into the cool air, ready for their journey.

"Are you alright with that, Zoe?" Andrew asked, glancing at her with a mix of concern and intrigue. "I think it might help you if we get off at Holborn. I can show you exactly where it happened—the platform where the shot rang out, where the man stumbled and fell onto the tracks, right in front of the oncoming train." He paused, letting the weight of the moment settle. "Then we can switch to the Piccadilly line to Hammersmith."

Zoe replied. "That actually sounds like a good idea, Andrew."

The trains were running smoothly and, for once, weren't too crowded. In no time, they pulled into Bank station, where Andrew and Zoe stepped off and made their way to the Central Line platform. As they waited, Andrew glanced up at the iconic Tube map, tracing their route.

"Just two more stops till Holborn," he said to Zoe with a grin. "Almost there."

As they stepped off the train, Zoe turned to Andrew with a hint of uncertainty. "Are we on the right platform?"

Andrew shook his head. "No, we need to go up this escalator and back down the other side. We need the train to Cockfosters—that's the line for Arsenal."

Wasting no time, they hurried towards the escalators, weaving through the sparse crowd. Moments later, they descended onto the correct platform, which was relatively quiet.

Andrew pointed ahead. "That's where Gino was sitting on the platform" he said. "And to his right, I mingled in the middle of the Arsenal fans."

Zoe took in the scene and smiled—this was going to be an interesting day.

Andrew described the tense moment when the train screeched to a halt—just after the gunshot rang out—its brakes slamming into action for an emergency stop. The sheer force of it left less than half the train outside the tunnel, the rest swallowed by darkness.

Zoe shuddered at the thought. "That must have been terrifying for everyone—on the train and on the platform. The deafening sound of the brakes, the train shuddering to a stop, and the eerie reality that the electric power was still running on the tracks, yet the train itself was lifeless. I guess that was to stop people from panicking and trying to escape—risking electrocution in the process."

" Yes Zoe, remember what we said in our report? We had to get out fast—before the place was swarming with ambulances, police, and fire crews."

"You were right, Andrew. The sooner you got away the better. I don't think either you or Gino would want to go through that again. So, Hammersmith next?"

"That's correct Zoe. We need to switch platforms and go back on the Central Line."

Zoe hurried to keep pace with Andrew as he weaved swiftly through the crowd, effortlessly gliding up the escalators. Within moments, they were on the train, their conversation growing more intense.

"We need to be smart about this," Zoe murmured, lowering her voice. "If we're not careful, we could walk straight into a trap. News spreads fast these days."

Andrew nodded, his expression serious. "Agreed. But how do we approach them without tipping them off?"

"That's the challenge," Zoe admitted. "Matt will send us more details, but from what we already know, they're running a highly sophisticated operation—wealthy clients, deep connections, and not just in the UK."

Andrew thought about it, considering her words. Then, with a small smirk, he said, "well, Zoe, you're probably right again. You always are."

As they arrived at Hammersmith Underground station, Andrew turned to Zoe with a grin. "Before we dive into my computer screens, let's call in on my favourite Greek deli. It's just around the corner from my apartment. Gino and I used to go there when we were working on the screens."

"That sounds great, Andrew," came the reply from Zoe "It will be a refreshing change from our usual staff canteen!"

It was only a short walk from the station when Andrew turned to Zoe with a smile. "Here we are," he said, pushing open the door with a welcoming gesture.

As they stepped inside, a towering man with a thick black beard and a spotless white apron suddenly appeared, his face lighting up with joy. With a booming laugh, he threw his arms around Andrew, lifting him slightly off the ground in a bear hug.

"Yassas! Kalimera, Andrew!" he bellowed, his voice warm and full of life. "It's so good to see you again! Ah, it's been too long! How is your lovely Chloe? And little Dimitris—he must be growing so fast!"

"Efcharisto Andreas! We're all doing well—Dimitris is always on the move these days. We'll all come over for dinner with you one evening, it'll be great to catch up!"

"Eudokeo Andrew! That sounds wonderful. What can I get for you both for lunch? Oh, and you haven't introduced me to this lovely lady yet!"

"Ah, my apologies, Andreas! This is Zoe, my colleague. We have some work to catch up on this afternoon, so I thought we'd have a lunch here before getting started. Are you staying here until the New Year?"

"Yes, until around March next year! Then, I'll be back in Cyprus for the whole summer, running one of my new restaurants in Limassol. When you get a holiday, you absolutely must come and dine at my new restaurant !"

"We'd love to, Andreas! I'll tell Chloe about it tonight."

"Perfect! Now, what can I get for you, Zoe and Andrew? I have some delicious toasted halloumi, served with a fresh Greek salad and warm, oven-baked pitta bread—fresh out of the oven!"

"Oh, that sounds amazing!" Zoe exclaimed with a smile. "I absolutely love that."

"Me too, Zoe," Andrew agreed.

Turning to Andrew, he asked with a playful grin, "So, are you still sticking to your usual—Coca-Cola with ice and a slice of lemon?"

Andrew chuckled. "You've got a sharp memory, Andreas."

"And what about you, Zoe?" Andreas inquired.

Zoe tapped her chin thoughtfully. "You know what? I'll have the same! A nice change from all the coffee I drown myself in every day."

As they waited for Andreas to bring out lunch, Zoe turned to Andrew with a curious smile.

"Do you speak Greek, Andrew?" she asked.

He chuckled, stirring his drink. "Just a little, Zoe. On my last case, we tracked a diamond smuggler all the way to Cyprus. That's where I met Chloe—my wife. We got married in Paphos, right by the sea." His eyes flickered with the memory. "I only remember a few Greek words, but they always come in handy."

Zoe raised an eyebrow, intrigued. "Sounds like quite a story, can you tell me a few words, later, I might persuade my partner to take me there next year."

"Yes you should Zoe it's a fantastic Island"

Andreas quickly bought out the lunch, prompting Andrew to grin and say, "Efcharistó, Andreas!"

Andreas chuckled, raising his glass. "I'm sure you will enjoy your lunch," he replied with a wink before toasting, "Yamas!"

"Cheers!" Andrew responded, clinking his glass against Andreas's.

After finishing their meal, they both agreed it had been delicious. As they stepped out of the deli, Zoe beamed and said, "Efcharistó, Andreas."

Andrew laughed. "You picked up that word fast, Zoe!"

Still chatting, they strolled around the corner towards Andrew's apartment, the afternoon sun warming the cobbled streets beneath them.

Andrew swiftly unlocked the apartment and silenced all the alarms, the soft beeping fading into the hum of his office. He gestured Zoe toward a seat by one of his large computer screens.

"Take a seat, Zoe. I'll get us both connected," he said, settling in front of the other screen.

Soon the displays flickered to life, casting a bluish glow over the screens. Andrew leaned forward, his fingers poised over the keyboard. "Alright, this isn't going to be easy," he warned. "We need to start with the CCTV footage from the Eurostar terminal at St Pancras. Our targets—one man, one woman—should be emerging from the station and heading towards the escalator for the Underground. Let's find them."

His eyes focused on lines of code on the video films scrolling past. The hunt had begun.

As they were scrolling through, the messaging app flashed—a new update had arrived. It was the latest information Matt had instructed his secretary to forward to Andrew and Zoe.

"I'll show it on both screens," Andrew said. "That way, we can each take a screenshot. We'll need it when we're out gathering information."

"Good thinking, Andrew," Zoe replied. "That'll make things much easier."

"Alright, let's see what she sent," Andrew said, tapping the message open.

Zoe scanned the details quickly. "Here—it shows the exact time and day they arrived at St Pancras. That was the day of the shooting."

"Right," Andrew agreed. "And we have a description of what they were wearing—Simon sent it over earlier. Let me check my report."

Andrew agreed. "Yes, the woman was dressed quite distinctively—a striking green cashmere skirt with a matching sweater, layered under a brown coat. Over that, she wore a snug black jacket, and on her feet, she had white Nike trainers.

She carried a small, lavish leather case, while the man accompanying her had a compact holdall."

"That's correct, Andrew. I agree," Zoe said.

Andrew's expression darkened slightly. "That's the leather case the bomb squad officer found. He handed it to me to take back to HQ, which I did. I then gave it to Simon."

Zoe said "Yes, that's right. Simon showed it to me before he took it to forensic for a fingerprint check before the armoury.

We were puzzled. Only three bullets in the case, and an empty indentation showed where three guns had once been. But the weapons were missing. Why?"

"This is what we have to find out, Zoe," Andrew said, his voice laced with intrigue.

"Yes, Andrew, it's a complete mystery!"

"And then, Zoe, there was the man. We couldn't forget him—the way he carried that sleek sports bag, how effortlessly he blended in with the crowd. Classic blue jeans, a crisp white polo-neck jumper, a black winter coat and spotless white Nike trainers. Who was he? And what was he hiding?

Do you have the photo of the clothes they were wearing on that day, Zoe?" Andrew asked. "Yes," Zoe replied.

Andrew forwarded the message to Zoe's phone, his eyes narrowing as new details emerged. A man's name, a woman's name. Both taken from their passports when the Railway Police checked them. The pieces of the puzzle were starting to fall into place.

"Zoe, let's capture screenshots of all this. The woman's name is Amelia Becket, and the man is Matthew Lawrence. We need to go through every second of the CCTV footage from all the underground stations and all exits.

I'm tracking their movements—figuring out how they got from St Pancras onto this train. We were told they're getting off at Holborn, which means they must have planned to visit one of the nearby hotels. A meeting with someone, perhaps? Let's find out."

A little further down, another message from the Railway Police popped up on Andrew's two screens —this one sent a few days ago. It contained two different passport names along with fresh CCTV images.

"Let's get these on our phones," Andrew said. "I'll print the ones we need so we can show them to everyone we need to question."

"Good idea," Zoe replied. Without hesitation, Andrew tapped a request for the photos, the latest arrival ones from St Pancras station.

"Here we go, Zoe," he said, "They've switched passport names again— Amelie Laurent and Matthieu Badeaux.. Both French."

"Well, that's a twist! We started with all Kurdish and Iranian names, and now we've got French ones?" Andrew raised an eyebrow. "I thought Matt was joking when he said we might have to go on the Eurostar to France!

"Do you speak any French, Zoe?" Andrew asked.

Zoe shook her head. "Just a few basic phrases, nothing useful."

"No worries. we've got Google to bail us out" Andrew replied, studying the list. "You know, it looks like they took their original English names and then gave them a French twist. Can you confirm if that's right Zoe?"

"Okay, Andrew, I'll look it up now," Zoe said, quickly pulling up an English-to-French translation on her phone. A moment later, she said. "You're right! The name Amelia in English becomes Amélie in French, and Matthew turns into Mathieu. But why does that happen? What's the reason for the change?" She looked up, intrigued. "Is it just pronunciation, or is there more to it."

"I have no idea why they changed their names, Zoe. Let me check the date… Ah, just as I thought—it was that day with Gino. Remember? When we raced after that Express Removals van, and he ended up in the Thames? Freezing, snowing, absolute chaos!"

"Yes, you're right, Andrew! That explains their change of clothing. The woman is now dressed in a snug blue woolly hat, a matching blue scarf, and a thick dark grey coat that shields her from the cold. She's also wearing blue slacks and a pair of crisp white Nike trainers. The man, on the other hand, has switched to a blue cap, a heavy black winter hoodie, and blue trousers, completing his look with the same white Nike trainers. We need to get some good photos of both of them." "Agreed, Zoe. I'll set up my printer now."

Andrew returned from the other room holding a stack of freshly printed photos. "Here you go, Zoe. Take a look—do they look alright?"

As he glanced towards the kitchen he added, "Oh, while I'm up, I'll get the coffee machine going."

"Great thinking, Andrew! You know I'm always up for coffee," Zoe said with a grin. She looked through the photos, nodding in approval. "These look good. So, what's our next move?"

"Well Zoe if we scrutinise the underground tube map we can work out where to start. Have you got a time of arrival at St Pancras on the first CCTV, the day of the shooting at Holborn Underground station?"

"Yeah, let me look it up." "That's fine, Zoe, I will go and get the coffee." In a few minutes Andrew brought in the coffee and biscuits. "Have you found the time of arrival Zoe?"

"Andrew, it's intriguing—they arrived St Pancras at 11:30 am. Was the shooting incident at 6 pm.?"

"Yeah, 6 pm, that was a Wednesday."

"Zoe, we need to track their movements. My hunch is they had scheduled appointments that day. If I'm right, the same pattern might repeat on their second arrival—that snowy day."

"Let's look into it. While I map out their route, can you compile a list of hotels? Start with the largest luxury ones first—we might find something interesting."

"Zoe, I bet they got on the Victoria Line to Green Park—it's just a stone's throw from Hyde Park, Knightsbridge, Bond Street, and Marble Arch. That area is packed with luxury hotels! Which high-end hotels can you find around there?"

Zoe soon produced a list. "Let's try these for a start," she replied.

The Ritz

The Savoy

Claridge's

The Beaumont Mayfair

The Chesterfield Mayfair

The Grand Royal Hyde Park

The Dorchester Hyde Park

"That should give us a good starting point in the morning, Zoe. I suggest we begin in Mayfair—what do you think?"

"Sounds good to me, Andrew. I'll meet you outside The Beaumont. What time works best for you?"

"I prefer an early start. How about 8:30 am?"

"That works for me. I'll send our plans to Ravi, along with a copy for Simon—he'll want an update on what we've accomplished today. It feels a bit odd being the one sending in reports when I'm so used to receiving them."

The next morning, at precisely 8:30 am, Andrew spotted Zoe waiting outside The Beaumont hotel. The crisp morning air carried the scent of freshly brewed coffee from a nearby café.

"Morning, Zoe," Andrew said with a friendly greeting. "Ready to get started?"

"Absolutely," she replied with a determined smile. "I noticed two concierges by the entrance. We could start with them, then check with the receptionist inside."

Andrew glanced at the uniformed staff, their polished demeanour exuding professionalism. "Sounds like a plan. Let's get started."

Zoe and Andrew strode up to the concierge desk, showing their warrant cards. Without wasting a moment, they spread out two sets of photos.

"Have you seen this man and woman on these dates?" Andrew asked, his tone firm but polite.

The concierges leaned in, looking at the images with furrowed brows. A moment of silence stretched between them before one of them shook his head.

"Sorry," he said, glancing at his colleague, who nodded in agreement. "Neither of them looks familiar."

Zoe exhaled, exchanging a quick look with Andrew. "Alright, thanks for your time," she said, slipping the photos back into her folder.

Zoe and Andrew went into the hotel lobby, showing their warrant cards to the receptionist. As they placed the photographs with the dates highlighted on the desk, Zoe leaned in slightly. "We need to know if this man and woman were here on either of these dates," she said, her tone firm but polite.

Andrew gestured toward the computer. "Could you check the hotel bookings for those days? Maybe they had an appointment with someone."

The receptionist studied the photos and both sets of names. "I'll check," she said, glancing towards her colleague who might recognize the faces.

Zoe and Andrew exchanged a glance. If these two had been here, it will be the break they were looking for.

The hotel receptionist and her colleague carefully examined the photos, looking through the booking records for both dates. Their brows furrowed in concentration as they scanned the pages, cross-checking every detail. After about 15 minutes, they exchanged a glance before shaking their heads.

"Sorry," one of them finally said. "We don't recall ever seeing this man or woman."

The other added, "and there's no record of either name in our booking registry." A dead end—at least for now.

Zoe and Andrew thanked both receptionists before stepping out into the crisp morning air. With determined strides, they made their way towards their next stop—The Chesterfield Hotel, Mayfair.

As they walked, Zoe glanced at Andrew. "What do you think, Andrew? Do you reckon we'll get lucky with our investigation today?"

Andrew gave a positive response. "I've got a good feeling about this, Zoe. If we get results, it'll be because of our hard work—and I have no doubt we will."

They soon arrived at The Chesterfield Hotel in the heart of Mayfair. A lone concierge stood on the steps, his uniform crisp, his posture attentive. As Andrew and Zoe approached, he offered a warm yet professional smile.

"Welcome to The Chesterfield. How may I assist you?"

Wasting no time, they launched into the same line of questioning they had used at The Beaumont Hotel. The concierge examined the photographs with great interest, his brow furrowing as he scanned the names and dates. A flicker of concentration crossed his face, but in the end, he shook his head.

"I'm sorry," he said regretfully. "I don't recognise either of them."

Zoe sighed but managed a polite smile. "Thank you for your time." Then Zoe and Andrew stepped inside the elegant reception, hoping their next lead would bring better luck.

Once again, Andrew and Zoe recounted everything, just as they had at the Beaumont Hotel. The receptionist listened intently. She was eager to assist and assured them she would check the booking register.

After about twelve minutes of scanning the records, she looked up with an apologetic shake of her head. "I'm sorry," she said. "Neither of them have stayed here."

She hesitated for a moment, then offered, "But here's what I can do—I'll jot down their names and take your contact number. If they should show up, I'll call you right away."

Her words carried a flicker of hope, and though it wasn't the answer they had hoped for, it was at least something.

"Thank you," Zoe said with a warm smile as she handed the receptionist her contact number. "That's very kind of you."

Zoe and Andrew both expressed their gratitude once more before stepping out of the hotel, waving in appreciation to the concierge on their way.

"That was really thoughtful of the receptionist to offer to contact us if they show up here," Andrew remarked as they walked down the street. "We didn't even consider that. Maybe we should leave our contact information with all the hotels we visit."

"You're right," Zoe agreed. "After we finish our next stop, I'll call the Beaumont Hotel and give them my number as well."

"Smart thinking, Zoe," Andrew said approvingly.

With renewed determination, Andrew and Zoe approached both hotels in Hyde Park, The Grand Royal and The Dorchester, explaining their situation once more. But, despite their best efforts, neither establishment could offer any assistance.

Zoe sighed, glancing across the street. "Well, no luck so far. But there's a Starbucks right over there. How about we grab a coffee and a snack before we try The Ritz, The Savoy, and Claridge's ?"

Andrew had a smile returning to his face. "Good idea. We'll need all the energy we can get."

They hurried across the road into the coffee bar, sat in a cosy corner booth and ordered two steaming coffees along with ham and cheese croissants, their golden crusts glistening under the café lights. As they waited Zoe took out her phone and dialled The Beaumont—the first hotel they had visited. Speaking in a low, urgent tone, she asked the receptionist if she could leave her phone number, along with both sets of names of the elusive man and woman they were tracking. Then if they should arrive at her hotel at any time would she please call.

After savouring the last bites of their buttery croissants and finishing their coffees they set off, ready to visit the three hotels they had pinpointed as potential locations where the mysterious man and woman might have stayed.

As they walked, Zoe took out her phone. "I'll give Ravi a call—keep her in the loop on our progress,"she said.

At the other end, Ravi's phone buzzed. Seeing Zoe's name on the screen, she quickly answered. She felt a wave of relief as she had been wondering how things were going with the hotel visits.

"How are you getting on with the hotel receptionists and the concierges Zoe? "asked Ravi.

"Well nothing positive yet, Ravi, though Andrew is very confident we will get a breakthrough. We had a busy morning and are now making our way to The Ritz, The Savoy and Claridge's. I will keep you informed."

"Thanks Zoe" replied Ravi.

Andrew and Zoe arrived at Claridge's. Andrew remarked "this looks pretty fantastic, I've never been here before." "Nor me Andrew" said Zoe.

Once again, they approached the two impeccably dressed concierges stationed at the grand entrance, their sharp eyes scanning Mayfair street. One concierge, with a smile, stepped forward.

"Good morning. May I assist you? Are you looking to stay at Claridge's?"

Zoe and Andrew exchanged a glance before smoothly showing their warrant cards.

"We are detectives," Zoe. stated, "We're investigating a case and need to know—have you seen this man and woman here on the days highlighted?"

The concierges were now tinged with curiosity.

Both concierges exchanged a glance before shaking their heads apologetically. "Sorry, we don't recognise either of them," one said. "You might want to check with the receptionists."

Hopeful, Zoe and Andrew approached the front desk, but the receptionists echoed the same response. Neither recalled seeing the man or woman from the photos Zoe had shown them.

Disappointed but determined, Zoe thanked them and handed over her contact number. "If they happen to show up—at any time—please call me," she urged. With that, she and Andrew stepped away, their search far from over.

"Well, Zoe, who should we try next?" Andrew asked, glancing at his partner.

Zoe's eyes lit up. "I have a feeling about The Savoy. Let's check it out."

"Good choice. It's not far from here," Andrew agreed.

As they neared the grand entrance of The Savoy, Zoe gasped. "Wow! Look at this place. A five-star hotel right on the River Thames—absolutely stunning!"

Andrew nodded in appreciation. "Impressive. Let's start with the concierge again. He looks sharp—probably knows everything happening around here."

"Agreed." Zoe straightened her jacket as they approached the concierge desk, where a well-groomed man stood, exuding professionalism.

As they had done at other hotels that morning, they presented their warrant cards and laid out the photos, dates clearly highlighted. Would this be the lead they were looking for?

The concierge leaned in slightly, his brow furrowed in thought. "Ah, yes! I do recognize these two. They were here around midday—on a Wednesday, I believe. I remember because it was the same day as that incident at Holborn Underground Station." He paused, nodding to himself as the memory solidified. "And they were back just a few days ago, when that heavy snowstorm blanketed London. Like everyone else, they were bundled up in thick winter coats."

He glanced towards the reception desk. "You should ask to speak to Davina—she was on duty at the time. If I'm not mistaken, they had an appointment with a gentleman who was staying here."

"Thank you, that's exactly what we needed," Zoe said, exchanging a glance with Andrew. Without wasting a second, they made their way to the reception desk where three women were stationed.

Zoe stepped forward. "We would like to speak with Davina. Is she available?"

A sharp-eyed young woman immediately straightened up. "That would be me. How can I assist you?"

Zoe and Andrew presented their warrant cards. "We're on urgent business," Andrew explained. "We're looking for a man and a woman who were apparently here for an appointment on the dates that are clearly highlighted on these photos."

Zoe leaned in slightly, her tone firm but polite. "The concierge was very helpful. He mentioned you were on duty when they arrived. We need to know everything you remember."

"Yes, that's right—I was on duty that day. I remember them clearly. They stood out—both exceptionally polite and dressed to impress," the receptionist said, nodding thoughtfully.

Andrew leaned in slightly, his tone firm yet measured. "And what can you tell us about the person they had an appointment with?"

The receptionist hesitated, her professional demeanour unwavering. "I'm afraid I can't disclose any information about our guests. Company policy." A pause, then a flicker of understanding in her eyes. "However, given the urgency of the matter, I could ask our Managing Director to speak with you. He may be able to provide some assistance."

"Thank you, yes please," Zoe replied with a polite smile.

"If you'd both follow me through the lounge, I'll set you up in one of our private rooms and see if Mr. Rishabh is available to meet with you. Would you like some coffee while you wait?"

"Yes, please," they answered in unison.

A few minutes later, a waitress entered, gracefully balancing a tray of steaming coffee. Zoe and Andrew both said, "thanks."

The waitress poured two cups, the rich aroma filling the room as she set them down.

About fifteen minutes later the door swung open and in walked a sharply dressed man, exuding authority with every step. His suit was immaculate, his demeanour confident.

"Good afternoon," he said smoothly, his voice carrying the weight of experience. "I'm Mr Rishabh, Managing Director of the Savoy. How may I assist you?"

His keen eyes flicked between them before continuing, "Davina mentioned that you're detectives—Special Branch if I'm not mistaken? She said your warrant cards confirm it. If you wouldn't mind showing them to me now, that would be most helpful."

Andrew produced his warrant card. "Yes, of course." Zoe did the same, placing hers alongside his before sliding two photographs across the desk—a man and a woman staring up from the glossy prints.

Mr Rishabh examined both cards briefly before looking up. "All right, thank you. Now, if you could explain the purpose of your visit?"

Zoe leaned forward slightly, her tone calm but firm. "Certainly, sir. Our primary objective is to confirm whether these two individuals have been here. We need precise dates verified by your staff and, more importantly, details on who they met. Were they accompanied by anyone? If so, for how long? We understand that your staff must adhere to confidentiality protocols, which is why we requested this meeting with you directly."

Zoe let the words settle, watching for a reaction.

"I understand you may be on a difficult mission, and I appreciate that. However, no one—not even me—is permitted to release any confidential information. What I suggest is this: I'll go to the reception and call the Metropolitan Crime HQ. If you can provide me with your Chief Commander's name, I'll personally verify with him that you are who you claim to be. I'm sorry for the inconvenience, but high-profile hotels in London have, in the past, been targeted for confidential leaks by unsuspecting employees. It's our duty to check—and then double-check." Zoe met Andrew's gaze before speaking with a calm confidence. "No problem, sir. ask for Chief Commander Matt Gibbons or Assistant Commander Simon Harris from Special Branch."

Mr Rishabh gave a hint of urgency in his expression. "I won't be long," he assured them before swiftly exiting the room.

About five minutes later, Mr Rishabh returned, this time accompanied by Davina. He offered an apologetic smile.

"Sorry for keeping you waiting," he said," I managed to get through to Simon Harris, and he had nothing but praise for both of you. To make things easier, I've brought Davina along. She'll provide all the information you need, and I'll stay with her to assist. If required."

"Thank you, sir," they replied.

Davina set her laptop down, the screen already glowing with data. She looked up and asked, "So, what do you need to know?"

"Well" Zoe said, looking forward with a sharp gaze. "From the photos, we've confirmed that the man and woman were here on the two dates we highlighted. Now, who did they meet, and for how long? Was this person seeing anyone else while staying here? And more importantly—can you give us a full name, mobile number, address, and any details about his appearance that might help us?"

Davina gave a knowing smile, "I figured you'd ask," she said, reaching for a folder. "I have all his details right here."

Full name Mr Robert Duvall

Address 4 River Drive Abbey Wood East London

SE26 4LM

Mobile 00794583001

Email robandgo@co.uk

He's a big man—physically and financially. At least, that's the impression he gives. I'd wager his wealth comes more from luck than sharp intellect; none of us think he's particularly well-educated. Still, he always pays on time and loves to flaunt his credit card as if it's a trophy.

But what really makes him stand out? The rings. A thick gold band on every finger, glinting under the lobby lights. That's why we call him *Gold Fingers*. And he lives up to the name—always bragging about his dealings in gold, as if he owns half the world's supply.

He has a chauffeur who shadows him everywhere, handling his briefcase and luggage like they hold the secrets to his empire. Oddly enough, he won't let our concierge lift so much as a shoebox for him. Something about him just doesn't sit right. If you ask me I wouldn't trust him as far as I could throw him.

"That's really helpful, Davina. Has he had any other visitors during his stay?"

"Yes, he's been coming here two or three times a month for the past six months. I could print out a list of dates for you if that would help." "That would be very useful, thank you."

"He's had quite a few visitors—mostly high-profile footballers and their wives or partners, along with some top businessmen and their spouses. He certainly keeps interesting company."

"Oh, and he's got a brand-new black and silver Bentley. We caught a glimpse of it pulling up outside, but before we could get a good look, the chauffeur drove it away. No clue where it's parked—if it even is. That's about all we've got so far."

"Thank you Davina. and thank you sir. We've now gathered a lot more useful information, so let's keep things moving. Before we go, can we run a CCTV check on his license plate?"

"Yes, of course. Davina, could you coordinate that with our electrician? He oversees all the CCTV cameras."

"And thank you, Davina. You've provided valuable information, for our two detectives, I've noticed this man around the bar area as well—as you described, with eight fingers adorned with gold rings. After a few drinks, he tended to get a bit loud."

Davina offered a polite smile. "I'll arrange for the CCTV photos, but it might take some time. Would you like more coffee?" She hesitated for a moment before adding, "It might also help if we get some shots of his chauffeur. We never liked him—arrogant and rude to us receptionists."

"Thank you again, Davina," Andrew replied sincerely. "We would definitely appreciate another coffee while we wait. Those photos could be a huge help in tracking down the man and the woman."

As soon as Davina and Mr Rishabh stepped out of the room, Zoe turned to Andrew, her eyes gleaming with excitement.

"Well, Andrew, I think we've just stumbled onto something huge. Don't you?"

Andrew agreed, a slow grin spreading across his face. "Absolutely. Things are about to move fast." He leaned back, deep in thought. "You know, I keep thinking about all that gold on his fingers... and Davina did say she suspected he was dealing in gold."

Zoe's brow furrowed. "Yes, so what's next?"

Andrew's voice dropped to a whisper. "What if those three guns and the bullets in that woman's small leather case aren't just ordinary weapons?" He paused, letting the idea sink in. "What if they're gold?

Zoe, can you call Ravi now? Bring her up to speed on everything we've uncovered today—Simon and Matt need to stay in the loop on how this case is unfolding. Also, ask Ravi to go down to the armoury and double-check that small leather case we retrieved from the underground train repair depot. It held three bullets and had indentations for three guns. They need to conduct another review. I recall it went to forensics for fingerprint analysis before it was handed over to the armoury, so let's make sure nothing was missed."

"Great, Andrew. That's certainly possible—but think about it. If someone were trying to smuggle guns through customs, would they really stop at just three? No, I'd expect them to bring in far more. Weapons usually arrive in the UK in much larger shipments. And if anyone knows the ins and outs of that world, it's Ravi. I'll call her now and have her record the conversation—just like I used to when you and Gino called me."

A sharp knock at the door broke the silence as the waitress entered, carrying a tray of steaming coffees. The rich aroma filled the room as she set them down gently.

"Thank you," Andrew said, handing her back the empty tray.

The waitress smiled warmly. "I also brought a tray of freshly baked scones," she said. "Davina thought you might have a long wait." Andrew's lips curled into a grateful smile. "That's very thoughtful of you. We really appreciate it."

Zoe ended her call with Ravi, who assured her that the <u>Operation Live Wire</u> report confirmed and checked by Val would be on her iCloud immediately. Without wasting a second she would head down to the armoury. Whatever these weapons were, they weren't standard issue—Ravi agreed. They had to be something special.

It wasn't long before Ravi called back, her voice tense. "You won't believe this—the case isn't in the armoury! It was never even recorded in the items received register!"

When I told Simon, he lost it. "What? What?" He shouted, "It must still be in forensics!" He grabbed the phone, called them straight away, and now they're searching for it.

"I'm heading there now to see if they've found it. Let's hope they have—because the moment they do, I'm personally taking it to the armoury. We need those three bullets checked urgently."

Zoe had her phone on speaker. "So, what do you think about that, Andrew?"

There was a brief pause before Andrew responded, clearly taken aback. "What... no one's ever followed up on this before?" His tone shifted, laced with intrigue. "Well, if the bullets and guns are gold, that's a game-changer. Just think about their value!"

He paused, "I have checked—today's gold rate it is £79.90 per gram. = £ 79,900.00 per kilo. Now, here's where it gets tricky. If you're carrying more than £10,000 worth, it has to be declared to HMRC. And without proper documentation of ownership and origin, well... let's say, things could get very complicated."

Zoe raised an eyebrow, the weight of his words settling in. "So, what you're saying is... someone might be sitting on a fortune without even realising it?"

Andrew exhaled. "Or worse—someone does realise it, and they don't want anyone else to know."

"Really, Andrew?" Zoe shot him a sharp look. "So that's why that man and woman had that special little leather case. I remember your report from the Neasden train repair depot—how the bomb squad engineer told you the case was lined with soft lead shielding. That's how they got past the security cameras, isn't it?"

"Yes, you're right, Zoe. If those three guns and bullets are really gold, they'd be worth well over £100,000!"

Zoe's phone buzzed. It was Ravi again. She answered quickly.

"Hey, you two! The leather case has been found—it was tucked away on a high shelf in forensics, hidden under a pile of white cloths. I took it straight to the armoury and waited while they ran the tests. It didn't take long to confirm… as we suspected—they're solid gold!"

"Well, Ravi, that's exactly what we suspected—especially after what we learned from Davina, the receptionist at the Savoy Hotel."

"So, what's our next move Ravi?"

"I've got a meeting lined up with Matt and Simon. I'll give you a call right after. The moment you get the CCTV photos from the Savoy, send them to me immediately—no delays."

"Got it. Davina said it might take a little while, but it shouldn't be much longer now."

Zoe and Andrew were deep in conversation, the last crumbs of scone clinging to their plates, coffee cups nearly empty, when the door burst open and Davina swept in, a triumphant grin on her face and a fistful of photos in hand.

"Sorry I took so long," she said, a little breathless, "but I think you'll be happy with what I've got." She fanned out the prints like a winning hand of cards. "Clear shots of Mr Duvall, his chauffeur, and that gleaming Silver Bentley."

"Thank you, Davina," they both said in unison. "That's incredibly helpful — it'll make a big difference for us."

Before heading out, they had a quiet word with the concierge, pulling out the CCTV photos Davina had shared. He took a close look, studying the images.

"No doubt about it," he said, tapping the photos. "That's the big guy — and that's his chauffeur. But listen, a word of advice." He lowered his voice. "Be very careful with the chauffeur. He's got a nasty streak, and honestly… I wouldn't be surprised if he's armed. I thought I saw the butt of a gun poking out of his back pocket when he was loading boxes into the boot."

Zoe and Andrew exchanged a quick glance, their eyes widening with surprise. "Wow—thanks for the information!" Zoe said, her voice a mix of curiosity and urgency. "We'll definitely be ready for him," Andrew added, already shifting into action. "We need to have a word with both, the chauffeur and Mr Duvall, his boss. This could change everything."

With a thank you, they turned to leave.

"Well, we'd better get going," said Zoe.

"Yeah—thanks again,"Andrew called out as they both stepped away, offering a wave. "Take care!"

"Let's go into Selfridges," Andrew said, pulling up his collar against the biting wind." It's freezing, and we're getting soaked. We need somewhere dry to sort out these CCTV shots for Ravi."

They hurried through the swirling rain, stepping into the warmth and hum of the store. The scent of roasted coffee drifted through the air. It didn't take long before they found a quiet corner tucked away in the coffee bar.

Zoe got to work quickly—snapping crisp photos of the footage, her fingers moving fast across the screen. Within minutes, the images were sent off to Ravi, their mission moving silently forward in the cosy calm of the café.

While they waited, Zoe stretched and sighed. "I've had enough coffee for one day."

"Me too," Andrew agreed, flashing a grin. "How about we have two Coca-Colas, with ice and lemon—sound good to you?

Zoe smiled. "Perfect. I'm okay with that."

Zoe was finishing up a call with Ravi. As he sat down, Zoe said "thanks for the drinks, Andrew."

Zoe looked up and added, "I have passed on everything we gathered today—verbally to Simon. And I have sent all the photos we had from the Savoy Hotel with my report to Ravi, she is now working on getting high-photo images of Mr Duvall's house from Google Earth. Simon asked her to check in with local estate agents and Rightmove to see if any properties on either side of No. 4 River Drive in Abbey Wood have recently been sold and, If possible, she'll try to get details from the local council as well.

Ravi also mentioned she'll be tied up for a while. Simon told her there's not much more he can do for now—he's scheduled a meeting for tomorrow morning, same place, 8:30 sharp. After that, he wants us to head over to Abbey Wood to have a recce in the area. So we can see what we can dig up on Mr Duvall and his chauffeur when we are there.

And Simon has his office staff contacting all the London Police record offices. He has a feeling Mr Duvall was involved in a gun smuggling case and he had a very expensive lawyer and he wasn't charged. If he is correct we will know more at our morning meeting."

"Well Zoe things are hotting up, it will be an interesting meeting tomorrow. We can make for home now, could we meet outside City Hall about 8:15 in the morning?"

"Yes, Andrew, that's fine with me. It's always nice to have a chat before Simon and Ravi get there," she said with a smile.

After their brief exchange they went their separate ways. Andrew made it home not long after, and Chloe's face lit up when he walked through the door.

"I've got something to tell you," she said, eyes sparkling. "But could you read to Dimitris first?"

Andrew nodded and headed upstairs. It didn't take long — a few pages in Dimitris's eyelids began to droop, and before he knew it the little one was fast asleep.

"You worked your magic again," Chloe said softly when Andrew came back down. "Though to be fair, he was completely worn out from running around all day."

Andrew looked at Chloe with curiosity. "So, what's the news?"

Chloe beamed. "Good news, Andrew—my mum's booked our flights to Cyprus for Christmas! We'll be flying from Gatwick to Larnaca and staying at her new hotel."

Andrew raised an eyebrow. "That sounds amazing. Are you sure the timing works? You know I'm knee-deep in this case..."

"I thought of that," Chloe said gently. "I hope it's okay. The flight's at 8:30 a.m. on the 22nd. I know how important your work is."

Andrew smiled, a hint of relief in his eyes. "If all goes to plan, we should have this case wrapped up at least two days before then. Fingers crossed, Chloe."

"We're getting very close now—two suspects are nearly within our grasp. If all goes well we should have them soon, and that would be quite the success." He paused, then added with a sly smile, "you might be amused to hear where our inquiries have taken us—only the finest addresses, of course. We've scoured The Ritz, Claridge's, The Beaumont, The Chesterfield, and The Savoy... the usual haunts of the high and elusive."

Chloe burst out laughing. "Oh, I see! And here I was thinking you had a difficult job."

The next morning, precisely at 8:15, Andrew and Zoe met outside City Hall, both sharp and ready for the day's meeting. The air was brisk, but a quiet tension buzzed between them.

"What do you think is going to happen today?" Andrew asked, casting a quick glance at Zoe.

She didn't answer right away, eyes scanning the street. Finally, she said, "Well, Andrew, I think Simon might be onto something about Mr Duvall's background. But honestly, it's the chauffeur I'm worried about. I've got a gut feeling he's going to be trouble once we start asking questions. We need to find out his name—fast."

"Sounds good, Zoe—you might be right, as usual," Andrew said with a grin. Right on cue, Simon and Ravi appeared. "Perfect timing," he added, glancing at his watch. "It's exactly 8:30."

Simon greeted Andrew and Zoe with a warm smile and led them into the buzz of the coffee bar. While Simon hunted down a spot with four empty seats, Ravi headed to the counter and placed their order: three coffees and one lime tea.

Once they were all settled in, Simon clapped his hands together and said, "okay let's get started."

"First off, let me say it—I was right. I had every department digging into Mr Duvall. We tracked him, cornered him, and finally got him hauled into court on a gun smuggling charge. But then, like clockwork, he brought in some top-tier lawyer, probably costing more than a year's salary, and—just like that—he walked. Not even a slap on the wrist.

I didn't buy it. Not for a second. I'm still convinced he's neck-deep in guns, cocaine, and now... designer gold firearms and bullets worth a fortune.

And with that, over to you Ravi."

Zoe shot Andrew a look that said it all—told you so!!

Ravi clutched a fresh stack of printouts she'd gathered from the local estate agents, Rightmove, and Abbey Wood Council. They were packed with details about the grand homes lining River Drive in Abbey Wood. Four impressive Georgian houses stood out—each boasting five or six spacious bedrooms, set behind tall iron gates with sweeping driveways leading up to the front entrance.

Behind each home stretched beautifully landscaped gardens, complete with sprawling lawns and sleek double garages tucked discreetly at the back. Security was tight, too—CCTV cameras watched every angle, giving the whole street an air of quiet exclusivity.

One detail caught Ravi's eye: House Number 4 was at the end of the row, enjoying a little extra privacy. And best of all? It was just a short stroll from Abbey Wood rail station.

"Great job, Ravi — you really put in the effort pulling all that information together for Andrew and Zoe. Now, you two, it's time to head over to Abbey Wood. I want you asking around about Mr Duvall and his chauffeur — don't leave any stone unturned. I'm eager to hear anything and everything you can dig up. Report everything directly back to Ravi, ASAP.

I need to get back—Matt's waiting. He wants to plan a raid on the house tomorrow. We'll be sitting down to finalize the details—number of units, how many cars, and the full scope of the operation. Everyone will be armed and suited up in bullet proof vests—including you two. Based on what you picked up from the concierge, there's a real chance this could turn violent. If the chauffeur's carrying a gun, we're walking into a live fire situation."

Ravi added something else has cropped up. See if you can find out whether Number 4 has a cellar. Ask the neighbours—quietly. I've got a feeling it's there, it maybe hidden."

Simon leaned in, catching the edge in Ravi's voice. "When we're back at the office, look out the file on Duvall. I want to know exactly what he was charged with—and whether they searched that house top to bottom."

"Alright, let's go," Andrew said with a grin, giving Zoe an excited look. "Taking the bus to Hammersmith will be faster." They waved goodbye to Simon and Ravi, their departure marked by the hum of the busy street, and within moments, they were on their way. Zoe glanced out of the window before turning to Andrew. "You know I was right about Simon, looking up the file on Mr Duvall" she mused, her voice thoughtful. Andrew said, "You're always right, Zoe,"

As they arrived near to Andrew's apartment they walked past Andrew's favourite Greek deli and Andrew said. "I don't think we will be able to stop for lunch today Zoe."

Zoe let out a weary sigh. "No, unfortunately. We've got to move—fast. We need to get over to Abbey Wood. That's the eastern terminus of the Elizabeth Line, isn't it?"

"Yeah, you're right" Andrew replied, "When you were checking the CCTV photos, didn't you spot that city gent? You tracked him to Reading and the guy in the Express Removals uniform—you could only trace him as far as Shoreditch. It's possible he switched to the new Elizabeth Line from there."

"Wait, are you saying Duvall's chauffeur might be the gunman from Holborn underground?"

"I'm saying it's not out of the question," Andrew replied, pulling on his bulletproof vest. "Once I get the Mondeo out of the garage, and we're ready to go, call Ravi. Ask her to take another look — compare the CCTV footage from the Strand with that first image from Holborn underground station CCTV." He paused, "from what I remember, the guy at the station had a black beard. Could've been real... or just a fake. I've worn one myself, from time to time.

Zoe tapped the postcode into the satnav, and before long, they were onto the main road. As expected, the traffic was crawling—typical for this time of day. Zoe glanced over at Andrew. "So, how does this car handle with the blue lights flashing?"

Andrew chuckled. "Like a dream. It's amazing how fast people get out of your way. Shame we can't use them now—we'd be there in half the time."

The slow pace gave them plenty of time to talk. Somewhere between the roundabouts and red lights Andrew asked Zoe, "what do you make of Ravi?"

Zoe didn't hesitate. "She's brilliant—sharp, professional, and she actually listens. Honestly, I wouldn't be surprised if Border Control tried to pull her back. She's got a deep understanding of how security works at every entry point in the UK.

Andrew was thoughtful. "Yeah... She's definitely got that edge about her."

It wasn't long before the satnav confirmed, "you have reached your destination." "Here we are, Zoe—River Drive," he said, easing off the pedal. "I'll swing around the back and keep well away from Number Four. No need to draw attention."

Andrew glanced in the rear view mirror, eyes sharp. "We'll park over by the fir trees, closer to Abbey Wood station. That spot should keep us out of sight. Then we can take a walk, sort things out."

He asked Zoe to use her codex mobile. "Send five and one. Ravi'll want to know we are here."

"These houses are ridiculously expensive-looking," Zoe remarked, eyes sweeping across the grand facades. "Georgian, double-fronted six-bedroom mansions with those heavy iron gates... Look at the size of them. And from the back, it's all so private—you can't see a thing. I'd bet every garden is perfectly manicured, too."

Andrew agreed. "Yeah. Let's walk around to number one at the rear entrance and make our way down towards number four."

They turned down a narrow lane running behind the row of imposing homes. And as they approached the back of number two, one of the tall black gates creaked open. A gardener's van slowly pulled out, tyres crunching on the gravel.

Without hesitation, Zoe stepped in front of it, holding up a hand. The van rolled to a stop. Both she and Andrew walked up to the driver's window and showed their warrant cards.

"We'd like to ask you a few questions," Zoe said, her tone firm but polite. "Regarding Mr Duvall at number four. Do you take care of his gardens?"

"I used to work for him," he said with a shrug. "Only lasted about six months. He doesn't keep anyone around for long—nothing ever seems to please him."

Andrew raised an eyebrow. "What do you mean? How difficult was he?"

"Let's just say... he had a voice like a foghorn and used it a lot. He once yelled at me for the way I mowed his lawn. Said the lines weren't straight enough or something ridiculous like that."

Andrew chuckled. "Sounds charming. What about his neighbours? Were they okay with him?"

"Well, the guy next door's abroad most of the time, lucky for him. His wife, though—she'd always be yelling at him to keep the noise down. He'd just swear right back at her. Honestly, I'm relieved I don't have to deal with him any more. Cutting his grass was the least of the misery."

"Thanks for that. What about his chauffeur?"

"Chauffeur? He's more of a bodyguard, really. Sticks to Mr Duvall like a shadow. I keep my distance—don't trust the guy. Carries a gun tucked into the back of his belt like he's waiting for trouble."

"Do you know his name?"

"Not exactly. Mr Duvall never uses his full name. Just calls him Malik. I've heard he's from Algeria, but that's all I've picked up."

"And what about Mrs Duvall? Is she around?"

"Hard to say. Back when I was gardening for him, there was always a different woman on his arm. Never the same one twice. Make of that what you will."

"One more thing—do you know if all four houses have cellars? Are they still used?"

"Well, I know they were all built with cellars, that's for sure. But whether they're still in use? No idea. They could be filled with wine or cobwebs for all I know. Sorry I can't be more help."

"Thanks so much — you've been incredibly helpful," Andrew said warmly. 'We didn't catch your name, though."

The gardener gestured toward the side of his van, where bold lettering read *Jim Haywards — Specialist Gardener Ltd.*

Andrew chuckled. "We completely missed that!"

"Only one more question," Zoe added, "Is there a coffee bar nearby?"

Jim replied, "closest one's over at Abbey Wood train station."

"Perfect — thanks again!" they both said in unison, stepping back as Jim gave them a friendly wave and pulled away in his van.

As the sound of the engine faded, Zoe turned to Andrew with a grin. "We were really lucky to catch Jim just as he was leaving. I don't think we would've got half that information from anyone else."

"I totally agree," Andrew said. "So... what's our next move?" asked Zoe.

"Well, Zoe, let's keep walking past number four and loop back along the front—maybe we'll catch sight of his Silver Bentley. It could be tucked away in the rear garages, but it's worth checking. Either way, I think we should take a few photos of the front gates and send them over to Ravi. That'll be useful for Matt when he's setting up the raid tomorrow."

The walk took them on a quiet circuit around the cluster of the four elegant Georgian houses. The neighbourhood had a hushed charm, with no one else in sight to interrupt their reconnaissance.

Suddenly, Zoe paused. "Look," she whispered, pointing. "The Silver Bentley's right there in front of the house."

Zoe quickly pulled out her phone. "I'll get some pictures of the car and those wrought iron gates—then I'll forward everything to Ravi along with the notes from Jim, the gardener. That should give her a clearer picture."

Zoe had taken a handful of stunning photos and was tapping away at her report when the heavy iron gates suddenly groaned open. The sleek Silver Bentley was already edging forward when Andrew grabbed her arm.

"Quick—this way!" Andrew whispered, steering her in the opposite direction, towards Abbey Wood station.

"We can't let him see us."

They hurried off as the Silver Bentley came out and turned right, cruising past house numbers three, two, and one.

Zoe let out a breath she hadn't realized she was holding.

"That was close," she murmured. "'Should we keep heading towards the station? I could use a coffee—and I still need to finish this report."

"Great thinking, Zoe—let's go," Andrew said, already picking up the pace. Abbey Wood station wasn't far, and within minutes, they had arrived. As Andrew queued up for coffee, Zoe put the finishing touches on the report and forwarded all her photos to Ravi.

While she waited, she glanced around, her eyes lighting up. "Wow," she breathed, taking in the sleek lines and gleaming surfaces. This station is incredible. So modern... so well-designed."

After they'd finished their coffees, Andrew said with purpose, "let's get back to River Drive. Maybe we can talk to the people at numbers three and two—see if they know anything else about Mr Duvall or his chauffeur, Malik."

As Zoe nodded in agreement, her phone buzzed. It was Ravi. She tapped the screen and put the call on speaker.

"Hey, guys," came Ravi's voice, upbeat but focused. "I've got all the photos and your report—everything's been uploaded by Val to the iCloud folder under Operation Live Wire. I have to say, your notes and that conversation with Jim, the gardener? Very intriguing...

I'm still digging through the police files, looking for the report on the previous search of his place. Honestly, I'm baffled—how did they miss everything? So, what's the plan now guys? You got lucky heading the right way when that car slipped out of the gates."

Andrew replied, "we're going back to River Drive. We will knock on the doors of numbers three and two—see if anyone's willing to talk." "Sounds good," came Ravi's response. "Keep me posted."

Ravi hung up and Andrew and Zoe made their way back to River Drive. They stopped at number three and pressed the button on the camera doorbell. A woman asked what they wanted and before either of them could speak, she shouted "leave the parcel by the gates!"

Andrew leaned towards the door bell. "Ma'am, we're police detectives. We'd like to ask you a few questions about Mr Duvall?"

There was a pause. Then her tone softened—just a little. "That's fine. I'll open the gates."

With a click, the tall iron gates creaked open. Andrew and Zoe exchanged a quick glance and stepped onto the property. As they followed the winding path down the drive, a woman stood waiting at the door, arms crossed.

Her first instinct was caution. She stepped back slightly.

"I would like to see your warrant cards, please," she said crisply. "And what exactly do you want to know about Mr Duvall?"

Andrew and Zoe exchanged a glance, then each produced their warrant cards without hesitation. The woman studied them closely before nodding.

Zoe took the lead. "Could we start with your name, please?"

"My name is Mrs Walker," she replied. "My husband's currently abroad on business—he won't be back for another month."

"Thank you, Mrs Walker," Zoe said, her tone polite but professional. "We have a few questions for you."

Zoe pulled out a small notepad and began,

"How long have you lived here ?

How long has Mr Duvall been your neighbour?

Does he live alone?

Would you say he's a good neighbour?

Does he get many visitors?

And lastly—do you know anything about his chauffeur?"

There was a brief pause, the questions hanging in the air like smoke. Mrs Walker looked from one officer to the other

Mrs Walker's voice was calm but clear. "I can answer all your questions," she said. "We've lived here for over six years now. Mr Duvall moved in about eight months ago. The previous owners were good neighbours—quiet, polite, the kind you miss when they're gone."

She glanced towards the window before continuing. "Mr Duvall moved in with a woman, but she disappeared after a month. We never learned her name. Since then, he's had the occasional lady visitor—usually only for the weekend."

Her tone shifted, a hint of irritation creeping in. "He's not exactly the friendliest neighbour. If you ask him to turn his music down he starts swearing. Frankly, we'd be relieved if he sold the place and moved out."

Mrs Walker hesitated, then added, "he gets visitors at odd hours. I've seen vans pulling in when he opens the gates. The drivers... they look foreign, mostly. It's all very strange."

"I don't like his chauffeur. We don't even know his name. He sleeps in one of the garages out at the back, and we think he might be from Iran or Algeria—though no one really knows for sure. Everyone keeps their distance. Sometimes, a van will drive round behind the house, and he'll be there with the driver, smoking something that smells awful. We've reported it to the police more times than I can count, but nothing ever comes of it.

Lately, though... it's gone quiet. I haven't seen that van in the last five days."

Andrew gave his thanks. "I appreciate your honesty."

He turned to Zoe. Their eyes met, and without a word, something passed between them.

Zoe raised her eyebrows. "Are you thinking what I'm thinking, Andrew?"

"Yes," he said, his voice low. "Exactly."

"We only have one more question, Mrs Walker," Zoe said,. "We would really appreciate any details you can recall about the van with the chauffeur. Do you remember what colour it was? Any distinctive markings on it?"

Mrs Walker replied. "Yes, I can tell you exactly. I see that van quite often when I come home in the evenings and park my car. It's a white van and on the back, it has Express Removals printed in bold letters."

Zoe's eyes lit up. "That's the best lead we've had all day—thank you, Mrs Walker, you've been extremely helpful. Before we leave, could I possibly have your mobile number? In case we need to contact you later."

Mrs Walker handed Zoe her mobile number with a warm smile as she opened the door. Andrew and Zoe stepped outside and made their way back to the car. They could hardly contain their excitement—that the Express Removals van had been here with Malik the chauffeur.

Once inside the car Zoe turned to Andrew, her voice buzzing with triumph. "No need to bother with houses two and one now—we've got everything we need."

Andrew nodded, grinning. "You're right. Call Ravi and tell her the good news before we file the report. Honestly, who would've thought? If we hadn't shown up at number three River Drive today, we'd still be chasing shadows."

Zoe finally got through to Ravi.

"Hey Ravi, you'll never guess what we have found out!"

"Oh, I'm intrigued. What is it—I've got some news for you too."

Zoe wasted no time. "Okay, so note this—Mrs Walker, Mr Duvall's neighbour, told us something very interesting. Apparently, she noticed an Express Removals van parked outside his place. At first it all seemed okay... until she noticed it was connected to the chauffeur. We only know his first name—Malik he might be from Algeria and he could be in the U K illegally."

Ravi paused. "Wait... what? That's serious. Why would a chauffeur be mixed up with a removals company?"

"Exactly what we were thinking," Zoe said. "There's definitely more going on here than meets the eye."

"Alright guys, after a thorough analysis of the CCTV footage from Holborn underground station, we've zeroed in on the guy—black beard, blue boiler suit, 'Express Removals' printed on his back. We've gone over every camera angle on that platform, twice. And here's the good news. We're confident he fired the shot—straight from his lunch box. We even digitally removed the beard from the image, and when you compare it to the photo you sent me of the chauffeur outside the Savoy Hotel it's a match. No doubt about it, it's the same man, 100 %.

Can you believe it? We never would've found out if you hadn't stopped by the Savoy and asked to check their CCTV footage."

"That's right, Ravi—can you log our latest report and the debrief with Simon and Matt? And let us know if there are any new instructions for the planned house raid."

"Absolutely, that's the plan. Simon's still waiting on confirmation of Mr Duvall's last charge, but so far, it's a dead end—no weapons, no drugs, not even one of those flashy gold guns. Honestly, I think we've got plenty from your investigation already. So, why don't you have another coffee while I tie up the loose ends? I'll report back as soon as I can."

"Okay, Ravi, it feels like we're finally closing in on all cases," Andrew said, his voice low but urgent. "Tomorrow's raid might get risky, though. We'll catch up with you later."

Andrew and Zoe decided to stretch their legs and walk back towards Abbey Wood station. Their car was tucked away discreetly, parked a short walk from the houses on River Drive. The cool afternoon air carried a hint of tension as they made their way to the same quiet corner café they had been to earlier.

They ordered two coffees and a pair of warm croissants, the comforting smell momentarily softening the edge of the day. As they settled at a small table near the window, the conversation naturally turned back to work.

"So Zoe," Andrew said, stirring his coffee, "what do you make of the raid planed on Number Four tomorrow?"

Zoe took a sip before answering."Honestly, I'm not sure yet. I'm guessing Simon will give us the full briefing in the morning, and knowing him, he'll want us right in the thick of it.

About fifteen minutes later, Zoe's phone buzzed. She answered quickly, it was Ravi. "Hi, guys. listen up—Simon has got his hands on the police reports from that earlier search, the one where they came up empty, and he is livid. Turns out, they had no idea the house even had a cellar. They didn't bother checking with estate agents or the council—unlike me.'

Everything's set for the raid tomorrow morning," Ravi said. "We move in between eight and eight-thirty. Matt secured the search warrant, and we'll have three squad cars, a police van, and an ambulance on site. All officers will be fully armed. The Chief Police Officer in charge has been briefed—especially about you two—and he knows to search the cellar thoroughly.

Simon wants you near the house before the team arrives. I suggest you get there by seven-thirty at the latest. If Mr Duvall tries to leave, call me immediately so I can alert the Police Chief. I'll be in my office from seven a.m. and monitoring everything. Okay now, go home, get some rest—we'll be in touch in the morning."

Ravi asked. "Any questions?"

Andrew and Zoe both replied. "No, that's fine with us, Ravi."

"Alright, Zoe, let's go," Andrew said, unlocking the car. "Do you want to drive back? Might be easier—you'll get a sense of the route, and I'll know exactly where to pick you up in the morning. Plus, we can time it from here."

"Good thinking," Zoe replied, getting into the driver's seat. "I bet you miss having Gino behind the wheel?"

Andrew chuckled. "Yeah, Gino loved driving—especially when we got to use the blue lights. Felt like he was in a movie half the time."

Zoe grinned. "Where's home for you, by the way?" asked Andrew.

"Camden Town, not far from Marylebone," Zoe replied pulling out her phone.

"Perfect," Andrew nodded. "I'll plug it into the satnav for tomorrow."

Zoe handed him her postcode and flat number. He tapped it in, and the car hummed to life beneath them.

"I've been thinking, Zoe, about tomorrow morning — it's going to be bitterly cold, maybe even some frost. We could swing by my unit near Borough Market and get a couple of ex-army combat jackets. They're all large, so they'll fit over our bulletproof vests — not only keeping us warm but giving us an extra layer of protection."

"Sounds like a smart move, Andrew, I'm all for it — even if we end up looking like the Michelin Men! Just point the way."

Andrew glanced at the GPS as they drove through the streets from Abbey Wood. "Actually," Andrew said, "we're not that far away now."

Ten minutes later, they pulled into Andrew's parking space. "Here we are," he added, after guiding Zoe around the back of the building.

Andrew unlocked the main door and they stepped inside. Then Andrew moved to a tall cupboard set into the wall. From it, he pulled out two heavy-duty ex Army combat jackets, their thick fabric ready for the cold-weather.

"Try this one " Andrew said, passing one to Zoe.

Zoe slipped into it and smiled. "Wow. These are solid, Andrew, like you said—we'll be warm and better protected."

Andrew grinned. "Told you. No point freezing out there when we've got kit like this."

Zoe looked around one last time, squinting thoughtfully at the pile of clothes. "Are we forgetting anything, Andrew?"

Andrew scratched his chin, then snapped his fingers. "Scarves! I've got a couple of oversized ones—let's bring two."

Zoe smiled, mischief twinkling in her eyes. "And Gino's dreadlocks? Think we'll need those too?"

Andrew burst out laughing. "Not unless you're planning on summoning a small storm tomorrow. I think we'll manage without them."

With a satisfied look around, Andrew turned and locked up his storage unit. The metal door groaned shut with finality. Then, casually putting the combat jackets over one shoulder, he placed the scarves and the jackets into the boot of the Mondeo.

"Ready for anything," Andrew said with a grin.

"Alright, Zoe, let's go. I'm keeping track of the time since we left—shouldn't be too much traffic," Andrew said, checking his watch as they pulled out.

Zoe handled the wheel with ease and in only fifteen smooth minutes, they were pulling into the quiet courtyard of Hazel Road Apartments in Camden Town.

Zoe parked and turned to him with a smile. "Here we are, Andrew. So... what time should I expect you in the morning?"

"Well, it took us forty-five minutes to get here from Abbey Wood," Andrew said, checking his watch. "Simon wants us there by 7:30 sharp, so I'll need to pick you up around 6:15. Traffic should be lighter that early—if not, we'll turn on the blue lights.

"Smart idea Andrew,we must make sure we turn off the sirens well before Abbey Wood, we don't want to tip off Mr Duvall. Things are going to get noisy enough when the police cars arrive at 8:30.

I've been thinking, Andrew, about Mrs Walker—Duvall's neighbour. Should I give her a call? Tell her to stay inside and lock up her doors?"

"Yes, Zoe, give her a call this evening—she was extremely helpful to us," Andrew said with a grateful smile.

Zoe stepped out of the car and Andrew waved goodbye before heading back to his Hammersmith apartment. It was only a fifteen-minute drive. When the Mondeo was locked in his garage Andrew hopped on a bus home.

Chloe greeted him warmly when he arrived, and little Dimitris shouted excitedly. Andrew scooped him up, carried him to his room, and soon had him settled.

As they relaxed, Chloe asked, "so Andrew are you any closer to wrapping up the investigation? We're flying out to Cyprus for Christmas soon, remember?"

Andrew said, "Yes Chloe, we're getting close now, we've narrowed it down to two potential suspects. But it's an early start tomorrow—I'll have to leave here before six am."

"Gosh, that's an early start, Andrew," Chloe said, raising an eyebrow.

"Yes," Andrew replied, a faint smile playing on his lips. "Fingers crossed everything goes smoothly. If it does, we'll have a solid result, and the cases can finally be closed."

"I hope so," Chloe replied. "I've read about plenty of crime operations where surprise was the key—early starts catch the suspects completely off guard. But for now, let's enjoy our dinner. You need a good night's sleep."

The next morning, Andrew was up before the sun. After a quick breakfast, he caught a bus to his apartment and went down to the garage. He packed both sets of firearms, ammunition, bullet proof vests and the two rugged ex-Army combat jackets, into the car boot.

Once everything was secured and ready to go , he stepped into the cool morning air, ready to drive to Camden Town to pick up Zoe and begin the operation.

As Andrew's car stopped outside the apartments, Zoe stepped out from the building. Andrew leaned over and pushed open the door for her with a grin.

"Perfect timing," Zoe said.

"Morning, Andrew. So... how are you feeling about today's Police raid?"

Andrew's smile faded, replaced by a look of steely focus. "I'm confident the police will bring both suspects in. And with any luck, the cellar's stacked with enough guns, drugs—or maybe even more of those gold guns—to bury him for decades."

Zoe gave a small nod, her eyes sharp. "I think we've almost got this case wrapped."

"You usually are right," Andrew said, shooting Zoe a quick glance. "Yes. Most of the time, Andrew."

"Did you call Mrs. Walker last night to keep her informed of what may happen today?" Andrew asked, glancing sideways as he kept his hands steady on the wheel.

"I did," Zoe replied. "She appreciated the warning. I told her to stay inside, lock all the doors. She promised she would."

Andrew checked the dashboard clock. "We're making good time—we should get there before 7:30."

He was right. They drove quietly into River Drive, parking out of sight behind the row of houses by some fir trees. Andrew deliberately avoided pulling anywhere near number four. Just like last time, he didn't want their car showing up on the house's CCTV.

"Alright, Zoe," Andrew said, opening the car boot for their gear. "Let's get geared up. Stick to the shadows—avoid the front and back of number four at all costs."

Zoe agreed and tapped a sequence—5 and 1—into her codex. A silent signal to Ravi: we've arrived and in position.

Within minutes, they were dressed up—bulletproof vests snug beneath worn ex-Army combat jackets. Zoe glanced down at herself and laughed softly. "I know I look like a tank," she said, "but honestly, I've never felt so comfortable."

Andrew, ever the cautious one, pulled a compact pair of binoculars from his pocket and scanned the area. "Let's take a look around—keep our distance, though," he said, his eyes looking through the lenses.

Zoe reached for the binoculars. " Mind if I have a look?

Smart thinking again Andrew. This way, we can stay out of range of CCTV and steer clear of any of the house alarms."

They scanned the area from a distance—number four was still and silent. No lights on inside. But in the double garage, a faint glow flickered, just enough to catch their attention. Fifteen minutes remained.

"We should keep watch,"Andrew said quietly. "If any of the garage doors open, we need to know right away."

"I'll cover the back," Zoe offered.

Andrew shook his head. "Stay in the car. The second you see that chauffeur guy come out, call me. I'll bring the officers around."

He handed Zoe the car keys. "In case things go wrong and you need to get out fast."

Zoe's phone buzzed in her hand. It was Ravi. She answered quickly.

"Hey guys, glad you made it in good time," Ravi said, her voice steady but low, like she didn't want to be overheard. "I need to update you—Simon and Matt had a meeting last night with the Chief Metropolitan Police Officer overseeing the ram raid at Number Four today."

Zoe exchanged a glance with Andrew. Ravi continued.

"His name's Clive Dawson. He's been briefed on everything. He has both your names, and he's going to speak to Mr Duvall to make sure he gets to see the cellar."

There was a beat of silence before Ravi asked, "what's your plan Andrew?"

Andrew hesitated, then spoke. "If the raid goes as planned?"

Yes, then leave the rest to Chief Dawson," Ravi said firmly. "Come straight back to the Station. Your names won't appear in any Police Officer's report. Understood?"

Zoe's pulse quickened. She looked to Andrew again.

"Crystal clear," Andrew said.

"Yes, Ravi—we've made sure our names are clear in every part of our investigation so far," Andrew said, trying to keep his voice steady. "Wait—hold on a second, Ravi. I hear sirens. They're getting closer."

He paused, glancing towards the flashing lights now illuminating the street.

"I'm now going out the front. Zoe's staying with the car around the back. We'll call you as soon as we can."

Within minutes three police cars screeched to a halt, their tyres spitting gravel as heavily armed officers spilled out, weapons drawn and eyes sharp.

Andrew quickly stepped forward, raising his hands to show he wasn't a threat. He spotted the Chief Police Officer among the other police officers and made his way over.

"I'm Detective Andrew Brown," Andrew said, introducing himself swiftly. "My colleague Detective Zoe Williams is waiting in our car behind the house —she's watching the double garage at the rear and she will call me as soon as she sees the garage doors open."

The officers arrived at the gate and pressed the doorbell — a sleek video doorbell camera blinked to life. The Chief Police Officer announced, with firm authority, "we have a search warrant."

The response crackled back through the speaker, laced with rage and expletives. "Bloody clear off!" the voice barked, followed by a string of colourful swear words. "You're not coming in here!" The Chief Police Officer in charge didn't flinch. "Right chaps," he said coolly, turning to his team. "Get the cutting tools. We're not waiting around."

It didn't take long, sparks flew as they sliced through the heavy-duty locks. With a final grunt of effort, the officers pushed the iron gates open and stormed inside.

The other two police cars had pulled up with a screech in front of the house. They stayed parked at the kerb, with all lights flashing, blocking the road and keeping curious neighbours at bay. The Police Officers were at the front door, pounding hard—first with knuckles, then with fists. The heavy knocks echoed through the quiet street.

After a tense few minutes, the commanding Chief Police Officer barked, "Okay chaps ram it!" The door resisted, thick and stubborn, but gave way under the force of the battering ram. It splintered open with a crash.

Inside, Duvall sat in the lounge, his face twisted with fury. He leapt up, shouting a stream of curses that filled the room like smoke. The Chief Police Officer stepped forward, holding up a document. "Search warrant," he announced firmly.

"Get out of my house!" Duvall bellowed, veins bulging in his neck.

Unfazed, the Police Chief turned to his team. "Search every room, now." And as the police were soon running up the stairs, the house was no longer quiet.

Andrew turned to the Chief Police Officer, his voice low but urgent. "Should we check the cellar sir? Ravi said there's a hidden door near the back exit, at the end of the kitchen. She mentioned she had confirmed it with the house builders."

The chief narrowed his eyes, then gave a sharp nod. "Okay, Andrew. Let's see what we're dealing with."

Duvall was still yelling from the hallway, his voice cracking with agitation. "I told you—there is no cellar! I don't have a damn cellar!"

Upstairs, the sound of boots thudding across floorboards echoed through the house as police tore through furniture, drawers, and closets. Every creak of wood seemed to deepen the mystery.

Andrew and the Police Chief stepped into the dimly lit kitchen. The air was thick with anticipation. Andrew tapped the screen light on his phone and held it out.

"According to Ravi's drawing, it should be right here," Andrew said, eyes scanning the wall ahead.

The room looked ordinary enough—no more side doors, visible only a massive dresser and an old bookcase standing like sentinels against the back wall.

"Only a back door exit" the Chief muttered, narrowing his eyes. They both knelt down, inspecting the floor. A faint seam ran beneath the furniture, just visible in the dusty light.

"It looks like the whole unit slides along the wall," Andrew said, his voice low with excitement. "This could be it."

They had just begun feeling around for the mechanism when Andrew's phone buzzed in his pocket. He checked the screen. It was Zoe.

"Andrew, hurry! The chauffeur's opened one of the garage doors! he is making his way to the train station down the foot path."

'Okay Zoe I'm on my way—don't get too close. Keep your distance, he might be armed," Andrew replied sharply.

The Chief of Police didn't waste a second. He ordered Andrew to take two police officers with him. The trio bolted out of the building, jumped into the patrol car, and raced down the side road with all sirens blaring and the blue lights flashing.

"Take the back route!" Andrew shouted over the noise, and the driver swerved left, tyres screeching as they raced to intercept. The police car stopped by Andrew's Mondeo. Andrew and the police officers raced down the path to catch up with Zoe.

Meanwhile, Zoe remained on the phone, her voice tense. "I'm still following him. He's heading towards Abbey Wood Train Station."

A gunshot rang out.

Zoe staggered as the bullet slammed into her chest, the force knocking her backwards onto the ground.

For a heart-stopping moment, everything was still. Then she stirred.

Miraculously, she was okay—the thick layers of her combat jacket and the bullet proof vest beneath had absorbed the full impact.

The Police officers and Andrew caught up with Zoe.

Andrew shot a quick glance at Zoe. "You okay?" he asked, barely slowing down.

"I'm fine!" she called back. "Go! He's heading for the rail station!"

One of the police officers stayed behind with Zoe while the other sprinted after Andrew. They were closing the gap fast—just as the suspect vanished into the station entrance.

Andrew didn't hesitate. He bolted inside, just a few steps behind. The man was heading for the escalator.

Thinking fast, Andrew slammed the emergency stop button. The moving stairs ground to a halt with a jolt. Without missing a beat, he dashed down the stationary centre escalator, overtaking stunned commuters.

The suspect glanced back, realising too late—Andrew was already at the bottom before him.

"Everyone stay still! Keep to the left!" the police officer barked from behind, navigating through startled passengers as the chase thundered on.

As the chauffeur hit the bottom of the stairs, he spun on his heel and bolted down the platform. Luckily, it was deserted. Without warning, he turned and fired a shot at Andrew—the bullet whistled past his head, missing by inches. But Andrew was faster. Gun already drawn, he squeezed the trigger and shot the man squarely in the right leg.

The scream that followed echoed off the walls as he collapsed, writhing and cursing. Moments later, the police officer sprinted up beside Andrew. While Andrew pinned the injured man to the ground, the police officer quickly called for an ambulance, his voice sharp and urgent. Then he dialled his Police Chief to give a rapid update.

Catching his breath, the police officer looked at Andrew and said, "I saw that shot—it nearly took your head off. You're lucky to be standing."

One of the ladies working at Costa had seen the whole thing unfold. Without hesitation, she rushed out with a bundle of towels for the police officer to wrap around the chauffeurs leg. The police officer, turned to Andrew and said with a half-smile, "Nice shot—you aimed, going for the leg."

Meanwhile, Andrew pulled out his phone and called Zoe. She picked up almost immediately. Andrew was concerned about her and asked how she was.

"I'm fine now," she said, her voice steady. "The other police officer walked me back to the car. I've taken off the ex-army combat jacket and the bullet proof vest. The bullet he fired at me got stuck between the two—didn't even leave a bruise. I have retrieved the bullet for forensic." "That's good, Zoe, I have his gun."

There was a short pause. "How about you?" Zoe asked

Andrew recounted the moment with sharp clarity. "Malik—the chauffeur—fired at me. Missed by inches," he said, his voice steady despite the adrenaline still humming beneath it. "Before he could take another shot at me I shot him— in the leg.

Now Malik is laying on the platform, writhing in agony, bleeding profusely, waiting for the ambulance to arrive."

"Thank God he missed you," Zoe said. "And thank you, Andrew, for insisting we call in your lock-up unit to retrieve those ex-army combat jackets. Who knows how this would've ended for me without them."

The ambulance arrived and the Paramedics managed to get the chauffeur Malik a stretcher and carry him up the escalator. The police officer had instructions from his Police Chief that he was to go with him in the ambulance, when they had bandaged up his leg. The police officer told the paramedics he was under arrest and must not be left alone at all times. One of the paramedics said he won't be walking or running for some time and from what he saw the bullet Andrew fired wouldn't be easy to get out and he will suffer with pain.

Andrew stood silently, watching as the ambulance pulled away, with Malik the chauffeur inside, flanked by the police officer. Before leaving, the police officer paused to thank the lady from Costa for the towels—her kindness a small but steady light in the chaos.

Andrew made his way back to their Mondeo, parked in the shadow of tall fir trees. As he approached Zoe stepped out, relief washing over her face.

"Hi Andrew. I'm so glad you're okay."

"Yeah, Zoe. We were both lucky," Andrew replied, "Come on—let's see what's happening at the front of the house."

Together, they walked around the building, tension knotting tighter with every step. As they reached the front gate, the scene unfolded before them: Duvall, handcuffed and scowling, was being ushered into the back of a police van. Blue police tape flapped in the breeze, cordoning off the entrance. Police officers held a firm line, blocking a swarm of reporters whose flashing cameras were met with stern warnings and outstretched arms.

As Andrew approached the police cordon, one of the officers did a double take. Recognition lit up his face.

"You're clear to go in—our Police Chief wants to see you. And who's the lady?"

Andrew gave a quick nod. "This is my colleague, Detective Zoe Williams."

"Alright, you're both good to go."

Andrew and Zoe made their way up the drive, the gravel crunching beneath their feet. At the entrance, Chief Police Officer Clive Dawson was waiting for them with a broad grin.

"Come in, come in, Andrew, Zoe! We owe you both. Without your relentless investigation, we wouldn't be standing here today— Duvall will be behind bars, and we found a massive stash uncovered in his cellar."

He gestured to both. "Follow me, I'll take you down to see it before it's all hauled away.

How are you both?" asked Clive Dawson, the Chief Police Officer, his tone a mix of concern and admiration. "I heard you both came under fire— Zoe taking a shot in the chest, the bulletproof vest and the extra combat jacket saved your life, and Andrew, I believe you got a clean shot at your target? Right in the leg, wasn't it? A smart move."

As Andrew and Zoe stepped into the kitchen, Andrew immediately noticed something was moved. The large dresser and bookcase had been shifted along the wall, uncovering a hidden door.

Clive Dawson appeared beside them. "Yes, thanks to you, Andrew—and to Ravi for looking up the building plans—we found the entrance. Come on down. Some of my guys have already started packing things up. Here's a rough inventory so far..."

Quantity 45 guns. 22 type 220 Swift and Glock 20.

Quantity 680 bullets.

Quantity 84 x 5 kilo bags of cocaine.

Quantity 12 Gold guns.

Quantity 24 Gold bullets.

"I'll have my office staff work out the street value and forward a report to Commander Matt Gibbons, with Simon Harris copied in," he said calmly. "As you probably know, we had a meeting about this last night."

Zoe stared at the figures, her eyes widening.

"Wow... that's going to be an incredibly high value, Sir," she said.

"Yes, Zoe, it's surprising, isn't it? You'd never guess, when we were strolling down River Drive, that something like this could be hidden away in a quiet house—or tucked into some abandoned warehouse. It's a real reminder that appearances can be deceiving."

He straightened his jacket, his voice firm again.

"Okay, you two can go home now. I'll make sure the reports we submit about today's events leave out any mention of either of you—for the usual security reasons."

"Thank you, Sir," they replied in unison, their voices steady but grateful.

As they left the drive and headed towards their car, Andrew and Zoe caught sight of the neighbour, Mrs Walker, strolling back from the station. She waved them down, her expression a mix of curiosity and relief.

"Thank you so much for warning me there might be trouble this morning," she said, her voice earnest. "I decided to spend the night at my sister's place in Wimbledon. I had on GB News—there was a shooting at the station and a police raid at Number four. Is it all true?"

Andrew gave her an apologetic smile. "I'm sorry, Mrs. Walker, but we're not allowed to discuss any details with anyone."

"I completely understand," she said. "No problem at all. You both take care. Goodbye!"

With a warm smile, she continued on her way, leaving Andrew and Zoe to exchange a glance before going to their car.

As they reached their car, Andrew turned to Zoe.

"Before we go," Andrew said, "we'd better call Ravi and update her."

"I'll do it now," Zoe replied, pulling out her phone.

Within moments, Zoe was on the line with Ravi, quickly recounting everything that had happened. Ravi was stunned when she heard they'd both been shot at—and even more impressed by Andrew's quick thinking in disabling the chauffeur, Malik, with a shot to the leg.

"I'll get in touch with the hospital where he was taken," Ravi said briskly. "Once I have his full name, I can confirm his nationality—and whether he's here illegally. Zoe, do you have the gun he used? And the bullet from your bulletproof vest?"

"Yes, Ravi," Zoe said. "We have both."

"Excellent," Ravi said. "Drop them off to me as soon as you get back. I'll personally rush them to the forensic lab and request an urgent comparison with the bullet we recovered from the Holborn underground shooting."

Andrew and Zoe cruised slowly past Number Four, where two policemen stood at the gates. A small crowd had gathered, craning their necks, whispering, desperate to piece together the morning's chaos. Cameras flashed from a cluster of reporters jostling for the best shot. As Andrew eased the car forward, the officers gave them a casual wave — a silent farewell to the morning.

Zoe said, "at least we won't be mentioned in any police reports," she said, relieved. "No names splashed across media channels, no stories on streaming sites, no front-page headlines."

Andrew gave a grim chuckle. " That's good," he said. "I'd rather Chloe didn't find out you were shot at point-blank range — or that I had shot a bullet in a man's leg."

Zoe leaned back in her seat and said, "are we driving straight to the station? We haven't had a drink since breakfast!"

"I was thinking the same thing," Andrew replied with a grin. "We can call in my lock-up on the way back — we will have to return these ex-army combat jackets anyway. We can have a coffee and a sandwich there."

"Perfect!" Zoe said, perking up. "I'm seriously missing my coffee. And honestly, thank God you suggested using those jackets — without them I'd be nursing a massive bruise right now. I definitely felt that hit!"

It wasn't long before Andrew swung the Mondeo into his usual spot behind Borough Market. As they approached the lock-up they passed the coffee bar, with the familiar scent of roasted coffee and fresh bread in the air. When Andrew had unlocked his unit they went in, Andrew shrugged off his jacket, placed it onto the rack, then held up Zoe's with a wry smile.

"I'm afraid yours is going in the bin, Zoe — bullet holes aren't exactly sold on the market."

Zoe laughed, brushing a strand of hair behind her ear. "Hey, better a hole in my jacket than a hole in me!"

Andrew locked up his unit and said, "it's time for coffee Zoe."

They shared a quick laugh before wandering over to the coffee bar, the warmth and chatter of the place wrapping around them. Andrew ordered a couple of coffees and sandwiches and they settled into a corner table, finally starting to relax.

As Zoe took her first sip, her phone buzzed across the table. She snatched it up — Ravi's name lit the screen.

"Hi guys," Ravi said, voice bright. "You okay? Are you on your way back yet?

"Yes, Ravi," they both answered. "We just stopped for a coffee — won't be long before we're back."

"Perfect," Ravi replied. "Listen, I need to tell you. I went into a meeting with Commander Matt and Simon. Matt's pretty confident he'll be able to close all cases tomorrow — and he's asked me to put a plan into action."

Ravi paused for a moment before continuing. "When you get back, meet me at the armoury, Zoe, I need to take the gun and the bullet from your bullet proof vest straight to forensics. They're going to compare it with the bullet from the Holborn underground station shooting — exactly like we hoped. I'll stay there while they run the tests.

You will both need to hand in your bullet proof vests, your weapons, and all remaining ammunition — except for that one bullet I will take to forensic. Can you take the Mondeo back to Tony at the police compound? He's already expecting you.

Matt asked me to tell you both to take the rest of the day off — you had an early start. There's a meeting scheduled for 9:30 tomorrow morning at City Hall, probably in the same room we used last time. His secretary has already taken care of the arrangements." "Sounds good," Andrew and Zoe replied in unison. "We'll give you a call as soon as we get to the armoury."

"Oh, Andrew, that's exactly what I thought would happen," Zoe said, a knowing smile on her face.

"You always do," Andrew replied, with a chuckle. "I don't know why I'm even surprised any more."

About fifty-five minutes later their car pulled up outside the Metropolitan Armoury. Zoe quickly dialled Ravi's number, and moments later Ravi hurried down the steps to meet them.

"Hey, sorry guys, I can't hang around," Ravi said, taking the evidence bag containing the gun and bullet. "I've got to get straight to the forensic lab. I'll see you both in the morning."

"No problem, Ravi," Andrew replied.

"Bye for now," Zoe added with a wave.

They watched Ravi disappear back inside.

They both carried their bullet proof vests, guns, and ammunition into the armoury. Andrew had to sign a form, officially declaring that he had fired a single shot. No one asked him why.

Zoe leaned in and whispered, "They probably already know. News travels fast around here."

Afterwards, they made their way to the police compound. As they pulled into the parking area, Tony Edwards, the Transport Manager, stepped out of his office to greet them.

"Hey, you two! Looks like you brought the Mondeo back in one piece—I'm relieved to see that," Tony called out, grinning.

He waved Andrew and Zoe over as Simon came by to pass along a message.

"Matt thinks he's onto some good information about the three cases. Looks like you might actually get some time off for Christmas," Simon said.

"Yes!" they both answered, visibly relieved.

Andrew laughed, giving the car an affectionate pat. "I'm going to miss the old Mondeo. Maybe you can hold onto it for us next time we need a set of wheels, Tony."

Tony laughed. "No problem at all—just as long as you promise not to put it in a ditch again!"

Andrew and Zoe waved a cheerful goodbye to Tony as they walked out of the police compound. Andrew turned to Zoe with a grin.

"Things are looking good for tomorrow's meeting. Shall we meet outside around nine?"

"Nine o'clock suits me perfectly," Zoe replied, smiling. "See you then!"

Andrew arrived home to find Chloe delighted by his early return. Dimitris squealed with joy as Andrew scooped him up, the two quickly lost in a lively game.

As they settled down, Chloe asked, "how was your day after such an early start? And do you think tomorrow might be your last day? Don't forget — our flight to Cyprus is booked for the following evening."

"It's looking very likely," Andrew said, his voice full of optimism. "We had a really successful day — a good outcome all around. Matt's called a meeting for tomorrow morning. We've already returned the police car to the compound, which is a good sign. If the meeting goes well, I should be home before lunchtime. Then we can finish packing and get ready to go."

"Perfect timing, Andrew — you couldn't have planned it better!" Chloe said with a grin, handing him a large envelope.

"Look at this, Andrew — it's from Italy! It must be from Gino and Sophia."

Andrew's face lit up. "Yes, it is! I'll open it now."

As he opened the envelope, something small and round slipped out and rolled across the floor. Chloe bent down and scooped it up.

"This fell out, Andrew," she said, handing it to him.

Andrew unwrapped the item and burst out laughing. "Well, would you look at this, Chloe! It's Gino's old penknife!"

Attached to it was a handwritten card:

"Have a nice Christmas, Andrew, Chloe and Dimitris, — from Gino, Sophia and the girls. Thought you might like my penknife, Andrew--- it might help you open a few doors!"

Andrew and Chloe shared a warm, laughter-filled evening and the next morning, Andrew left for his meeting looking bright, cheerful, and carrying a little extra item in his pocket.

Zoe and Andrew met outside City Hall at precisely 9 a;m, their breath misting in the cool morning air as they swapped stories about the chaotic events of the previous day. Both had smiles, and they were thankful to have come through it all without a scratch.

"I think Matt's going to wrap everything up today, don't you?" Zoe said, brushing a strand of hair from her face.

Andrew agreed. "Yeah, I think so too. Oh—look, here they come."

Matt, Simon and Ravi appeared around the corner, their strides purposeful. Without wasting a moment, the group made their way into the City Hall offices. Inside, Matt, looking unusually pleased with himself, gestured toward a cluster of chairs.

"Everyone, please take a seat," he said. "My secretary's arranged coffees—and one lime tea."

As they settled in, a smartly dressed lady swept in with a tray of steaming cups, setting it carefully down before slipping away. Matt clapped his hands together, his eyes twinkling with anticipation.

"Right," he said, his voice cutting through the hum of conversation. "Let's get started.

1) A major breakthrough: The Duvall Case

I want to talk about Duvall, who is currently behind bars awaiting trial. The Police Officers uncovered his massive stockpile of cocaine, firearms—type.220 Swifts, Glock 20, and 9mm, ammunition—and, astonishingly, several gold guns with gold bullets.

Simon and I had a meeting the night before the discovery. We were surprised by how Duvall had previously evaded charges when an earlier search of his home turned up nothing. If it wasn't for Ravi's sharp eye when thoroughly checking the house plans, we might never have known about the hidden cellar.

It was Andrew and Chief Police Officer Clive Dawson who finally discovered the cellar door. Inside, they found contraband valued at an incredible £4. 85 million. All items have now been seized and are in police custody.

This is a tremendous victory. Mr Duvall is set to spend a very long time in prison—and needless to say, he won't be flaunting those flashy gold rings any more!

2) His chauffeur, in a desperate attempt to escape, fired a shot at you, Zoe. Luckily, you avoided serious injury — no broken bones, just a few bruises. How are you feeling now, Zoe?"

"I'm fine, thank you, Sir," she replied steadily.

"Good, good — we're all relieved to hear that," he said warmly, before turning to Andrew.

"And you, Andrew — you had an even closer call. Clive Dawson informed me that the bullet aimed at you passed alarmingly close to your head. It's a miracle you weren't hit. Quick thinking on your part — shooting him in the leg to neutralize the threat without taking a life. Very wise, Andrew.

3) Ravi, what can you tell us about the chauffeur? All I know is what Andrew and Zoe reported — his name's Malik."

"That's right, sir," Ravi replied. "I contacted the hospital where he was taken. He's now under 24-hour police guard. I managed to get his full name — Malik Jazairi. He's from Algeria, and after checking with Border Control I discovered he's an illegal immigrant. But that's not all. He's also wanted for shooting a man on a French beach — the victim had tried to stop him escaping in a rubber dinghy. On top of that, he's wanted by Manchester's Moss Side police for drug dealing and gun running."

"Interesting," Matt said, leaning back in his chair. "Simon, get on the phone to Chief Constable Alan Edwards in Manchester. Pass on what we've got about Malik Jazairi — I expect he'll want to send a couple of his detectives down here to have a word with him."

Ravi continued, her voice steady and clear.

"Andrew and Zoe recovered the gun used by Malik Jazairi, along with the bullet he fired at Zoe—the very one that struck her bulletproof vest. Our forensic team compared it with the bullet extracted from the Jewish imposter who was shot in the back at Holborn underground station. Their analysis is conclusive: both bullets were fired from the same weapon.

But that's not all. Andrew and Zoe also obtained footage from the CCTV cameras at the Savoy Hotel. When we matched it against the CCTV images captured on the station platform the night of the shooting, it was an exact match. There's no doubt about it—Malik Jazairi pulled the trigger that evening."

4) "Now Ravi what about the man and woman who are smuggling gold guns from France, travelling undercover on the Eurostar. The question is — where are they now? What's the latest, Ravi? What have you found out about where these weapons are ending up?"

"Sir, I've uncovered something intriguing. These gold guns and their matching gold bullets are being discreetly sold — not to criminals or arms dealers, but to the wives of top footballers, as a bizarre form of 'protection' while their husbands play abroad. Some high-powered executives' wives are also buying them, flaunting them as twisted status symbols.

The guns themselves are masterpieces: authentic-looking, exquisitely detailed, and paired with slender, solid gold bullets. After speaking with contacts in the UK Border Control's Ammunition Division, I learned that each gun is engineered to fire only a single shot. After that, the firing mechanism locks permanently — one bullet, one chance.

That's why the briefcase found by the bomb squad on the London underground train only had three solid gold bullets inside. They had sold three guns — and not all the customers intended to use them to kill. Some just wanted to own the ultimate luxury weapon.

Hidden beneath his home, in the cellar Duvall kept a secret arsenal: a glittering stockpile of gold guns stored deep in his cellar. At the luxurious Savoy Hotel he held clandestine meetings with the smugglers who brought the weapons into the UK, and with the wealthy clientele eager to buy them. Duvall was the brilliant architect behind the entire scheme, poised to amass a fortune as each exquisite gold firearm fetched between £20,000 and £25,000 — with a single solid gold bullet commanding an astonishing £2,000.

Before we left for this morning's meeting I received a call from French Border Control at the Gare du Nord Euro station. They had intercepted our targets — a man and a woman travelling under the false names Amélie Bequette and Matthieu Badeaux. Hidden in their luggage was a small case containing three gold guns, each paired with a single solid gold bullet. In addition, the man was caught with four bags of crack cocaine concealed in his holdall, each wrapped meticulously in foil to evade customs scanners. It was the sharp nose of a sniffer dog that ultimately unravelled their plan. Both suspects are now in custody in Paris, awaiting trial."

"Thank you, Ravi, for the latest update. Thanks to all for your hard work — I can now officially close all three cases with confidence. You've all worked incredibly hard to achieve these results, so take some well-deserved time off and enjoy the Christmas holidays. I look forward to seeing you all refreshed in the New Year!

Oh, and before I forget — a little something from yesterday's events at Abbey Wood. When the police searched the double garage behind Number 4, they discovered a box hidden in the loft. Inside were five blue boiler suits, each printed on the back with the name **Doughnut Delivery. "**

Naturally, all eyes turned to Commander Matt, who couldn't keep a straight face. Laughing, he admitted, "Sorry —it's a joke! They actually were printed **Express Removals.**

And with that final twist, we now have confirmation — Duvall was indeed the man behind it all"

THE END

Acknowledgements

My special thanks to Elaine and Keith Sharp

I could not have completed this book without the many hours of Elaine's time in proof reading and correcting all my grammar.

Also to Elisabeth Bizzie White for her valued advice on publishers, copyright, book layout, and amendments.

I really appreciate everything they have done for me.

And of course my lovely wife Gill and my two daughters. Carolyn and Angela for all their support.

Malcolm C. Brooks Author

About the Author

Malcolm Brooks was born in Buckinghamshire in 1938, he served with the RAF for 3 years mostly in Cyprus and was awarded the National Service medal and Active Service medal.

His working life consisted of 5 years at BMC mini assembly at Oxford then after marriage he secured a job for an electronic company as purchasing manager, then UK Sales manager for another company which involved a move to Wiltshire.

Malcolm wrote his first book during Covid and most of his time is now spent playing and coaching the fast growing sport of Petanque.